Bolan's thoughts turned to CLODO's leader

He was the brains behind a number of attacks on computer manufacturers and related businesses during the past several months, and much more than computers had been destroyed.

Bombs, stray bullets and other collateral damage were always the result of warfare. But with terrorists, it became the objective rather than an unfortunate by-product. Since its reorganization, CLODO's bombings, machine-gunning and other terrorist strikes had claimed hundreds of lives.

The Executioner's jaw tightened as the bloody sight before him generated anger. He wasn't responsible for the death and destruction at this CLODO safehouse.

Pierre Rouillan was responsible for the deaths of his men.

Don Pendleton's Mack Bolan®

Killing Game

A GOLD EAGLE BOOK FROM
WORLDWIDE®

TORONTO • NEW YORK • LONDON
AMSTERDAM • PARIS • SYDNEY • HAMBURG
STOCKHOLM • ATHENS • TOKYO • MILAN
MADRID • WARSAW • BUDAPEST • AUCKLAND

Recycling programs
for this product may
not exist in your area.

First edition November 2009

ISBN-13: 978-0-373-61533-9

Special thanks and acknowledgment to
Jerry VanCook for his contribution to this work.

KILLING GAME

Printed in U.S.A.

At least two-thirds of our miseries spring from human stupidity, human malice and those great motivators and justifiers of malice and stupidity…
—Aldous Huxley,
1894–1963

The stupidity, motivation and flawed thinking of certain individuals never cease to amaze me. We must stand on guard and protect the innocent from their deranged plans of carnage. Whatever it takes.
—Mack Bolan

CHAPTER ONE

Paris, France

Mack Bolan, aka the Executioner, glanced up at the sliver of moon in the otherwise darkened sky. Then, dropping his line of vision, he took another quick survey of the one-story suburban house in front of him and his black-clad companion. This house looked little different than the other homes lining both sides of the street in this upper middle-class Parisian residential neighborhood, but it *was* different.

This dwelling housed terrorists.

The Executioner pointed Russian Intelligence agent Marynka Platinov toward the side of the house, then tapped his wristwatch with the same hand. "Thirty seconds," he whispered.

The beautiful blond-haired Russian agent glanced at her own watch, nodded, then took off in a jog around the corner.

Bolan couldn't help but let his eyes fall to her hips as the well-developed muscles in her buttocks tightened. Platinov—often shortened simply to "Plat" when Bolan spoke to her—wore the same stretchy black battle coveralls, known as "blacksuits," as him.

She and the Executioner had worked together several times in the past—first when she'd been a new KGB officer and later, when she'd emerged from the ashes of the Soviet Union to rise in the ranks of the newly formed Russian Intelligence Bureau—and Bolan was one of only a handful of people who knew her whole story. He and the beautiful Russian woman had developed a solid working relationship.

The Executioner glanced at the weapons and other equipment that hung from Platinov's blacksuit. A double shoulder rig with a matching pair of Colt Gold Cup .45s was stretched across her back, and a 1911 Government Model .45 rode on a curvaceous hip.

The Executioner glanced at his watch as his partner turned the corner. Twenty seconds remained. He pulled back the bolt of the Heckler & Koch MP-5 submachine gun hanging from his shoulder on a sling, chambered the first round and flipped the selector switch from the safety position to 3-round-burst mode. As he methodically readied the weapon, his thoughts turned on Platinov and the only real area of disagreement that always stood between them.

The Russian woman was as loyal to her country as Bolan was to the U.S. And on rare occasions—even when their end objective was the same—those two loyalties conflicted. When that happened, problems arose. The Executioner didn't foresee any such problems on the horizon for this op, however. The leader of CLODO—Computer Liquidation and Hijack Committee—and the rest of his newly vivified terrorist organization that they sought, were an equal threat to both countries. Yet, Bolan reminded himself, he would have to keep one eye on the enemy and the other on Platinov.

Bolan started up the concrete steps to the front porch of the CLODO safe house, taking them two at a time. At precisely the thirty-second mark, he slammed his right boot into the door just to one side of the dead-bolt lock. Wood cracked then splintered as the framework around the door exploded like a hand grenade filled with wooden shrapnel. A fraction of a second later, he heard a similar noise at the rear of the house and knew Platinov had entered the back entrance.

The front door swung open, crashing into the wall and rebounding back toward the Executioner as he raised the submachine gun to waist level. He pushed the door back again with his left hand. As the noise died down, the house went eerily silent for a second.

During that lull, the Executioner had time to quickly assess the interior of the house. He found himself standing on a ragged carpet in the living room. A soccer game was playing on a large-screen HDTV in the far corner, and set into the wall next to it was a fireplace.

Men, close to a dozen and many dressed similarly, sat around the living room on couches and in reclining chairs, watching the game, rifles, shotguns, submachine guns and pistols scattered throughout the area.

Platinov stood between the fireplace and a kitchen table in the far corner opposite the HDTV, her own MP-5 hanging from the sling over the shoulder of her blacksuit. Just to her side, Bolan could see a small breakfast table and chairs. The rest of the kitchen, he knew, had to be hidden behind the wall to his left.

The Executioner noted a dining-room table also to his left, with more men clustered around it, playing cards. Poker chips were stacked in front of each man. The terrorists cursed and dived for their weapons.

The Executioner triggered a 3-round burst of hollow-point rounds at the CLODO gunner directly in front of him. The man wore a blue beret, a tan short-sleeved shirt and brown trousers.

Hal Brognola, the director of the Sensitive Operations Group based at Stony Man Farm, had briefed Bolan and Platinov via satellite phone during their flight from Washington, D.C., to France. Along with the location of this only known CLODO safe house, the Executioner and Platinov had learned that the beret, shirt and pants were a sort of "unofficial" CLODO uniform. There was nothing particularly militant-looking about the garb and, indeed, many men on the streets of Paris who had nothing to do with this anticomputer terrorist organization wore basically the same clothing. But these specific items of clothing—always in the same colors and combination—were the first step in helping the terrorists identify one another. The next step was a series of coded, and frequently changed, nonsensical questions and answers to make sure that they had not just bumped into some non-CLODO-aligned Parisian on his way to a bocce game in the park.

Members of the CLODO organization had come to be known as CLODO men by all who opposed them. That included America, Russia and most other civilized countries of the world. CLODO had been active during the late 1980s, then had seemed to fizzle out, until a few weeks earlier. Then, all hell had suddenly broken loose with car-bombings, random machine-gunnings at shopping malls and other public places, and drive-by shootings at computer manufacturing plants, distributors, wholesalers and retail stores.

Another—and perhaps the most important—bit of intel that Bolan and Platinov had obtained was the name of the man who had revived CLODO—Pierre Rouillan. Now in his thirties, Rouillan would have been a child during the eighties, and the Executioner couldn't help wondering what had turned the young man toward the all-but-dead organization and driven him to reanimate it.

Bolan dived to the floor as return fire sailed over his shoulder, coming to rest on his side directly against the back of a long, leather sofa.

Using the sofa for concealment, the Executioner raised the MP-5 with one hand, thumbed the selector from 3-round burst to full-auto and stitched the remaining rounds back and forth into the couch. Screams and moans met his ears from the other side of the sofa, and he saw a bloody mist rise up into the air.

The 9 mm RBCD total fragmentation rounds didn't just penetrate their human targets, they shredded them.

Bolan hesitated only long enough to drop the empty 9 mm magazine from his weapon and ram home a fresh one. On the other side of the couch, he could hear more 9 mm fire that he knew had to be coming from Platinov's subgun.

Though he was hidden from view of the men in the living room, the sofa was concealment rather than cover, as the Executioner had proved himself only moments earlier. In another second or so, the terrorists still standing on the other side of the sofa would realize where he was and begin firing into the couch. The four men who had sat there would obviously be dead, so the chance that they might accidentally hit one of their own would not hinder them in the least.

But an even more imminent problem faced Bolan. While he was still hidden from the men in the living room, he was on full display to the card players.

The Executioner rolled away from the sofa, flipping the H&K's selector into 3-round burst mode, and rose to one knee. He opened fire, the first two 9 mm rounds striking a terrorist in the chest an inch apart. Bolan had allowed the subgun to rise slightly with the recoil of the second round, and the third hit the same man just above the nose in his forehead.

From the corner of his eye, the big American could see that Platinov had dropped to one knee as well. The ancient, antique-looking rocking chair behind which she knelt offered neither concealment nor cover, but it did distort her body enough to at least slightly confuse the gunner's aims. The Russian agent had opened fire a split second after Bolan, and her first target had been a man who had taken cover from behind a chair against the wall, a SiG-Sauer pistol in his hand. Both she and the Executioner were using RBCD ammo, and a red mist hung in the air, floating slowly toward the floor in front of the dead body from which it had come.

As the Executioner opened fire again, he continued to eye Platinov from his peripheral vision. Two more of the card players fell as Bolan watched his Russian ally knee-walk swiftly up behind a man with his back to her. The terrorist was leaning forward to reach for a shotgun between his feet. But before his fingers could find the cold metal or wooden stock, Platinov had leaned forward and pressed the barrel of her weapon into the back of the man's head at the base of his neck.

Bringing her left forearm up to cover her eyes, Platinov pulled the trigger. The contact shots caused almost as much blood and other gore to blow out the entrance holes as that which exited the terrorist's forehead.

The terrorist fell forward onto the floor on his face. Or at least what was left of it.

Platinov, the Executioner knew, had covered her eyes to keep the residual blood out. She could hardly afford to "go blind" with blood obscuring her vision in the middle of a gunfight. It was a good strategy. Except for one thing.

By covering her eyes with her forearm, Platinov *had* temporarily blinded herself.

One of the gunners who'd been sitting on a couch against the side wall noticed her vulnerability and tried to take advantage of it. He raised what looked like an old Luger toggle-bolt pistol and stepped into a classic Weaver shooting stance. As she squinted slightly, the muscles in his hands and arms tightened as he pushed the pistol forward with his right hand and pulled it back toward him with his left. At the same time, he did his best to drop the Luger's front sight on Platinov. The man, Bolan thought, looked as if he'd just received his certificate for completing one of the many shooting schools that had popped up around the world. Attendees shot hundreds of rounds as they went through these courses, always being trained to make sure the front sight was "flashed" on their target before squeezing the trigger.

They emerged from such schools as experts.

Experts, however, at putting holes in paper silhouette targets or making steel plates ding. *Not* experts at gunfighting by any means.

Again, from the corner of his eye, the Executioner saw the man began to gently squeeze the trigger.

The soldier turned his weapon toward the man, pointed it and shot him.

Saving Platinov from the unseen attack had meant the Executioner had to momentarily ignore the return fire from the card players. As bullets and buckshot sailed past him, Bolan opened fire again, lacing one of the gamblers standing sideways from belt to armpit with three rounds into his ribs.

The gunner was already dead and on the ground by the time Platinov had fired the contact shots into the back of the other terrorist's head. Now, she dropped her arm.

She would never know just how close to death she had come from the man who had drawn the Luger. Or that it had been Bolan who had saved her life.

Bolan decided not to press his luck any further with the surviving card players. He had already taken out the man who had sat with his side toward the Executioner, and now he dived to the side as return fire continued.

The Executioner rolled once, then came up on one knee again. Even this slight movement forced the hardmen to redirect their aim.

Bolan cut loose with another 3-round volley into the heart of a gunner wearing a beret. The man had been doing his best to gain target acquisition on the Executioner's new position. That task was abandoned as deep, thick, red blood spurted from his chest, accompanied by the now-familiar mist that had become the RBCD rounds' personal signature. At least one of the totally fragmenting rounds had also pierced a lung, and the man dropped his Uzi, twisted in the air with a scream and fell on top of his own weapon, his chest sucking up and down in dying breaths.

Bolan sought another target, zeroing in on a man wielding a Beretta 92. The round missed him by millimeters, coming so close to the Executioner's ear that he could feel its heat.

But this was no game of horseshoes. "Close" didn't count.

Bolan pumped another trio of rounds into the gunman, practically ripping his chest away from the rest of his body. He fell backward onto the table, his legs dangling down to spasm as if in some bizarre, predeath, dance ritual.

The gunner who had sat next to him had grabbed a sawed-off shotgun from somewhere beneath the table, and now he brought the shortened pump-action weapon around and racked the slide, chambering a shell. But he had no time to pull the trigger.

Bolan angled the H&K his way and cut loose with another 3-round burst, aiming at the man's chest. But at the last second, the gunner crouched instinctively and all three 9 mm rounds sank into the top of his head, like electric drills boring down through his skull and into his brain.

So it didn't make too much difference. The man was still as dead as disco before he hit the floor.

The card players were all dead now, and Bolan turned toward the living room, assisting Platinov as they rid the world of the final two CLODO terrorists. As the gunfire died down, Bolan's thoughts turned again to Pierre Rouillan. The file he and Platinov had studied during their flight had contained several pictures of the man who had been responsible for CLODO's revival. He was a little over six feet tall, dressed conservatively and appeared to have a strong attraction to beautiful women, wine and the finer things in life. He was also the brains behind a number of attacks on computer manufacturers and related businesses during the past several months, and much more than computers had been destroyed.

Bombs, stray bullets and other collateral damage were always the result of warfare. But with terrorists, it became the objective rather than an unfortunate by-product. Since its reorganization, CLODO's bombings, machine-gunnings and other terrorist strikes had claimed hundreds of lives.

The Executioner's jaw tightened as the bloody sight before him brought on anger rather than the frustration or fear or nausea that it might have inspired in a more common man. It was not he, or Marynka Platinov, who was responsible for the death and destruction at this CLODO safe house.

It was Pierre Rouillan who had brought about the deaths of his own men.

PIERRE ROUILLAN'S EYELIDS lifted the second he heard the doors crash open. As gunfire thundered in the other rooms, he swung his legs off the bed, grabbed his shirt and leaped to his feet. Silently, he thanked a God he didn't believe in that he had not taken off his pants. Snatching the 9 mm Kel-Tec PF-9 compact pistol off the nightstand, he stuck it in his belt and hurried toward the window.

A moment later, he was in the backyard, half-expecting to suddenly be tackled and thrown to the ground by men dressed in SWAT-type gear.

He frowned when he found the backyard deserted.

The firing behind him was in full swing now.

Rouillan slowly drew the pistol from his belt and held it close to his leg as he walked toward the open back door, curiosity getting the better of him. From several yards away, he could see that the back door had been kicked open. Moving to a window next to the door, he gazed at the flash-fire that accompanied each round. Rouillan would make his escape in a moment, but first, he had to know who had learned about the safe house and was now attacking it.

The back door opened directly toward the kitchen table, which meant the living room stood out of his line of vision. Dropping to both knees, Rouillan peered through the opening and angled to see around the corner, his nose almost dragging across the hard concrete of the single step that led to the entrance. As his eyes focused on the back of a blond-haired woman wearing black combat gear, he saw her lean forward and shoot.

He looked past her. Standing on the tiles by the front door was a tall, broad-shouldered man dressed in an identical blacksuit. And, just like the woman, he was firing an H&K MP-5 submachine gun. He also carried two pistols—one was in a shoulder holster beneath his left arm and looked like it was long enough to have a sound suppressor threaded onto the barrel. The other gun—in a holster on his right hip—was huge. Rouillan wasn't close enough to identify it.

The terrorist leader started to pull his Kel-Tec around the corner, then paused. Shooting the woman in the back would be easy. And the big man at the front of the house hadn't noticed him yet, either. Rouillan might even be able to pump a couple of rounds into him as well.

On the other hand, he didn't want to risk having the shot miss. While Rouillan knew he was a good shot, he wasn't ready to gamble his life on the Kel-Tec. The hollowpoint rounds did not always open up after they'd left the short barrel, and the muzzle-flash in the doorway might well catch the attention of the big man at the front of the house.

And even though his face was deadpan as he fired his MP-5, there was something about the big, black figure that screamed at Rouillan to be careful.

This man was deadly.

No, the Frenchman thought, it was a chance better not taken. Better he make his escape while he could. After all, he had worked hard reestablishing CLODO. And without his leadership, the still-fragile organization was likely to crumble and then disintegrate altogether.

Another quick thought suddenly entered his mind, but Pierre Rouillan immediately pushed it out of his head. That thought was that he might not be all that concerned with CLODO, and that he might just be a simple old-fashioned coward, worried more for his own safety than the good of the organization.

That uncomfortable idea was pushed out of his head as quickly as it had come.

Rising to his feet, the CLODO leader replaced the pistol in his belt and took off at a jog across the grass toward the chain-link fence at the rear of the backyard.

He had plenty of other men, and plenty of other safe houses, where he could hide out until it was time for the big strike.

He doubted that he would ever even see the big man and blonde woman again.

Rouillan smiled as he grabbed the top of the fence and swung his legs up and over the barrier. He jogged across the backyard of his neighbor's house. CLODO was still known primarily for the bombing of the Phillips Data Systems in Toulouse in 1980, but his new CLOCO master plan was coming up.

When *it* detonated, nothing would explode.

But the whole planet would shut down in a screeching, screaming halt.

EMPTY BRASS CASINGS crunched under Bolan's boots as he made his way toward Platinov, who stood in the center of the living room. He kept the H&K up and ready. Too many "dead" men had magically come back to life during his career for him to let his guard down yet. And when he looked at the Russian agent, he saw that she had learned the same lesson over the years.

Marynka Platinov's submachine gun was still gripped with both hands, her right index finger on the trigger.

"We're not going to have much time," Bolan said as he knelt next to a body in the middle of the floor. "Neighbors will have already called the cops."

"I'll check the back rooms," Platinov suggested.

Bolan nodded as he began going through the pockets of the man on the floor, who wore a blue beret like some of the others. But, otherwise, he was dressed in faded blue jeans, high-topped hiking boots and formerly-white T-shirt, now soaked crimson with blood. His pockets contained everything from a little .22 hideout Beretta to a receipt from a local laundry. In the left front pocket, Bolan discovered a small Spyderco Clipit knife being used as a money clip. It contained at least a thousand euros. Although he had unlimited operational funds from the U.S., the Executioner saw no reason to waste taxpayers' money for his war chest. It was always a bonus to use the money of America's enemies to finance their own destruction.

By the time he had finished searching the man in the vest, Platinov had returned to the living room. "I didn't find anyone else in the house," she said. "But there *was* someone."

Bolan frowned as he waited for more information.

"The bed in the back," Platinov went on. "The sheets are still warm."

The Executioner nodded.

"And the window into the backyard is open," she added. "He, or she, must have heard us come in and booked out of here." She paused. "I couldn't have missed him by more than a couple of seconds."

Bolan knew such coincidences sometimes happened. They were the fortunes of war. "Rouillan himself, maybe," he speculated.

Platinov shrugged. "Maybe. Maybe not. No way to know." She paused for a moment, then added, "And you won't believe what I found in another bedroom."

"What's that?" Bolan asked.

"A computer."

"Why is that so unbelievable?" he asked.

Platinov stared him in the eyes. "Cooper," she said, using Bolan's cover name, "That's what this whole group is about, remember, they are against computers. Their famous quotation is 'Computers are the favorite instrument of the powerful. They are used to classify, control and repress.'"

Bolan nodded. "I remember it," he said. "But all that a computer in the back room of this house means is that CLODO has modernized since the 1980s. They've learned that if you want to defeat the enemy, you have to first know him."

"Yes," Platinov replied. "But I still find it ironic."

The Executioner agreed. "Help me search the rest of these bodies," he said. "And be quick. We're going to have to take off the second we hear the first siren."

Platinov dropped to her knees on the carpet and began to go through the pockets of one of the corpses.

Hurriedly, and never leaving his knees, Bolan moved from corpse to corpse, going through the pockets of slacks, jeans and work pants, as well as shirts, vests and coats of all types. He found mostly the typical items that might be found on any man: money, keys, cell phones, cigarettes and a variety of paperwork. He had just come across another small hideout weapon—this one an old Baby Browning .25—when they suddenly heard the sirens of approaching Parisian police cars.

The Executioner had dropped everything that he'd

found in the dead men's pockets on the carpet next to them, and now he produced a folded canvas bag from a zippered pocket on the thigh of his blacksuit.

Platinov saw what he was doing, read his intentions and began scooping up everything from papers to loose change and wristwatches from the carpet.

Twenty seconds later, the bag was filled and Bolan was zipping it shut again. He handed Platinov his H&K, then slung the canvas bag over his shoulder. "Let's go," he said. "We'll go through this stuff as soon as we're out of the area."

The Russian woman nodded, then turned to follow Bolan out the back door she had kicked in less than five minutes earlier.

As the sirens neared, the two black-clad figures took off, sprinting across the grass, disappearing into the night.

THE EXECUTIONER and the Russian agent came out from between two houses and spotted the Nissan exactly where they'd left it. Bolan pulled a key ring from his pocket and pressed the vehicle's unlock button twice with his thumb. Both the driver's and passenger's doors clicked, and the headlights flashed on and off as they approached.

Yanking open the driver's door, the Executioner tossed the canvas bag into the back of the Nissan as he slid behind the wheel. Between the houses, on the street a block over, he could see the flashing lights of the Parisian gendarmes. Good. As he'd suspected they would do, the French police had only blocked in the streets immediately around the safe house. He and Platinov had gotten out of their enclosure by the skin of their teeth.

Bolan stuck the key in the ignition as Platinov strapped herself in with the seat belt. The Russian agent had both of their MP-5s held between her thighs with the barrels resting on the floorboards.

A second later, the Executioner threw the vehicle into Drive and they drove quietly out of the neighborhood.

When they had crossed a bridge spanning the Seine River and were nearing the world-famous Paris-Sorbonne University, Platinov finally broke the silence. "Where are we going now?" she asked.

"We need to find a room somewhere," Bolan said from behind the wheel. "Someplace out of the way where we won't be conspicuous. And where we'll have the privacy to go over all of the stuff in the bag."

The Russian agent nodded. "Yes," she agreed. "But I believe we are going to be a little conspicuous no matter where we go, dressed as we are." Without waiting for an answer, she unbuckled her seat belt, brought one of her shapely legs over the console between the seats and then used her arms to pull herself on into the back of the car.

Bolan heard the click as Platinov unsnapped the ballistic nylon gun belt from around her waist. His eyes rose briefly to the rearview mirror when the click was followed by a long, zipping sound that meant the Russian woman's blacksuit was coming off.

Platinov met the Executioner's eyes in the mirror. "Go ahead and look," she said teasingly. "There is nothing here you haven't seen before."

Bolan chuckled as the woman behind him slipped out of her battle suit. He caught a quick glimpse of red thong panties—apparently the only underclothing she had worn beneath her blacksuit—as his eyes returned to the road. He heard another zipper as he drove on and knew Platinov had to be rummaging through one of their equipment bags for a less conspicuous outfit to put on.

A few minutes later, she climbed back between the seats to the front. As her legs crossed over the console, the Executioner saw that she had retained the red thong beneath a pair of flesh-colored pantyhose and a beige skirt. Above the skirt, she wore a matching jacket with a nondescript white blouse beneath it.

"Your turn," the Russian woman said, ignoring her seat belt this time.

Bolan had turned onto a side street, crossed a bridge and knew he was nearing the Notre Dame area. The sidewalks were crowded with men, women and children taking in the nighttime beauty of the Seine and bartering with the vendors at the dozens of used-book and souvenir stands along the way. Traffic had all but halted anyway, so Bolan stopped the Nissan in the middle of the street, threw the transmission into Park and turned to Platinov. Without speaking, he twisted in his bucket seat and climbed into the back of the Nissan.

Platinov swung her legs over behind the wheel.

Quickly, the Executioner removed his own gun belt and shoulder rig, then stripped off the blacksuit. From one of the black nylon equipment bags, he pulled a folded, light blue dress shirt, a navy blue sport coat and a pair of carefully pressed khaki trousers. From another bag, he produced a pair of soft-soled hiking shoes and a dark blue socks. After buttoning the shirt and tucking it into his pants, he lifted the nylon shoulder rig that bore his sound-suppressed 9 mm Beretta 93-R and slid into it, fastening the retainers at the bottom to his belt. A close-fitting plastic belt holster went onto his hip, and he removed the .44 Magnum Desert Eagle from the web belt he'd worn over the blacksuit and snapped it into place.

Extra magazines for the Beretta, and a TOPS SAW— Special Assault Weapon—knife, in a sheath—hung under his right arm, helping to balance out the weight of the Beretta and sound suppressor. Pouches on his belt carried spare .44 Magnum magazines. He covered all of the weapons with the sport coat, then slid back between the seats as Platinov had done a few moments earlier.

By the time the Executioner had taken the passenger's seat, the Russian woman had guided the Nissan out of the Notre Dame district into a quieter part of town. People still walked up and down the sidewalks, but those sidewalks were lined with hostels, hotels and bed-and-breakfasts.

"Where do you want to stop?" the Russian agent asked.

"One's as good as another as far as I'm concerned. Just find a place to park."

Platinov let a tiny laugh escape her lips as she spotted an open space along the street and pulled up to the side of the car in front of it, preparing to parallel park.

"Did I miss something?" the Executioner asked.

"Only something in my mind," Platinov said as she twisted the wheel and her neck, backing up into the open space before pulling forward again. "I was just thinking about the fact that everywhere else I go, and everyone else I go there with, takes orders from *me*. When I am with you, however, I seem to automatically follow your lead."

When Bolan didn't respond, Platinov added, "I wonder why that is?"

Bolan still remained silent.

"Perhaps it is because we have slept together," Platinov went on as she twisted the key and killed the Nissan's engine. "I do not sleep with every male I work with, you know," she added somewhat defensively as she pulled the key out of the ignition.

"I never thought you did," Bolan replied. "Now, let's get checked in and see what leads we can find in that bag, okay?"

Platinov nodded. "Okay," she said simply and exited the vehicle.

Bolan and Platinov entered the lobby of a hotel directly in front of their car. Letting the straps from their nondescript equipment bags slide onto the hardwood floor as they reached the front desk, Bolan stared at an open door behind the counter. When no one appeared, he tapped a bell on the countertop.

A surly faced, unshaven man wearing a coffee-stained white undershirt and dark trousers appeared in the doorway, then waddled to the counter. The shirt stretched across his immense belly as tight as one of the Executioner's own blacksuits, and the ribbed stitching threatened to burst apart with every bounce brought on by the man's steps. The stub of a cigarette hung from the corner of his mouth, sending wisps of smoke upward into the air. Without bothering to greet them, the man in the filthy undershirt reached beneath the counter, pulled out a registry card and slid it across the slick top.

Bolan registered them as Mr. and Mrs. Josh Murphy, of Enid, Oklahoma.

The unshaven man dropped a key attached to a large wooden stick on the countertop and said simply, "Passports."

Bolan reached into one of the bags and pulled out a pair of the blue booklets. They had been made up for both him and Platinov by experts at Stony Man Farm, the top-secret counterterrorist installation with whom the Executioner sometimes worked.

The man in the dirty clothing glanced at the pictures inside the passports. As the Executioner and Marynka Platinov moved toward the elevator, Bolan noticed him leering at the Russian woman's buttocks as she walked.

Platinov appeared to notice it, too. A slightly disgusted frown spread across her face.

A few minutes later, Bolan unlocked a door beneath

the number 307. Holding it open for Platinov, he looked in to see the sparsely furnished room. A threadbare brown plaid bedspread was stretched tightly across the twin bed, and a chipped wooden table and two chairs set against a wall. Other than that, the room was empty.

"You always take me to the nicest places, Cooper," Platinov said, dropping her bags on the bed.

"Thanks, Plat," he said simply. He dropped his own luggage on the ragged rug on the floor. But immediately, he picked up the canvas bag that contained what they had collected from the corpses at the safe house. Setting it on the table, he took a seat in one of the splintery wooden chairs.

Platinov sat down across from him.

Bolan unzipped the bag, then turned it over, dumping the contents onto the tabletop. Out came a wide variety of objects, from key rings and more hideout guns and knives, to folded papers, receipts, chewing gum wrappers, billfolds, money clips and broken cigarettes. One man had been a cigar smoker, and a leather cigar case carried three medium-sized cigars with Cuban wrappers.

Bolan examined the cigars, careful not to touch the label, which might retain a fingerprint. Rising to his feet, he dropped the cigar and moved to the bed. From one of the black, zippered cases he produced a small fingerprint kit and a package of blank index cards. He returned to his chair.

"Separate everything that might hold a print," he told Platinov. "And get the laptop up and ready."

The Russian woman rose to her feet as Bolan unscrewed the lid off of a small bottle of black fingerprint powder. Setting it down carefully, he did the same with a bottle of white powder.

The dark powder would be used on light-colored objects such as the keys. The white was for the cigars, the smooth leather cigar case and other darker items.

Fifteen minutes later, the tabletop was covered with both white and black powder. But the Executioner had lifted seven full prints and fourteen partials from the items that had been in the terrorists' pockets. Two of the best had come from the cigar case itself.

"Is the computer up and running?" Bolan asked as he pressed the clear plastic tape of the last print onto its index card.

"Ready," Platinov replied. She took the stack of index cards he pushed across the table to her and began to scan them via the mini-scanner plugged into one of the laptop's USB ports.

Pulling his satellite phone from the front breast pocket of his blazer, the Executioner tapped in the number for Stony Man Farm. The call took several seconds to connect, bouncing off numerous satellites and running through various dead-end numbers to throw off anyone who might be trying to tap in to the call.

It was a precaution that everyone associated with Stony Man Farm always took.

Thirty seconds later, though, the Executioner heard Barbara Price's voice on the other end of the call. "Yes, Striker?" she said.

"Tell Bear I'm getting ready to send him seven full fingerprints and fourteen partials," Bolan answered. "I want him to run them through AFIS. But he also needs to hack in to the similar systems in Europe. Especially France."

"Affirmative, Striker," Stony Man Farm's honey-blond mission controller replied. "Send them on."

Bolan shut the phone and dropped it back into his coat pocket, then reached across the table and took the laptop from Platinov. Then, one by one, he called up the files and e-mailed them to Stony Man Farm.

Five minutes later, the laptop beeped and a mechanized voice said, "You have mail."

Bolan tapped the appropriate keys to open the e-mail from Aaron the "Bear" Kurtzman, Stony Man Farm's computer wizard.

When he had read the message, the soldier said, "We've got a hit. It leads to another safe house address." He grabbed a large canvas-and-leather portfolio, which looked little different than a shoulder-carried bag any tourist or French businessman might have. Quickly, he unzipped it and pulled out a long, triangular-shaped canvas case with a zipper that ran three-fourths of the way around.

"What is that?" Platinov asked as he dropped the case into his shoulder bag and turned back to her.

"I could tell you—" he said as they started toward the door again.

"But then you'd have to kill me," Platinov finished the tired, overused cliché as she rolled her eyes.

The Executioner chuckled as he led the way down the hall to the elevators, then pressed the down button.

A minute later, he and Platinov were striding out of the lobby of the hotel and back to the Nissan.

CHAPTER TWO

Bolan kept the Nissan just under the speed limit as he and Platinov made their way toward the next safe house. He had just checked in with Stony Man and learned that what had begun as mere rumors that CLODO was working up toward some kind of large-scale terrorist attack had now been confirmed by two independent CIA informants. And while Bolan wasn't, and never had been, employed by the CIA—or any other government agency for that matter—he *did* retain an "arm's length" relationship with Stony Man Farm. And Aaron Kurtzman, the wheelchair-bound computer genius at the Farm, regularly hacked through all of the Central Intelligence Agency's security safeguards to obtain the intelligence information the "spooks'" field agents collected.

Word in the terrorism underground was that CLODO was building up to something big. Something, according to one of the CIA snitches, that would reputedly make the attacks on September 11, 2001 seem like a Fourth of July fireworks display by comparison.

Bolan knew it was true. He could feel it in his gut. Though not rigged for war, he had adequate weapons for the hit. In addition to his pistols, he had brought along his TOPS SAW knife, which was sheathed at the small of his back. Platinov had slid into the double horizontal shoulder rig that bore her twin Colt Gold Cup .45 pistols. Inside her skirt, she had the other 1911 Colt .45, and several spare mags that would fit any of the three pistols.

After crossing the Seine and traveling some distance, they arrived at a residential area of the city. While there were still lights on in a few of the house windows, the streets were devoid of pedestrians.

Bolan turned onto the Rue de Jeanette as Platinov pulled a small flashlight from her purse and unfolded a map of the city. Frowning in the semidarkness, she asked, "Can you see any of the house numbers?"

Bolan nodded. "There's 1112," he said. The Nissan continued to roll past the next house. "We're at 1116."

Platinov nodded back. "Good," she said. "We're going the right way. It should be about three blocks farther down on the left." She cleared her throat. "Don't you think it's about time you told me the game plan?" She glanced over her shoulder at the Executioner's bag, where the mysterious canvas case was hidden.

Bolan nodded. "Yeah." He indicated the back of the vehicle with a twist of his neck, then said, "Grab the case I stuck in there."

Platinov twisted between the seats and pulled the triangular object out of the Executioner's bag.

"Unzip it," Bolan said as he slowed, then stopped at a stop sign.

The sound the zipper made was loud inside the vehicle, which added to the rising tension as they inched their way down the dark and lonely Parisian street. When Platinov pulled the top cover back to reveal a giant revolver with a scope mounted on top of it, she burst out with, "Are we expecting these CLODOs to be elephants?"

The Executioner chuckled. "No. But by now, word of what we did at the other safe house will have reached this place. They'll be on their guard, so the element of surprise is already lost to us. I think we should take out as many of them as possible from long range."

"Well, this should do it," Platinov said. "What is it? I've never seen one before."

The former Olympic track and field star might never have seen that particular model of Smith & Wesson wheel gun, but she'd seen enough S&Ws to know how they operated. Pushing the latch on the side of the weapon with her thumb, she swung the cylinder away from the mammoth frame.

"It's a 500 Smith and Wesson Magnum," the Executioner said. "Meaning .50-caliber on Smith's new X-frame."

"It's big, all right," Platinov said. "But it holds only five rounds."

Bolan drove on through the intersection as he said, "Imagine how big it would have to be to hold six."

"Point taken," Platinov agreed. "What you have here is a rifle disguised as a pistol."

"Exactly," Bolan agreed as he cruised slowly past the next block. "It was created for long-range silhouette shooting and big game hunting. But it's easier to carry and conceal than a sniper rifle, and for what we're about to do it should be more than accurate enough."

Platinov agreed. "We don't need the pinpoint accuracy of a true sniper rifle from across the street," she said, nodding. "How long is this barrel?"

"Eight inches," Bolan said. "But the last inch, you'll notice, is actually a recoil compensator."

"I expect it still has quite a kick," the Russian agent said, turning the weapon around in her hand to stare at the compensator holes.

"Well, I think you'll know you've fired something. There's factory ammo on the market with bullets up to 500 grains. But since we're after men instead of dinosaurs, I've got it loaded down with 325-grain hollowpoints."

"I suspect I'll still feel quite a jolt," Platinov said.

Bolan laughed. "It doesn't scare you, does it, Plat?"

Platinov looked up from the gun, a quick trace of anger on her face. "Of course not," she said.

One of the many things the Executioner had learned about the beautiful Russian woman over the years was that she couldn't stand her courage, or dedication to an assignment, being questioned. Another was that while her days of Olympic stardom might have ended, she had retained the same competitive mind-set that had won her the gold medals.

Bolan stared ahead but watched Platinov out of the corner of his eye. Almost as quickly as the grimace of anger had appeared, he saw it disappear, leaving her face deadpan. "No, it doesn't scare me," she said again in a voice that betrayed only a slight degree of irritation. "Have *you* shot it yet?"

The Executioner nodded.

Platinov's smile was as plastic as a smile could get. "Then it should be quite easy for me," she said with phony pleasantry.

Bolan let the Nissan roll on as he suppressed a smile. One of the things he liked most about working with Platinov was her competitive nature. He didn't know whether she'd been born with it or had it taught to her as she grew up in one of the Soviet Union's "athletic schools," but she definitely had it now. It made no difference whether she was sprinting or running hurdles in the Olympics, or helping him take down a terrorist cell during a firefight, Marynka Platinov was going to win.

Platinov broke the icy silence by saying, "Okay, that childish little outburst of ego was my fault and I apologize for it. Now—" she paused to draw in a deep breath "—does all this imply that *I'm* the one who's going to be shooting this monstrosity?"

"That's right, Plat," Bolan said. "I'm going to park somewhere down the block, then give you time to find a decent place to snipe from. I'll make my way up next to the house before you start shooting, then hit them up close and personal."

Platinov nodded. "Makes sense. Is that all there is to it?"

"No. Couple of other things." He twisted at the waist and reached into the bag in the backseat. Pulling out a plain brown paper bag, he set it in his lap, opened the top and pulled out a round steel object with .500 Magnum rounds sticking out from it in a circle. "The .500 wasn't designed as a combat weapon," he said. "And nobody makes speed loaders for it. So I had a friend do a little gunsmithing on it. He had to bevel out the holes in the cylinder so the moon-clips would fit. But now you can load all five rounds at the same time."

Platinov frowned, tipped the big pistol up in her hand and caught the 5-round bundle already loaded as it fell out. She nodded as she skillfully stuck it back into the weapon, then took the sack filled with full moon clips from the Executioner. She began transferring the extra ammo from the sack to the side pockets of her jacket.

"There's one other thing," Bolan said as he drove on. "And it's the most important of all."

Platinov waited.

"Once I enter the house, I'll be close to your targets. Don't shoot me by mistake."

Platinov laughed. "If I ever shoot you, Cooper," she said, "it will not be by mistake." Now her smile turned seductive. "Besides, I have other plans for you. And I'll need you alive for them."

Bolan grinned. It seemed there was no getting around the attraction between them. "Then it sounds like I'm safe until then," he said.

"Yes, certainly until then."

Bolan slowed the Nissan as they passed the address Kurtzman had sent them. It was a split-level clay house, at least a century old. Nothing unusual about it. Nothing that made it stand out from any of the other older dwellings up and down these residential streets.

Except for the fact that an oversized picture window was set in the front of what Bolan expected would be the living room. The curtains were tightly closed, but a light glowed brightly behind the draperies.

And unless there was some kind of party going on inside the house, there were far too many vehicles in the driveway, and along the curb, for it to be occupied by just one family.

Bolan circled the block, passed the safe house again, then pulled over to the curb as soon as he found an open space just past the other parked vehicles.

The Russian agent got out of the car, then paused, looking back in. She held the huge S&W 500 in her right hand, and the side pockets of her jacket bulged with the extra moon clips. "I'm going to see if I can get up on top of that house without waking anyone inside," she said, pointing to the darkened structure directly across the street from the safe house. "From there I should have a direct shot into the living room through that front window." She paused a second, then said, "Get that curtain out of my way as soon as you can."

"I've got a better idea," Bolan stated. "Signal me with your flashlight when you're in place and ready."

"I will. But what—"

The Executioner held up a hand to cut her off. "I'll signal you the same way when I reach the corner of the house." He paused a moment, thinking through his strategy once again. "When you see my beam, take out that front window with your first shot. Then wait. I'll be diving through the broken glass and, with any luck, taking the curtains down to the floor with me when I land inside. That should not only get me in, but give you a wide-open view of the inside of the house at the same time."

Platinov quietly closed the car door and headed out.

Bolan turned toward the safe house. Every so often, he glanced to the house across the street, waiting for the flashlight to tell him it was time to go into action.

Five minutes later he saw a light flash on, then off, atop the roof of the house where Platinov had taken up her post. A couple of seconds later, he saw the signal once again.

Show time.

The Executioner got out of the Nissan slowly, closed the door behind him, then sprinted across the street. Seconds later, he was over the curb and up on the grass of the yard next to the safe house. He ducked into the shadows and pressed his back against the wall.

All of Bolan's senses went into high gear as he waited to see if his movement had been noticed by anyone keeping watch over the safe house. It was not unusual for at least one member of a terrorist cell to remain outside to keep watch over the house's exterior. But as he watched, listened and even noted the smells around him, Bolan saw no indication that that was the case here. If there were outside sentries, however, they would already have alerted the terrorists inside the house via cell phone or walkie-talkie that something strange was going on. There was no sense in wasting any more time, either way.

Bolan sprinted from the house next door to the corner of the safe house nearest the picture window. Then, pulling a small flashlight from the side pocket of his blazer, he pointed it across the street and flashed it on and off twice.

A second later, he heard an explosion erupt atop the house across the street, then saw at least three feet of flames burst from the barrel of the big S&W. At the same time the picture window next to him all but disintegrated.

The Executioner wasted no time. Rounding the corner of the safe house, he dived into the curtains, the fingers of both hands grabbing the velvety material as he flew through the air. A screeching sound rent the air as the metal curtain rod above him was pulled from the wall, and then he fell to hardwood floor, entangled in the mass of material and thin steel. The soldier drew the SAW knife with his left hand, the Desert Eagle with his right. It would take far too long to find his way out from inside the curtains, which meant that the only sensible action was to create his own opening.

Bolan rose to his knees. Thrusting the knife tip through the curtain material directly in front of him, he sliced down as far as he could. Then, still holding the knife and the big .44 Magnum pistol, he reached forward and grabbed the sides of the opening, clutching them between his fingers and the two weapons.

Ripping both hands apart, Bolan caught his first glimpse of light since diving through the window. A man wearing a blue beret and brown slacks was bringing a British Sten submachine gun to bear.

Pulling the Desert Eagle's trigger, the Executioner caught the terrorist in the chest, driving him back.

Another mammoth blast came from across the street, covering fire from Platinov, but another enemy gunner fired on Bolan, rounds tearing through the curtain missing his left ear by a millimeter.

He had to get out of these curtains of death, and he had to do it now. Bolan rose from his knees to his feet as first his head, then his shoulders, and finally his legs came up and out of the curtains. Then he stepped away from the tangled material as the real battle began.

The Executioner took in his environment in a heartbeat. Just as he'd guessed, he was in the safe house's living room. He could hear a television almost directly behind him. Against the other three walls were sofas and chairs, and the time it had taken him to untangle himself from the curtains had given the terrorists time to push away from the walls and take cover behind the furniture.

Bolan knew it hadn't been him who had prompted such actions. Had he dived through the window and into the curtains alone, the hardmen inside the living room would have had only to draw their weapons and send a massive hailstorm of gunfire into the disarrayed clump of curtains. It had been Platinov's fire from the roof across the street that had saved his life. The terrorists now taking cover were doing so to avoid the thunderous assault that was coming from somewhere outside of their house.

But now that they could see Bolan, and the giant pistol in his hand, they turned their attention his way.

The Executioner fired another round directly into a stuffed armchair behind which he had seen the top of a balding head. The 240-grain Magnum round easily penetrated the leather cover material and stuffing, then hit the man behind the chair somewhere critical enough to send him sprawling out to the side in instant death.

Return fire suddenly poured from the other men around the room as they recovered from their initial shock. Covered on three sides in the living room, Bolan knew it could only be a matter of seconds before he'd be nailed.

To his side, an archway led from the living room into a dining area. Firing two more quick rounds from the Desert Eagle, Bolan heard the springs inside one of the sofas sing out as the bullets shredded through them and took out another terrorist hiding behind them. The man had just enough life left in him to stand up, but not enough to lift the heavy Thompson submachine gun in his hands before he fell forward over the back of the couch.

As soon as he'd pulled the trigger the second time, Bolan dived toward the archway. He had not yet had time to sheath his knife, so he tucked both the blade and the Desert Eagle flat against his chest. The shoulder roll took him out of the living room into the entryway behind the front door, and he rolled back to his feet at the foot of a staircase that led to the second floor of the house.

The Executioner ducked and pivoted back around as gunfire sailed over his shoulder. The men in the living room had now been forced out from behind the couches and chairs in order to get into a position from which they could attack. And as yet another sonic boom sounded from across the street, Bolan watched one of the men's heads totally disintegrate atop his neck.

Bolan leaped to the third step of the staircase. He had seen no one at the first landing of the split-level home, and could see no one at the top, either. This unconventional tactic provided him with no cover or concealment, but it made the men trying to kill him pause for a few tenths of a second.

Which was more than enough of an edge for the Executioner.

Bolan had finally sheathed his knife, and now he drew the Beretta 93-R. Thumbing the selector switch to 3-round-burst mode, he cut loose with a trio of 9 mm rounds that stitched another CLODO terrorist from navel to neck. The man's eyes widened in disbelief, then he fell forward onto his face, dropping the .357 Magnum Taurus 8-shot revolver he had been about to bring into play.

The Executioner's unorthodox movement had worked

once. So he reversed it, jumping downward, landing on his rubber-soled hiking shoes with the grace of a cat. But the roar that came out of the Desert Eagle was that of a lion as he pressed the big pistol's barrel directly into the chest of a young terrorist, pulverizing his heart.

Bolan ducked back from the archway, climbing up one step again to avoid the torrent of lead that zipped his way. When he leaned back around with the Desert Eagle, he spotted another younger terrorist sprinting toward the window.

The Executioner raised the Beretta to fire, but another loud blast kept him from wasting his ammunition as Platinov sent yet another 325-grain semijacketed hollowpoint into the man's chest.

Bolan watched him hit the floor on his back like a sack of potatoes falling off the back of a truck. The young man had just enough strength left to crane his neck up and look at his ruined chest.

Then he closed his eyes forever.

According to Bolan's count, Platinov had fired all five of the rounds in her weapon. Now, she would have to reload the big X-frame wheel gun and, even with the full moon clips, that would take time.

Time during which he couldn't count on getting any cover fire from her.

Only two CLODO men remained in the living room, and the dining room across the entryway appeared empty. The Executioner pulled the triggers of both pistols at the same time. A .44 Magnum round ended the life of a French terrorist when it drilled through his black T-shirt and into his even blacker heart. At the same time, a left-handed 3-round burst of 9 mm slugs cut through the ragged tweed sport coat of another hardman.

Bolan dropped the nearly spent magazine from the Desert Eagle as he transferred the Beretta from his free hand to his armpit. Jerking another box mag of .44 Magnum rounds from his belt, he jammed it into the butt of the huge Israeli-made pistol.

He had seen the glitter of brass at the top of the ejected magazine as it fell from the Desert Eagle's grips before hitting the floor. He had not been able to keep count during this battle, but the mere fact that at least one round was left in the discarded magazine assured him that another was already chambered in the .44.

No sooner had he reloaded the Desert Eagle than the Executioner's fine-tuned ears heard movement above him, at the top of the staircase to his side. His head jerked that way and he saw yet another terrorist in a blue beret. The man wore the same brown slacks as many of the others. But it looked as if a tie-dyed T-shirt covered his chest—at least at first glance. As he turned toward the threat and got a closer look, the Executioner realized that the man was actually shirtless. His chest and belly had been completely covered with tattoos.

And he was aiming a Mossberg JIC—Just in Case— 12-gauge shotgun down the steps.

The Mossberg—with a stubby eighteen-inch barrel, pistol grip and no stock—came as close to being the perfect close-quarters-combat firearm as any one gun could. But it was as useless as a stalk of dry spaghetti if a bullet took the shotgun's wielder before he could pull the trigger.

Twisting at the waist, Bolan let the Desert Eagle rise, as if on its own accord, to shoulder level. He stopped as soon as the heavy barrel pointed at the nose of the man atop the steps.

The terrorist had obviously trained in the "competition style" of shooting, in which the shooter always tried to superimpose the front sight over the target before squeezing the trigger. There were several drawbacks to that style of shooting when it came to a real gunfight rather than a pistol match at a gun range. First of all, it went completely against human nature, during times of life or death, to focus on anything but the threat itself. The rear, ancient, primordial part of the brain literally screamed at the defender to look at the threat rather than the front sight or anything else.

Trying to find the front sight under such emotional strain was further complicated by the fact that the eyes got the message from the brain as well, and fought against focusing on the end of the gun when it was the target that was about to kill him.

And last, but hardly least, was the theory that the trigger should be gently squeezed rather than pulled. Under such tension, the human body's small motor functions shut down and sent blood and adrenaline flowing to the larger muscle groups to increase strength. A death grip was automatically taken on the gun, and the trigger was pulled, not squeezed, regardless of what the shooter had been capable of doing during practice.

A true life-or-death gun battle was as different from a practice session at a gun range as a karate tournament was from a street fight. And, as he pulled the trigger of the big .44 Magnum pistol, Bolan thought of the moronic firearms instructors he had heard say that the stress of losing a pistol match duplicated the stress of a true fight to the death.

Such range "masters" had obviously never been in a real gunfight themselves. They might have trophies filling their living rooms and dens which they could show off to their friends, but they had never shot at anything that was shooting back at them.

The Executioner's 240-grain, point-aimed, RBCD total fragmentation round drilled through the tattooed man's nose and angled up into his brain before exploding. The now familiar pink mists shot out of the terrorist's head from the front, back and both sides, hanging in the air for a moment like a quartet of crimson clouds. The terrorist dropped the shotgun, which bumped down the stairs, coming to a halt directly in front of the Executioner as if to say, "Use me."

Bolan holstered both the Desert Eagle and Beretta, then reached down and lifted the shotgun in both hands. Racking the slide back far enough to see that a shell had already been chambered, he flipped off the safety with his thumb and stepped to the side to allow the near-headless body of the Mossberg's former bearer to tumble down past him.

Behind him, the Executioner heard the explosion of Platinov's 500 S&W Magnum revolver from across the street again. Good. The Russian woman had successfully reloaded the mammoth handgun and begun sniping again. But all of the men on the ground floor had been eliminated by now, so he had to guess she was taking potshots through the curtained windows of the floors above him. His suspicion was confirmed a second later when he heard the tinkling sound of broken glass above him.

Bolan raised the Mossberg's stumpy barrel up the steps just as another pair of hardmen appeared on the landing, both armed with AK-47s. The man on Bolan's right was right-handed and prepared to shoot that way. The terrorist to the Executioner's left was a southpaw.

Standing side-by-side as they were, they looked almost like mirror images of each other.

Raising the shotgun to shoulder level, Bolan sent a load of double-aught buckshot into the throat of the man on his right. Rivers of crimson shot from the arteries in the man's neck, and his head fell to his right shoulder, still attached to his body but only by the few tendons and ligaments.

The man to the Executioner's left screamed out loud as his partner's blood sprayed his face. Panicking, he pulled the trigger of his Soviet-made assault rifle and sent a fully automatic burst of 7.62 mm rounds flying high over Bolan's head.

The big American took his time, steadying the shotgun, his eyes planted firmly on the blood-covered terrorist's chest—just an inch to the right of center. A second later, he pulled the trigger and the 12-gauge buckshot spread into a tight, inch-and-a-half grouping as the lead balls struck home.

Both corpses fell headfirst down the steps past the Executioner to join their fellow terrorist at the foot of the steps.

Bolan racked the slide of the Mossberg to chamber another round. So far, he had fired two of the double-aught shells. The magazine held only five, so he had either three or four rounds left in the weapon, depending on whether the man who had introduced the shotgun into the fight had topped off the magazine after chambering the first round.

At this point, the Executioner had no way of knowing. What he did know was that he'd have to be ready to drop the scattergun and draw one or both of his pistols at a second's notice.

The firing from across the street had ceased, which meant Platinov had come down off her perch to join him in the ongoing battle. Between the roars of the firearms, Bolan had heard enough noise above him to know there were more terrorists upstairs, on the second level and maybe even the third.

One thing was for certain. The fight wasn't over yet. Not by a long shot.

CHAPTER THREE

The smell of spent gunpowder burned the Executioner's nostrils as he mounted the steps of the CLODO house, grasping the grip and fore end of the Mossberg JIC. He kept the barrel aimed slightly upward, roughly at waist level, ready to raise or lower his aim with lightning speed should an enemy face or body appear in the doorway or the window next to it. By the time he was a quarter of the way up the steps to the house's second level, he could see half of the next set of stairs that led to the third, and top, tier of the dwelling.

The rooms on the second landing were all to his right. At the top step the Executioner dropped to one knee and inched an eye around the corner. The layout was simple. A bedroom stood just to his right. Another, next to it, faced him. And across the hall, he could see a bathroom.

The doors to all three rooms were wide open, which didn't necessarily mean they were empty.

The Executioner knew there were plenty of hiding places. He would have to search them all, and any hidden enemies would see him long before he saw them. They might even get off a round or two before he pinpointed their location.

Switching the shotgun's pistol grip to his left hand, Bolan rose to his feet and stepped around the corner. Slowly, and as silently as the aged wood allowed, he pressed his back along the hallway wall and moved to the first bedroom. When he reached the open door, he halted, waiting, listening, trying to hear anything that might give away the presence of anyone inside the bedroom.

For a moment, the Executioner's thoughts drifted to Plat. Where was she? It had been several minutes since he'd last heard the roar of the 500 S&W Magnum, which meant she'd had plenty of time to scramble down off the roof and join him inside the house. Yet he had seen no trace of her. And there was another possibility.

There might have been one or more hidden outside sentries whom they both had missed. If that was the case, Platinov would have been mere child's play to locate when she fired the gargantuan S&W. One or more of the terrorists could easily have slipped up onto the roof behind her and taken her out while her attention was on the house across the street.

As far as he could tell, there had been no small-caliber shots fired from across the street—just the Magnum booms of the .50-caliber revolver. But there could be many explanations for his not hearing more gunfire, and the Executioner forced those thoughts, too, away from his mind. Platinov was either alive or dead. But either way, there was nothing he could do to assist her at this point, and worrying about her would do nothing but distract him from what he had to do himself.

Still holding the Mossberg left-handed, Bolan suddenly stepped into the doorway. A brief glance into the bedroom revealed a man wearing a blue beret. The terrorist made no attempt whatsoever to hide. He sat confidently, his lips almost smiling, with his back against the head of the bed.

Bolan pivoted away from the threshold, recognized the weapon propped between the man's legs, and aimed at the doorway. The Browning .50-caliber machinegun was identifiable by the spade handle grips, plain-sided receiver, canvas cartridge feed belt and the open top of the ammunition box on the tripod upon which the giant rifle rested.

He also IDed the rifle by the deafening roar it made as the .50-caliber rounds—longer, and even more penetrative than the 500 S&W Platinov had been using—shot through the open door and then moved to the wall as he hit the wooden floor on his belly.

White dust and chunks of plaster rained on the Executioner's head as the big .50-caliber slugs tore the wall to shreds above him. The gunner inside the bedroom kept up a steady stream of fire, shooting blindly, obviously counting on the probability that at least one of his stray rounds would find the Executioner.

What he didn't consider was that the giant holes he was making in the wall could work both ways.

Bolan rolled onto his side, placing the JIC on the floor next to him and jerking the Desert Eagle from his hip holster. So far, the machine gunner had fired all his rounds at waist level or above. But the Executioner knew it would be a matter of seconds before he began shooting lower—assuming that if the man he'd seen in the hallway was still alive, he would have taken to the ground.

Bolan wasn't wrong.

A few seconds later, the giant chunks of plaster began to blow out holes closer to the floor. Bolan waited, breathing in through his nose, then out through his mouth, in order to remain calm and collected for the task he knew he had to perform.

Finally, a giant, ragged hole appeared in the wall three inches above the Executioner's line of sight. Exhaling another deep breath, he peered through the new opening.

In an instant, Bolan saw that while the hole was large enough to see through, or shoot through, it wasn't big enough to do both. The big frame of the Desert Eagle would block any view he tried to take as soon as he stuck the barrel through the opening. So, frowning as his brain took a mental "photograph" of the exact angle of trajectory from the hole to the chest of the man on the bed, Bolan dropped low again, raised the .44 Magnum pistol above his head and stuck the barrel through the opening. The angle was awkward, and required him to twist his wrist and put his thumb on the trigger instead of his index finger. But the Executioner was used to improvising, and as the random .50-caliber blasts to the wall continued, he used the picture he had taken in his head to angle the .44 at the man on the bed.

A second later, the Executioner pulled the trigger with his thumb.

And a second after that, the machine-gun blasts from inside the bedroom halted.

Bolan withdrew the Desert Eagle, holstered it and picked up the short-barreled shotgun once more. Rising to look into the same hole through which he'd just shot, he saw that his blind aim had been slightly high.

The .44 Magnum round had taken the terrorist in the throat rather than the chest.

Not that it mattered. The man had already bled out and was staring lifelessly at the wall he had all but demolished.

The roar in his ears had barely died down when the Executioner heard the creak of wood behind him. During the duel with the Browning, he had been forced to concentrate his efforts there and turn his back to the rest of the second level of the split-level safe house. But now, he rolled over so he could view both the other bedroom and bathroom.

And he did so none too soon.

Obviously assuming that their comrade would end the threat with his Browning, two men in the second, smaller bedroom had stayed out of sight. But they were not amateurs, and had been well-trained in one of the many terrorist "boot camps" operating throughout the world. Now that the firing had ceased, and the last roar they'd heard had come from a pistol, they could tell that the fight had not gone their way. And now they both stepped into view through the doorway, holding Barrett M-468 assault rifles.

Looking somewhat like the standard M-16 series, the M-468s were chambered for the newer, more powerful, .270-caliber cartridge. But as Bolan had already proved several times during this encounter, calibers didn't fight calibers.

Men fought men.

It didn't matter a bit that the two terrorists held the latest technology in small-arms warfare after the Executioner had ended both of their lives with a pair of old-fashioned 12-gauge shotgun shells.

The Mossberg JIC either had one round left in it or none. But either way, the Executioner decided it could no longer serve as his primary weapon. Letting the short-barreled shotgun fall to the floor, he drew the Desert Eagle with his right hand, the Beretta 93-R with his left. Pushing the big .44's safety lever forward with his thumb, he moved the smaller 93-R's selector switch to 3-round-burst mode.

Bolan moved cautiously toward the staircase that led to the top level of the house. Below him, on the first floor at the rear of the house, he heard more pistol fire—what sounded like 9 mm and .45s. His guess was that Platinov had now abandoned the huge 500 S&W Magnum gun and circled the house, coming in some back entrance with her top-of-the-line .45-caliber Colt Gold Cups. Whoever she was shooting it out with down there had to be welding the 9 mms.

When he reached the corner, the Executioner inched an eye around the barrier, the Beretta in his left hand hanging at the end of his arm in front of him, ready to rise and fire if he saw any sign of the enemy. He didn't, and another step around the corner found him slowly, and cautiously climbing the final flight of stairs.

A thin, well-worn carpet ran down the middle of the stairs, leaving a foot or so of exposed wood on either side of each step. Bolan stayed on the carpet, both pistols in front of him, ready to send a .44 Magnum RBCD total-fragmentation round or a 3-round burst of the same "exploding" bullets in 9 mm, up the stairwell. The carpet muffled the sounds of his hiking shoes. But the ancient wood still creaked with every step.

Bolan knew there were more CLODO terrorists upstairs, and they knew he was on the way.

Just before he reached the top step, the Executioner stopped and dropped to his knees, leaning forward to peer around yet another corner. He could see roughly half of the room, and it looked like it had been set up as a young boy's bedroom by the previous owners. Posters of rock bands and rap groups covered the walls, European, American and Japanese. He could also see two half doors against the far wall that reached from the floor to the point where the ceiling sloped downward.

Closets, the Executioner realized, with latch locks to keep the doors closed.

But although the doors were both closed, the latches hung straight down, unlocked. It didn't take a genius to assume that if there were terrorists on this floor of the house, they'd be inside the closets.

The Executioner straightened and took the last step to the landing just outside the top bedroom. He peered around the last corner, surveying the other half of the room. It appeared devoid of human beings, but the front wall of the room contained one more of the odd, slanting closets

Bolan stepped into the room. The floor was bare wood, and he took advantage of the soft rubber soles of his hiking shoes to make the least amount of noise possible as he moved to the closet to his right. A large window looked out over the backyard next to the unlatched door, and he glanced that way for a second.

The light had been on in the upstairs bedroom when he'd arrived, adding to his suspicions that the room was occupied. That meant that his vision out of the window into the backyard was limited, while anyone behind the house could see him clearly.

But no one fired at him, which told the Executioner that Platinov had taken out any of the terrorists who might have been in the backyard.

Holstering the Desert Eagle, Bolan transferred the Beretta 93-R to his right hand and stepped just to the side of the closet door. The way the roof angled downward, he was forced to stoop slightly and bend his knees. From this uncomfortable, semibalanced position, he reached out with his left hand, grasped the door latch and swung the door open.

A second after that, a hailstorm of gunfire blew out of the opening just to his side. Bolan waited for the blasts to die down. Then, during the lightning-fast millisecond when the shooters wondered why they saw no dead body in front of them, he curved his arm around the corner into the short closet, blindly spraying four 3-round bursts up, down and to both sides.

With only four rounds left in the Beretta, Bolan dropped the magazine and inserted a fresh 15-round box. Inside the closet, he could hear a soft moaning and the deep intakes of breath. He kept the Beretta close to his shoulder as, still stooped, he leaned around the doorway and angled the pistol inside the tiny room.

Lying on the floor were four CLODO terrorists. Three wore the tan shirts and brown trousers that the group used for identification purposes. The fourth was dressed in blue jeans and a T-shirt that bore the likeness of the American comedian Jerry Lewis.

Two of the men, both wearing these unofficial CLODO uniforms, lay on the floor, obviously dead. They were as still as rocks, having taken the frangible 9 mm rounds in their heads. The third man in brown and tan lay across them. It was he who was doing the moaning as he clutched his lower abdomen with both hands.

A 3-round burst into the man mercifully ended his moaning.

Shotguns, pistols and rifles were scattered across the floor and on top of the bodies.

Bolan knew that the men in the other two closets had to have heard the gunfire. So as he backed out of the room, trading the Beretta in his right hand for the Desert Eagle. This time, he moved in front of the door of the second closet but fired an entire magazine of Magnum rounds through the splintery wood before reloading and holstering the big .44, all the while keeping the door covered by the Beretta.

The wood of the door was now splintered and warped, so rather than open it, the Executioner lifted a foot and kicked. Sharp pieces of wood flew into the closet ahead of him as the door disintegrated. Forced to bend his knees and stoop again, Bolan stepped forward and surveyed the contents of the closet. Only two of the terrorists had chosen this tiny room in which to take refuge, and both lay dead on the ground.

There was no reason to waste any more time, or ammo, here.

The Executioner turned toward the third closet, which was set into the wall facing the front of the house. He still hadn't checked under the bed but now he saw an arm reach out from beneath the bedspread holding a 9 mm SiG-Sauer.

Bolan aimed at the weapon and shot it out of the hand holding it. The gunner beneath the bed screamed in pain and jerked his arm back beneath the bed. The soldier dropped to the floor, facing the bed. Beneath the box spring, he could see the man with the bloody hand as well as two more of the CLODO terrorists. He wasn't surprised.

But having their attacker drop down into firing range shocked the men under the bed, which caused them to hesitate.

And hesitation cost them their lives.

Bolan peppered the underside of the bed with 3-round bursts as the men tried to bring their weapons into target acquisition. It was a losing battle for them, and a second later they, too, lay dead in an ever-spreading pool of mixed blood.

The only place left that could have hidden a CLODO man was the final closet. The Executioner bounded back to his feet and squinted at the door. Its latch was down, too.

The roof in the front wall of the house was higher, so this door and closet were not as slanted as the other two had been. The Executioner moved swiftly now, speed having taken precedence over stealth.

This time, he didn't have to open the door himself. It flew forward on its own, and a terrorist stepped out, aiming a 12-gauge Remington autoloading shotgun at the Executioner.

Bolan dived to the floor, as a heavy load of buckshot sailed over his head, missing him by millimeters. He twisted on the slick hardwood floor, then slid to the foot of the bed and turned onto his shoulder, the Desert Eagle aimed upward.

A moment later, two .44 Magnum rounds had destroyed the intestines and heart of the man with the Remington. He fell backward as the Executioner sprang to his feet again, ready to take out the next terrorist who came out of the closet.

But there were no more.

As the roar of the gunfire faded and the smell of cordite settled into his nostrils, Bolan heard footsteps on the stairs just outside the bedroom. A moment later, they stopped and a heavily Russian-accented voice said, "Don't shoot, Cooper. It's me." Without waiting for an answer, Marynka Platinov stepped into the room. She had discarded the jacket that, along with the matching skirt, formed her suit. Both of her Colt Gold Cup pistols hung at the end of her arms, aimed at the floor.

The enormous Smith & Wesson 500 was tucked into her waistband along with her third .45.

The Russian quickly took in the dead men in the room, then turned to the Executioner. "You leave a trail of bodies that make finding you as easy as following bread crumbs," she said, referring to the old fairy tale.

"Yeah," Bolan said. "But how could you be sure it was me still alive up here?" Bolan asked her.

Platinov chuckled. "I have worked with you several times now, Cooper," she said, "and you always seem to come out on top."

Before Bolan could reply, the sound of distant but rapidly approaching police sirens broke the stillness on the top floor of the split-level house.

"We'd better search these guys for leads, and do it fast," the Executioner said.

"Yes," Platinov agreed.

The Executioner dropped to his knees and began going through the pockets of the last CLODO man he had killed. He pulled a wallet and a key ring out as he said, "How'd you like the 500 Magnum?"

Platinov tapped the Pachmayer grip covering the butt of the colossal revolver, which still stuck up out of the waistband of her skirt. "I'm keeping it," she said. "You'll have to get another one." Then she sank to her knees and began helping Bolan with the search.

THE NISSAN PASSED several approaching police vehicles as Bolan and Platinov made a slow-speed, nondescript getaway from the split-level safe house. Just as they'd done before, they had hurriedly gathered all items of interest from the men's pockets into a pair of sturdy canvas equipment bags and pulled away from the curb only seconds before the first flashing lights had appeared.

The French police would be operating off of the vague information given to them by their dispatcher, which would have originated from the telephone call of one of the neighbors. At this point, it would be thought of no differently than any of a half-dozen "disturbance" calls that they'd probably already worked that evening.

So as Bolan and Platinov looked at the two gendarmes, and the gendarmes returned the look as the vehicles passed each other, no one was stopped, questioned, or searched. Instead, all four heads within the vehicles nodded polite "hellos."

The two drove on in silence as they headed back toward their hotel to go over the contents in the bags. Something had been bothering the Executioner ever since the first gunfight at the other house, and that concern had grown while they'd filled the bags with possible evidence. Now, as he turned onto Rue de La Foyette, what was bothering his unconscious finally surfaced in his mind.

It was not anything that he and Marynka Platinov had found at the two CLODO safe houses that bothered him. It was what they hadn't found.

Platinov had evidently been thinking along the same lines because as they neared the hotel, she said, "Correct me if I am wrong, but the last time CLODO did anything big—I mean really big—was when they bombed the Phillips Data Plant way back in the 1980s, right?"

"Right," Bolan said, pulling the Nissan into the hotel's parking lot.

"And since Rouillan revived them a year or so ago, everything they have done has involved explosives of one kind or another. Correct?"

Bolan could tell she was headed in the same direction he'd been thinking. "Or guns," the Executioner said. "Bombings and random machine-gunnings at train stations and other public places are pretty much their trademark."

"Then why haven't we found any bomb-making supplies at either of the safe houses we've hit?" Platinov asked bluntly. "Or weapons? Oh, we've found these men's personal weapons. But we haven't found either stores of arms and ammunition or the ingredients it takes to make bombs."

Bolan nodded. "You're right," he said. "All we've come across are personal arms. The biggest and 'baddest' thing so far was that lone Browning on the second level back there." He hooked a thumb over his shoulder. "Where are they storing their other rifles, hoarded ammunition, and everything else along that line if not at the safe houses? If CLODO's really back in business, and going to war with the computer companies and everyone who uses computers, what are they planning to destroy everything with? Sledgehammers?"

The last suggestion had been meant to be sarcastic and Platinov took it as such. "That is bothering me, too," she said. "Do you believe it is likely that their other weapons and explosive materials are hidden at some other location we haven't come across yet?"

"That's one possibility."

For a moment, silence reigned over the Nissan again. Bolan parked the car, they got out, and he opened one of the rear doors. Then Platinov said, "Your tone of voice indicated that you believe there are other possibilities." She opened the back door on her side of the vehicle.

"There are," Bolan answered as they each pulled out one of the canvas bags and started toward the main entrance of the hotel. "But let me mull them around a little longer before I tell you about them," he said. "I'm not all that straight with it myself, yet."

Platinov had slipped back into her suit jacket to cover her double shoulder rig and now she shrugged. "Okay."

Bolan shook his head at the bellmen when they

hurried down the steps to help them with their bags. A moment later, Bolan and Platinov were picking up their key at the front desk, then boarding the elevator toward the third floor.

Once in the room, Bolan took a look at his watch. It was nearly 0200 hours in Paris, which would mean it was around 9:00 p.m. back home in the eastern States. Pulling his satellite phone from the inside pocket of his jacket, Bolan dialed the number to the Farm.

Barbara Price, mission controller at Stony Man Farm, answered. "Hello, Striker," she said, using his mission code name. "What do you need?"

"Nothing at the moment." He gave her a quick rundown of what had happened since their last conversation, then said, "I'll probably be calling you back with more after we go through these bags." He glanced at the two canvas bags that contained all of the evidence they'd taken from the safe house. "In the meantime, pass what I've just told you on to the Bear and see if he can make use of any of the information. He not only speaks, he *thinks* in computerese, so he may come up with some way to use some of this intel that would never cross the rest of our minds."

"Will do, Striker," Price said. "May I assume that you're still working with Agent Platinov?"

There had been no trace of jealousy in Price's voice. And no one who had heard the question would even notice that a tiny amount of resentment had even been in the question. But Bolan knew Barbara Price better than anyone else in the world, and he had picked up on it.

Barbara Price was a world-class beauty in her own right. And while both she and the Executioner were far too professional to allow their mutual attraction to interfere with the Farm's operations, on the rare nights when he was able to stay over at Stony Man, Price had his undivided attention.

Finally Bolan said, "It's still a joint op between us and Russia, but I'll be the one who calls you."

"Affirmative," Price said. "Stony Man out, then."

"Striker clear," the Executioner said before tapping the "call kill" button. He looked across the bed to where Platinov sat cross-legged. She had already kicked off her shoes and dumped the contents of the canvas bags onto the bed in front of her. In her hands, she squinted at a scrap of paper that looked to have been folded and unfolded dozens of time.

Bolan joined her, and they came across the usual things found in men's pockets—billfolds, keys, a few French Lagouille pocketknives. Hideout weapons such as fixed blade knives in ankle holsters, and one tiny .22 short North American Arms minirevolver. Some of the terrorists had carried several sets of IDs in different names—passports, driver's licenses and other picture identification cards. When he had finished inspecting everything in his bag, Bolan frowned. There was a lot of stuff here. But as far as he could tell, none of it would lead them on down the trail toward Rouillan, his revived terrorist organization, or their upcoming big strike that was rumored to soon take place.

As he had searched the contents of the canvas bag,

the Executioner had seen Platinov out of the corner of eye as she dug through her own pile of personal effects. But when he looked up now, he saw that the woman was again holding the same folded, then unfolded, scrap of paper he'd seen her looking at earlier.

"Got something?" he asked.

"I don't know," Platinov said. "Maybe, maybe not."

"Let's see," the Executioner said.

Platinov had moved up on the bed to rest her back against the wall and sat cross-legged, looking as if she might break out in some yoga mantra at any moment. But the posture had caused her skirt to ride up.

Forcing his eyes down to the scrap of paper, Bolan studied it. It looked to have come from a yellow legal pad and had been torn off rather than cut. It read: Chartres—Achille LeForce, 4:00 p.m. At the bottom of the scrap of paper was a date.

That very day.

Bolan looked up at Platinov. "Whatever it is, it takes place this afternoon," he said.

"LeForce is a common French name," Platinov said. "So is Achille, for that matter. And Chartres is a village in the province of Touraine. It's southwest of here."

Bolan stood up, walked swiftly to a leather briefcase on top of the other equipment bags they had dropped in the corner of the room and brought it back to the bed before opening it. Pulling out a manila file envelope, he shuffled through the papers contained inside.

"What are you looking for?" Platinov wanted to know.

Bolan held up one hand to silence her as he continued to sort through the intel reports. A moment later, a hard smile curled the corners of his lips.

"What is it?" Platinov demanded again.

"We had limited time to go over this file during the flight to Paris," he said. "But one little detail—a detail that seemed insignificant at the time—evidently stuck in my head."

"What's that?" Platinov asked.

"Chartres is Rouillan's home town. He was born and grew up there."

"Then it is likely he might pick Chartres for whatever that scrap of paper indicates," Platinov said. "He would be familiar with the area. And know all of the possible escape routes if something went wrong."

Bolan nodded. He knew the area, too, from past missions. Several roads led in, and out, of the small French village that was famous for the Cathedral of Our Lady of Chartres. This structure ranked right alongside Notre Dame as an example of the greatest Gothic architecture in the world. The cathedral was particularly noted for its lavish stained-glass windows. "That's the 'up' side of things," he said almost under his breath.

But Platinov's hearing was acute. "What is the 'down' side you are insinuating with that remark?" she asked.

"Everyone in Chartres will know him," Bolan said, replacing the file in the briefcase and closing the latches. "And some will be his friends."

When Bolan hadn't spoken again for several seconds, Platinov finally said, "So…do we go there or not?" She uncrossed her legs but made no effort to pull down her skirt.

Slowly, Bolan nodded. "We go there," he said. Staring straight ahead at the wall, he added, "We don't have much to go on and the odds are stacked highly against us. Chartres isn't very big. But it's big enough that we'll have to find some way of locating Rouillan once we're there. And as soon as we start asking questions, word will be out all over town that we're looking for him." He stuffed the paper into the side pocket of his jacket. "But, the way I see it, it's all we have at this point."

Bolan turned to face Platinov now, and saw the same "come hither" smile on her face that he'd seen so many times before. The beautiful Russian woman's skirt was still hiked up almost to her waist, and the muscles in her Olympic sprinter's legs all but rippled through her transparent hosiery.

"Whatever this note means," Platinov purred seductively. "It will not take place until four in the afternoon. We have nearly twelve hours, and Chartres is only a short drive from here." She cleared her throat with a husky sound. "I wonder how we could pass the time between now and then?"

Bolan stared at her. He was only human, and he and Marynka Platinov had been attracted to each other like magnets since the first time they'd met. For a moment, he was tempted to take the Russian woman up on what was a blatant offer of pleasure.

But then the warrior in the Executioner's soul took charge of him again.

Bolan stood up next to the bed. "I think the best way to spend that time is to get to Chartres and start snooping around. We need to find out what's supposed to happen at four o'clock and where it's supposed to go down." He cleared his throat and glanced at his watch. "We may not have enough time already."

Platinov's smile turned to a slight frown and then a sigh escaped her lips. "You are hard on a woman's ego, Cooper," she said as she stood up, lowered her skirt, then smoothed it out again by running the palms of her hands up and down her thighs.

Bolan laughed softly. "Don't take it as a rejection," he said. "It's just that finding Rouillan has got to come first."

Platinov had taken off her jacket but left the shoulder rig carrying her twin Gold Cup pistols in place. Now, she lifted her Model 1911 from the nightstand where she'd set it earlier, and returned it—along with the inside-the-waistband holster—to the rear of her skirt.

Bolan watched her run her fingers around the waistband, making sure that the Spyderco Military Model folding knife was clipped in place. As she slid her arms into the suit jacket, she said, "Business before pleasure, I believe is the way that you Americans put it."

The Executioner nodded.

"Then let's go," the Russian woman said. One at a time, she pulled out all three of her .45s, checked to make sure a round was in each of the chambers, then returned them to their hiding place. Bolan did the same with the Desert Eagle and Beretta.

The Executioner made one final check at the small of his back. The TOPS Special Assault Weapon, or SAW as it was more commonly called, was clipped in place in its sheath.

They were ready. A moment later they were out of the door.

And a moment after that, they were on their way to Chartres.

CHAPTER FOUR

It was just as the Executioner had feared it would be as he guided the Nissan down Chartre's main street. As he and Platinov passed, everyone on both sides of the street looked up to take note of them.

They were strangers. And just as it was in small towns all over the world, strangers were duly noted by the locals, which meant that he and Platinov stood out.

Mentally, Bolan shrugged. There was no sense worrying about it because there was nothing he could do to change that fact. All he could hope for was that they could pass themselves off as tourists. The problem with that was the majority of such visitors arrived on tour buses or by train. Driving a car put them in a whole new minority of what was already a minority.

Bolan lifted his satellite phone from his lap and tapped in the number to Stony Man Farm. When Barbara Price answered with, "Yes, Striker?" he said simply, "Put the Bear on."

A moment later, the call had been transferred to Aaron Kurtzman in the Computer Room. "What can I do for you, big guy?" the computer wizard asked.

"You can hack your way into the French police files," Bolan said. "I need anything you can get on Achille LeForce from Chartres."

"Easy enough," Kurtzman said. "Hang on. I'll put you on the speakerphone while I search."

A moment later, Bolan heard a click. Then the tapping of fingertips on a computer keyboard. Thirty seconds later, Kurtzman was back. "Found him," he said.

"Never dreamed you wouldn't."

"Achille LeForce," Kurtzman said. "Five feet ten inches tall, two hundred and forty pounds. Brown curly hair, and a scar on the left side of his forehead. Quick summary—small-time criminal. Arrests for burglary, drug dealing, firearms and parole violations. Never served more than three months on any of them." The wheelchair-bound computer genius paused to take a breath. "But the part that'll interest you is his known associates. Any idea who tops the list?"

"Pierre Rouillan."

"Well, if you smoked cigars I'd buy you an Arturo Fuente Gran Reserva," Kurtzman said.

Bolan chuckled. "Give it to Hal," he said, referring to Stony Man Farm's director, who usually had a stubble of cigar in his mouth.

"He'd just chew it up," Kurtzman said. "That's about it on LeForce. Anything else I can get for you?"

"You find an address for him?" the Executioner asked.

"Got more than two dozen," Kurtzman replied. "Most current is six months ago. You know how it is— small-time crooks are the same the world over. They never stay in one place very long."

"I hear you, Bear." Bolan had known that a current address was improbable but it had been worth a try. "Talk to you later." He hung up.

As they had driven down the street, both Bolan and Platinov had looked at the faces they passed. Men, women and children glanced up, frowned slightly, then returned to whatever they'd been doing before. The frowns told the Executioner that these citizens were noting that something was different about the two people in the Nissan. They didn't know exactly what. But they knew.

Bolan knew it was going to get worse. As soon as he and Platinov started asking about Rouillan, they'd be branded as police, or intelligence officers, or some other branch of the French or another government looking for the newly infamous terrorist. Word of their inquiries would spread like wildfire and reach Rouillan's ears if he was anywhere near Chartres.

They were already running against the clock. If Rouillan heard about them, he'd be gone quicker than a flash of lightning.

Platinov stared out of her side window, doing her best to look like a rubber-necking sightseer. They had stopped at Versailles to gas up the automobile, and the

Executioner had decided at the last minute that a change of clothing was appropriate. So, within the confines of the gas station's unisex rest room, he had traded his blue blazer and slacks for a baggy green T-shirt and khaki cargo shorts. With his broad shoulders and narrow waist, he was able to leave the Desert Eagle in the close-fitting holster and jam the sound-suppressed Beretta into his waistband on his other side. The TOPS knife stayed at the small of his back, and he filled the cargo pockets of his shorts with extra magazines for both pistols. The low-cut hiking shoes he'd worn with the blazer and slacks worked just fine with his "new look" as well.

Drawing his pistols and reloading would be slower than if he'd worn the weapons openly, but for their visit to Chartres, blending in as much as they could with the scenery took a much higher priority than speed.

His mission, at this point, was to gather intelligence on Rouillan. He wasn't expecting to run into a gunfight.

But he was ready if one came running at him.

Bolan turned a corner off the main downtown street. As he began looking for a place to park, the Executioner glanced again at Marynka Platinov. The Russian beauty drew attention no matter where she was, or how she was dressed. He had done his best to keep his eyes to himself while they'd changed clothes back at the gas station. But he couldn't avoid an occasional glimpse of her naked breasts after she'd shed the suit jacket, white blouse and bra, and replaced it with a blue short-sleeved sweatshirt that read Sorbonne and featured the world-famous

French university's logo. The sweatshirt had been cut off just below her breasts, and what was left of the tail now hung straight down at least three inches from her bare midriff. Platinov, too, now wore khaki cargo shorts. But unlike the Executioner's, which extended almost to his knees, the Russian woman's shorts barely covered her posterior. Her hosiery had gone back into a suitcase, and white Puma athletic shoes were tied at the end of her shapely, well-muscled legs. Platinov had threaded a leather belt through the belt loops of her shorts, but the cut-down sweatshirt barely hid her breasts, let alone any weapons. So she had been forced to put her matching Gold Cup .45s and the extra 1911 pistol into a canvas bag. It would be slung over her shoulder, and she could even keep her hand out of sight inside the bag, holding one of the guns, if they sensed danger.

The Executioner turned another corner onto a side street, still looking for a place to leave the car. He knew there were other items in Platinov's bag as well. He'd watched her drop both Russian-French and English-French language dictionaries in to cover weapons from sight should anyone get close enough to look directly down into the bag. He wondered for a moment what they were for. He had heard Platinov speak French on numerous occasions, and her command of the language was impeccable.

The Executioner's thoughts were suddenly interrupted when he spotted an empty parking spot along the side street. Pulling up next to the car in front of it, he backed in to parallel park, then turned to Platinov as he twisted the key to kill the engine. "You ready?" he asked.

"Aside from feeling like a complete fool in this ridiculous American-tourist-geek getup, you mean?" she answered. "I feel like I should be wearing mouse ears at Disney World."

Bolan grinned. "Yeah. Besides that. Any ideas where to start?"

Platinov turned to him and frowned. "We know that something is supposed to take place here at 1600. And we know—or at least think we know—that it involves Rouillan's friend Achille LeForce. And we hope it involves Rouillan."

The Executioner nodded. "The trail's thin, I admit," he said. "But it's all we've got. We don't know whose pocket that scrap of paper came out of before we found it, and it probably wouldn't do us any good if we did. Maybe one of the dead men back at the house was supposed to meet Rouillan and LeForce here. It could be that LeForce is bringing in that cache of weapons or bomb-making materials we speculated about earlier. Or he might have cocaine, or heroin, or ice or crack or any of a number of other drugs, the profit from which Rouillan uses to finance CLODO. Or there could be a bomb set somewhere in town that'll detonate at 1600 hours. The possibilities are endless."

Platinov nodded. Twisting in her seat, she reached behind her and grabbed the leather briefcase Bolan had opened back in their room and set it in her lap. Flipping the latches, she opened the file on Rouillan and began

shuffling through the pages. Finally, she pulled out a
photo of Rouillan. In it, the French terrorist was talking
to another man. The picture had obviously been taken
with the aid of a long-range, telescopic lens. But it
showed Rouillan's face and the other man's quite
clearly.

Bolan's brow furrowed. "You think that's LeForce
with Rouillan?" he asked. He had seen the picture
before when they'd traded Russian and American files
during the flight from Washington. But as far as he
could tell, the other man in the picture remained unidentified.

"I don't know who it is," Platinov said. "We were
never able to ID him. But now, along with what your
'Bear' just told us, it's my guess that this other man is
LeForce."

"It could be," Bolan said, squinting slightly at the
photo. All that could be seen of both men were their
heads. But the unidentified man's curly brown hair and
thick, muscular neck fit Kurtzman's description. "Drop
it in your bag and let's get going. Unless I miss my
guess, these French 'home boys' are going to have
strong feelings about a guy like Rouillan. They'll either
love him or hate him. But there won't be any in
between."

Platinov nodded, dropped the photograph into her
canvas bag along with her third .45 and the other items,
then twisted again and returned the briefcase to the
backseat. The Executioner got out of the driver's side
and pressed the button on his key chain to lock the

doors. Now, he noticed that they had parked directly in front of a small boutique that appeared to sell Christian-related souvenirs.

The soldier looked at his watch. It was almost one o'clock. They had only three hours to find out what the scrap of paper referred to and stop it.

And with luck, kill Pierre Rouillan and his sidekick LeForce during the process.

This Christian souvenir store in front of them was as good a place to begin their search as any other. And Bolan doubted that the proprietors—assuming that they were Christians themselves—were less likely than the average man or woman to lie and shield a terrorist. He glanced at Platinov. Her face told him similar thoughts were going through her head.

Bolan walked to the shop's glass front door and pulled it open, letting Platinov walk in first just like any other gentleman tourist would have done. But the threshold was where their covers would have to end. He was going to have to ask if the shopkeepers knew Achille LeForce or Pierre Rouillan, using both men's names. And he might also have to show them the picture.

At that point, there would be no turning back to their "pretend tourists" roles.

The shop was filled with crucifixes of all sizes, statues and wooden carvings of saints, particularly Our Lady of Chartres, medallions and similar items. At the back of the small room the Executioner saw an older man standing behind a counter. Directly behind him, mounted on the wall, was a life-sized crucifix carved out of what looked like cedar.

The little man had a fringe of white hair above his ears and on the back of his head. He smiled pleasantly as Bolan and Platinov walked toward him.

"You take the lead on this one," Bolan whispered to Platinov as they walked down an aisle toward the counter.

The Russian agent nodded. She knew that the old man was far more likely to open up with a beautiful younger woman than he was with a battle-scarred warrior like the Executioner. He wouldn't care what Bolan thought about him. But he'd want to impress Platinov. In Bolan's life-long battle with evil, he had learned that you took advantage of every weapon you had.

And many weapons had absolutely nothing to do with bullets or blades.

Just as he'd guessed, the old man ignored the soldier as Platinov began speaking to him in broken French. Bolan busied himself, pretending to look at a display of medallions next to the counter. He knew now why Platinov had brought the translation dictionaries along. She was pretending to know far less French than she actually did, and as she conversed with the delighted older man she occasionally looked up a word in the book, then held it with one hand for the man to read while she pointed to it with the index finger of the other hand.

Bolan continued to look at nearby souvenirs, busying

himself as if he didn't understand a word of what they were saying. Maybe they would be able to hold on to their assumed identities longer than he'd guessed they would. In any case, it didn't hurt to try.

Finally, after roughly two minutes of mildly flirtatious small talk, Bolan heard, "LeForce, Achille LeForce," come out of Platinov's mouth. Bolan was standing with his back to the counter, trying on different pairs of sunglasses. The stand holding the sunglasses held a small mirror at the top, and all it took for the Executioner to see the fringe-haired man's reaction to the name was a slight adjustment of that mirror.

What he saw in the reflection was fear.

Suddenly, not even Platinov's sensuality was enough to get the old man to talk.

Bolan turned and walked toward the counter.

It was now his turn to interrogate.

The white-haired man looked even more afraid when Bolan joined Platinov at the counter. The soldier wished that he didn't have to scare the man further, but he had to weigh temporarily frightening a kind old gentleman against whatever scheme Pierre Rouillan had underway; a scheme that might take hundreds or thousands of other innocent lives.

"Let's stop pretending here," the Executioner said in French. He glanced at Platinov. "Put your dictionary back in the bag." He turned to look directly into the white-haired man's near-panicked eyes. "She speaks your language better than you or me." He paused a moment, then asked, "What's your name?"

"Geraud," the little man choked out fearfully.

The old man had stepped away from the counter and now had his back against the wall behind it. Three feet to his side was an open door that appeared to lead into a storage room.

Bolan saw the old man glance toward it. The big American raised his T-shirt with his hands, letting the proprietor see the grips of both the Desert Eagle and Beretta before dropping the shirt again. "Don't even think about that door, Geraud," he said. "You'll never make it."

"What…what is it you want?" the elderly gentleman squeaked out. "The only money I have is here in the cash register." He moved toward the machine on the counter top.

Bolan stopped him with an upraised hand. "We're not here to rob you," he said.

Geraud froze with his arm still extended toward the cash register. "Then what is it you want?"

"What I want first," Bolan said, "is for you to understand something. You cooperate with us, you won't get hurt. And I'll make sure your name doesn't get out on the streets for talking." He paused to clear his throat. "You understand?"

"*Oui*," the tiny man said in a tiny little voice.

"Do you know either Achille LeForce or Pierre Rouillan?" Bolan asked.

The white-haired man glanced to Piatinov. The expression on his face told the Executioner that Geraud was hoping she might intervene for him now. But in his peripheral vision, Bolan could see that all hints at coquetry had left the Russian woman's face. Her features were still beautiful, but now they were beautiful in the way they might have looked had Michelangelo carved them out of marble or stone.

"She's not going to help you," Bolan said. "And I'm going to ask you only one more time. If I don't get an answer I believe, things are going to get ugly for you. Now, do you know either LeForce or Rouillan?" he repeated. The Executioner waited, hoping the man was too frightened to call his bluff. He could never really hurt an innocent old man like this.

But the innocent old man didn't know it.

The little shopkeeper nodded sharply, the white hair around his ears dancing like the fringe on a buckskin jacket. "Both of them," he said in a squeaky voice. "Since they were young."

"Are they here now?" Bolan asked. "Do they still live here in Chartres?"

"LeForce does," the white-haired man said. "Rouillan, I hear, comes in and out. Mostly at night, since he's wanted by the gendarmes."

Bolan leaned forward. Had the little man with the white fringe of hair around his head been a criminal or a terrorist, he would have grabbed him by the throat by this time. But since he was simply a poor old man, unfortunately caught up in the middle of things, the soldier simply laid a hand on his shoulder.

That was enough. Bolan didn't even have to ask any more questions.

"The rumor is that he stays with a woman when he's in town," Geraud blurted out. "I do not know her name or address, but I know where she lives. I can take you there. I can point it out." He had said it all in one breath, and now he stopped, his mouth opening wide to gasp for more oxygen. Geraud's frail chest expanded and contracted as he tried to catch his breath.

"Close your shop," Bolan said, removing his hand from Geraud's shoulder. "You're a good man, and you're doing a good thing, Geraud."

The old man closed his eyes for a moment, perhaps in prayer. When he opened them again, Bolan said, "We'll go out the back door so no one sees us together."

The little man nodded, then hurried down the aisle to the front door. He flipped the sign that faced the street, telling his potential customers that the shop was closed, then he twisted a dead-bolt lock bar into the door.

Geraud came scurrying back to Bolan and Platinov just as quickly as he'd run to the door. "I will take you there," he said again. "It is only right that I do so because both LeForce and Rouillan are criminals. But please do not make me go into the house with you. I am not a fighter." He lifted his hand and made the sign of the cross on his chest.

Again, Bolan felt sorry for the little old man with the white fringe of hair. Scaring him had been necessary for the greater good. But fear was no longer needed.

The Executioner reached out and placed his hand on Geraud's shoulder once more. But this time, the little

Frenchman could tell it was a reassuring, rather than a threatening, gesture. His face relaxed slightly.

"I'm not going to make you go in," Bolan said. "In fact, as soon as we get close enough that you can point out the house, I'll cut you loose." Now that Geraud was more sure of himself, Bolan dropped his hand to his side again. "You can come back here, reopen your store and forget all about us." He watched even more of the tension evaporate from the little man's face. "And you'll know you did the right thing. Know you did your part to rid the good people of the world of a pair of terrorists."

The little man nodded animatedly again. Without speaking, he led the way through the open doorway he had looked at earlier when he'd hoped to escape. Bolan and Platinov followed him through a storeroom stacked high with boxes and shelves of Christian-oriented souvenirs. Most were related to the Cathedral of Our Lady of Chartres, only a couple of blocks away.

Twisting the back door, Geraud held it open for both Platinov and Bolan and let them step into the alley behind his shop. Then he turned to lock the door again with a key he produced from his pocket.

"You lead the way," the Executioner told the little shopkeeper. "We'll stay about ten yards behind you so it doesn't appear that we're with you."

Geraud's head bobbed up and down gratefully. "Thank you," he said. "I will be able to point it out from a corner," he said. "Then I can go?"

"Then you can go," Bolan said.

A moment later, Geraud was out of the alley and onto the sidewalk at the end of the block.

And a moment after that, ten yards behind him, just as the Executioner had promised, Bolan and Platinov turned the corner onto the same sidewalk.

PIERRE ROUILLAN KNEW he was vain, but that knowledge didn't bother the Frenchman one bit.

Rouillan stepped out of the shower and grabbed a dry towel from Colette's towel rack, briefly rubbed his hair—it would not set right if it was too dry or too damp—then quickly dried the rest of his body before wrapping the towel around his waist and tying it. He hurried toward the mirror above the sink.

Rouillan smiled at his reflection. He was handsome—there was simply no other word for it. An old girlfriend had once told him he reminded her of the famous French film star Jean-Paul Belmondo. Another woman had told him he looked better than Belmondo.

In his opinion, the latter was correct.

Taking a small hand towel from the ring on the wall next to the mirror, Rouillan rubbed his hair a few more times. Then he shook his head vigorously back and forth. When he felt he had achieved the correct balance between wet and dry, he pulled open a drawer to his side and found his comb. Slowly, methodically, he combed his hair. The cowlick in back was in full bloom today, so he twisted the lid off a jar of setting gel and plastered it down. Then, satisfied that it would hold, he opened a cabinet door next to the drawers and pulled out the hair dryer. Setting it on low, he used the comb to section off different areas of his hair, blew them until they were just shy of completely dry, then used the comb to hold each section in place as he set down the dryer and spritzed his head with hairspray.

Rouillan continued to stare into the mirror with a critical eye. But it didn't take long for the frown of discretion to become a grin. Yes, along with a superior mind he had been gifted with superior looks, not to mention charm, that few women had been able to resist over the years, and he had used all three natural endowments both for sex and in his reorganization of CLODO.

As if acting on stage for an audience, Rouillan lifted his hands, palms up, to the mirror, then said out loud to himself, "Hey, you use what you have, no?"

He chuckled at the words, but it was time to check the rest of his face now, so he squinted critically again at his reflection. The "scruffy" look of two-to-three days growth of beard was still in throughout Europe and America, and it had been three days since his face had last seen the razor. Perfect.

Well, almost perfect.

Rouillan could see that a few more of his facial hairs had turned white, as well as several in his mustache and beard. The sight brought a mild depression to his soul. He might be brilliant, good-looking and engaging, but he was still human. Time stood still for no man. So, pulling out the drawer just above the one where he'd found the comb, the head of CLODO dug through Colette's makeup until he found the mascara. Still looking at his reflection in the mirror, he twisted the small brush out of its pencillike cover, then blotted it slightly on a tissue from the box next to the sink. He needed to have exactly the right amount of mascara on the brush when he applied it. Too little would not change the color from white to brown. Too much would smear, and give away the fact that he had doctored the stubble.

It took a good five minutes, and washing his face again twice, to get it just right. But when he did, he smiled into the mirror again, quite pleased with himself. A few crow's feet had begun to form at the corners of his eyes, but Rouillan did not consider them to be a liability. In his opinion, they added maturity and character to his otherwise unblemished skin. Someday, he supposed, he might need to begin using a moistening agent on his skin. And sometime after that, an eye-tuck or even a face-lift might come into play.

But for now, Pierre Rouillan was pleased with his appearance.

Unwrapping the towel from his waist, he dropped it in the middle of the bathroom floor. Colette would pick it up. That was *her* job, not his. Walking naked from the bathroom to the bedroom, the CLODO leader began dressing in the clean clothing he had laid out on the bed before showering. A white, three-button pullover polo shirt went over his head and he left all three buttons undone to exhibit his chest hair—none of which had yet begun to lose color. His underwear was of the finest silk, and he took note of its smoothness as he stuck his feet through the leg holes. Silk briefs were the only type of undergarments he ever wore—he liked the way they allowed his pants to slide around with every movement he made. And he was reminded of that fact as he donned the gabardine slacks that had rested, still on the hanger, on the bed next to the shirt. They were pleated in front, and in combination with his shirt, looked nothing like the "unofficial uniform" the rest of his CLODO men often wore.

The fact was, few of his own men even knew what he looked like. His orders went through his life-long friend, Achille LeForce, and he stayed in the background most of the time. The real reason he had come up with the short-sleeved tan shirt and dark brown trousers with a blue beret was so they could be readily identified should Rouillan find himself in a position where he had to "throw sheep to the wolves." The "wolves" in this case, were the police. The "sheep" were his own men. So far nothing like that had happened. But if it ever did, he wanted something to keep those ignorant gendarmes busy while he made his escape.

Rouillan glanced at the bed as he slipped into a pair of Gucci loafers. There was no blue beret sitting there, either. Berets—or headgear of any kind—would negate all the time he put in on getting his hair just right.

The leader of CLODO had just finished dressing when he heard the front door open. Walking out into the living room, he stepped off the waxed hardwood floor and onto the brightly colored Oriental carpet beneath the glass coffee table in the center of the room. From there, he saw Colette, dressed in her white nurse's uniform, close the front door and drop her keys back into her purse. He glanced at the Rolex watch on his wrist and saw that it was 3:30 p.m.

His meeting with LeForce would take place in a half hour.

Rouillan forced a smile to his face. "You are home early from your shift," he said as if delighted to see her.

Colette's eyes sparkled with the love he knew she felt for him. She knew he was wanted, but he had convinced her that he had been framed on all charges. She was one hundred percent loyal to him, and had helped shelter him from arrest on more occasions than he could remember.

"I developed a migraine," Colette said, the grin on her face telling him that the headache was pure fiction. "And one of the other nurses had arrived early. Her husband is out of work, and they need the money, so I gave her my hours."

Rouillan stepped forward and wrapped his arms around her. "You are an angel," he said.

Colette pulled away just far enough for him to see the seductive smile on her face. "Take me into the bedroom and I'll show you just how wrong you are," she purred.

Rouillan picked her up and carried her down the hall to the bed that had held his change of clothing only a few minutes earlier. He continued to smile down into her face. But the smile was forced. He had counted on

Colette being at work when LeForce arrived. This woman knew nothing of his true business and connection to CLODO, and he wanted to keep it that way.

Laying the beautiful nurse on the bed, Rouillan quickly disrobed as he watched Colette rid herself of all but her white stockings and garter belt. She knew he liked them, and her wanting to please him brought a sharp pain of remorse to his heart for what he was about to do. He pushed the feeling out of his brain as quickly as it entered. What had to be done had to be done. It was that simple.

Easing onto the bed, Pierre Rouillan embraced Collette, then quickly began to make love to her, glancing at his watch occasionally as he did.

The woman noticed his distraction and said, "Are you taking pills, Pierre? Late for an appointment, perhaps?"

Rouillan could tell she was irritated, but he had nothing to say. So when he felt himself about to finish, he glanced at his watch one last time, then wrapped the fingers of both hands around Colette's throat.

At first, the woman looked surprised—cutting off the oxygen was a form of lovemaking with which they had never experimented, but then she smiled, fully believing that Rouillan was trying to intensify her pleasure.

The smile didn't change to a desperate facial grimace and a wild, leg-kicking and arm-flailing attempt to live until just before she died.

Rolling off the dead woman, Rouillan lay on his back, his forearm across the bridge of his nose, his chest heaving up and down as he caught his breath. It was unfortunate, he thought. He had liked Colette. Perhaps he had even loved her—he didn't know. In his entire life, with hundreds of women in his past, he didn't think he had ever experienced what others called "love."

He was not sure he was capable of it, and a little voice in the back of his brain told him he was right.

The front doorbell rang as Rouillan finished dressing again and slid back into his loafers. "Just a minute!" he shouted out as he left the bedroom and walked down the hall to the front door. Glancing quickly through the peephole just to make sure, he saw his lifelong friend, Achille LeForce standing on the porch. LeForce was shorter and stockier than Rouillan, as strong as a bull and not much more attractive than one, either. But as he gazed through the peephole at LeForce, he knew he was looking at the one man on the planet he could fully trust. LeForce had been the brunt of many a grade school practical joke until Rouillan had befriended him. From then on, he was respected. And Achille LeForce was not the kind of man who forgot such a favor.

In short, Rouillan realized as he twisted the dead bolt and reached for the doorknob, he could get Achille LeForce to do anything he wanted the man to do, no matter how dangerous or degrading. LeForce had "taken the fall" for many of the crimes they had committed during their youthful days. It had been quite easy to convince the stocky man that there was no sense in both of them being punished, and that since they were to be a lifelong team, it would be advantageous if one of them, at least, had a clean record.

And that "one of them," of course, should be Rouillan.

Rouillan shook his head slightly as he opened the door. The man he was about to allow into Colette's house was an idiot, but a very useful idiot.

Rouillan stepped back as LeForce crossed the threshold. "You have brought the materials?" the CLODO leader said without greeting.

"In the back of my pickup," LeForce replied. "Secured in the camper."

"The boxes are not marked?"

"Of course not," LeForce said. "I am not an idiot, Pierre."

The irony of his last thought about the man's intelligence, and the fact that LeForce had just used the same word to deny the unspoken question, was not lost on Rouillan. Yet, for a moment, he felt as if the man was truly his brother. Pierre Rouillan might not know if he had ever loved a woman, but he was certain in his brotherly love for Achille LeForce. "Please accept my apology," he said, and meant every word of it. "I had my mind on other matters." He motioned for his friend to take a seat on the sofa in the living room.

"If it is all the same to you," LeForce said, "I would prefer to unload the shipment and be on my way." He paused for a moment, then said, "I have other things that must be done this afternoon." His brow furrowed slightly, then he added, "Colette's car is in the driveway. She is home?"

Rouillan nodded. "She is, but she will be no problem." He paused, then added, "She developed a migraine and is asleep."

LeForce's eyebrows lowered even more on his face. "You trust her not to talk to anyone about our business?" he asked, obviously confused. "You never have before."

"I do now." Pierre smiled and saw that his words only baffled his friend even more. He shrugged. "Our relationship has changed." Without speaking further, he opened the door and led the way out to LeForce's pickup. He watched his squatty friend unlock the rear door of the camper, and they began hauling cardboard boxes into the house.

When they had finished, LeForce said, "That is all. Now, unless there is something else you need, I will be off."

"Actually," Rouillan said, "there *is* one other thing."

"What's that?" LeForce asked.

"I have some trash that needs to be disposed of. I was hoping you could take care of it."

"Fine," LeForce said in his best always-eager-to-please voice. "Just show me to it."

"Gladly, old friend," Rouillan said. "But first, move the coffee table, then roll up the rug and bring it with you."

Yet again, LeForce looked perplexed. But, like a good and obedient dog, he did as he was told.

Then he followed Pierre Rouillan down the hall and into the bedroom.

BOLAN AND PLATINOV didn't have far to walk, but they stayed behind Geraud until the tiny little white-haired man stopped at a corner just two blocks from his shop.

A row of houses—one almost identical to the next—stood across the street.

When he motioned to them, Bolan and Platinov walked forward. "It is the sixth house on the right," Geraud whispered, although no one else was around. "The one with the car and the pickup-camper parked in the driveway." He paused, then said, "Now may I please go before someone sees me?"

Bolan pulled a roll of euros out of his pocket and handed several to Geraud. "For your trouble," he said.

Geraud shook his head. "I did not do this for money," he said. "I did it because it was the right thing to do." His hand rose and he crossed himself again, then he glanced to the side.

Bolan followed his line of sight. Two blocks over, the Executioner could see the twin steeples of the Cathedral of Our Lady of Chartres towering over the other buildings. He peeled off several more bills, then forced them into Geraud's hand. "If you don't feel right taking it, then give it to your church." He nodded toward the steeples.

Geraud smiled for the first time since Bolan had met him. *"Merci,"* he said. "That I will gladly do."

"Now get lost," the soldier said. "You've done a good deed here."

Geraud nodded, pivoted away from them, then hurried off back in the direction of his shop.

"What a strange little man he was," Platinov said as soon as the shopkeeper was out of earshot.

"He's a man with a mission," Bolan replied. "Not exactly like ours but not so different, either. We're all trying to accomplish the same thing. Just in different ways."

"And what is it we are after?" Platinov asked.

"Peace," Bolan said.

Platinov nodded. "Yes," she said. "Dream on."

Bolan understood the Russian woman's sarcasm. Crime, terror, evil of all sorts—it was never going to be completely erased from the face of the earth. But that didn't mean that warriors such as he and Platinov weren't supposed to keep trying.

"Now," he said, taking her hand to make it look like they were just another couple of tourists out to see the sights, "let's do a little recon of this house. Two vehicles, which means a minimum of two people inside. Probably more than two. With any luck, it might be LeForce or even Rouillan himself."

"And how do you plan for us to sneak up on the house in the middle of the day?" Platinov asked, lifting a hand to shield her eyes from the sun that burned down on them.

"By not sneaking at all." With his hand still holding hers, Bolan started down the cracked sidewalk with the beautiful Russian woman. "We just pretend to be lovers on vacation in France."

As the two strolled on, they continued talking, occasionally stopping to point at something that caught their eye for the benefit of any other eyes that might be watching through the window.

They were still two houses from the one Geraud had pointed out to them when two men carrying the ends of a rolled-up carpet appeared at the back of the pickup-camper. They set the carpet down long enough to open the tailgate, then slid the roll into the back of the camper.

"I can't believe this," Platinov said in a quiet voice. "Can you ID either of them?"

Bolan nodded. By now they were walking arm in arm. "The one guy—he fits Rouillan's general description," he whispered. "And the other one could be LeForce. But they're still too far away to be sure."

"Let's walk a little faster, shall we?" Platinov suggested.

"Yeah," Bolan whispered, and they picked up their pace. By now they were only one house away, but the stockier of the two men was already behind the wheel of the vehicle and pulling out of the driveway.

The other man had started back to the front door of the house and had his back to Bolan and Platinov. A positive ID on either one didn't look like it was going to happen.

The Executioner gritted his teeth in disgust. He could easily take out both men with either the Desert Eagle or the Beretta, but he had never killed an honest man by accident. And he wasn't about to start now.

The man returning to the house walked up the steps to the porch, then stopped to open the storm door on the outside of the structure. Then, suddenly, as if feeling

Bolan's and Platinov's eyes on the back of his neck, he twisted toward them.

As he started to turn, all doubt as to the man's identity fled the Executioner's soul. Instinct had told him this man was Pierre Rouillan.

Now eyesight confirmed it.

Dropping Platinov's arm, Bolan's hand went under his shirt for the Desert Eagle.

And at the same time that Platinov drew one of her Colt Gold Cup .45s, Rouillan pulled a small black 9 mm Kel-Tec from the back pocket of his gabardine slacks and opened fire.

CHAPTER FIVE

The pickup was already a block away by the time the Executioner took aim and sent a double-tap of .44 Magnum rounds into the camper shell. At the same time, Platinov dropped one of her .45 hollowpoint slugs through the shell's back window. The projectiles' only effect was to make the driver increase speed, then the vehicle disappeared around a corner.

Almost simultaneously, two rounds popped from Rouillan's compact Kel-Tec as the Frenchman used his other hand to open the door to the house. He dived inside a half step behind Bolan's next behemoth .44 Magnum round, which was closely followed by another .45ACP from Platinov's Gold Cup.

The house wasn't old, but it wasn't new, either, and the wooden doorframe which was struck by the bullets, had begun to rot. Splinters of wood sailed from the frame, making it look like it had been hit by a hand grenade or mortar fire filled with wooden shrapnel.

By the time Bolan could shoot again, the door slammed shut.

"Spread out a little," Bolan whispered just loud enough for Platinov to hear. Crouching slightly, the Desert Eagle leading the way, the soldier moved cautiously toward the porch. He could see the door ahead. It was solid, and the large, panel-paned windows—with the blinds closed—concerned him more.

The Russian agent headed toward the same door, but from a different angle.

The Executioner kept one eye on the multipaned picture window, the other on his surroundings. But with the sun where it was in the sky, all of the small individual windowpanes might as well have been one-way mirrors in a police interrogation room. All they revealed were distorted pictures of the houses across the street.

Suddenly the sound of shattering glass filled the air and a rifle barrel appeared in the bottom right-hand frame of the window.

Both Bolan and Platinov hit the grass on their chests as the glass square exploded and sent tiny pieces flying out into the yard, sparkling like crystals under the bright sun. A second later, the bolt of an AK-47 followed the barrel through the jagged glass, and a steady stream of 7.62 mm NATO rounds swept from right to left across the yard, mere inches above the heads of the big American and the Russian agent.

Bolan squinted at a face through the unbroken panel just above the rifle barrel. Nearly pressed against the glass, the face of the man shooting the weapon was no longer hidden by the reflection of the sun. The wooden frame around the face made it look strangely like a photograph, and it was just as clear as any picture.

There was no mistaking who was in the house, wielding the 7.62 mm Soviet assault weapon.

Pierre Rouillan.

Bolan raised his arm off the grass high enough to angle a lone .44 Magnum round through the glass. But a millisecond before his finger squeezed the trigger, Rouillan pulled the AK-47 back out of the broken windowpane and disappeared from sight.

Bolan's .44 round took out the glass, but it was a fraction of a second too late to include the French terrorist in its path.

As soon as the man and rifle barrel disappeared, the Executioner was up and running toward the porch. As he hit the concrete steps another volley of 7.62 mm rounds drilled through the thin front door.

From the corner of his eye, Bolan could see Platinov. She had been right behind him, but had now halted on the steps, one of her Gold Cup pistols aimed at the door.

A new volley of fire broke through the windowpanes, but Platinov was covered by the angle of the steps. Bolan had now worked his way inside Rouillan's field of fire in front of the door.

Platinov looked to her partner for instructions.

With his back pressed against the wall between the door and windows, Bolan turned to face her. He held his index finger to his lips, then silently mouthed the word, "Wait."

The Russian nodded her understanding.

The Executioner knew that the solid wood door would be hard to take down, and the only reasonably safe time to do that was while Rouillan wasn't shooting. He wasn't likely to do that until he had to reload his weapon, and that would give the Executioner and Platinov a few seconds of "safe time" to burst through the opening.

Assuming a kick or two would even clear the door.

Bolan couldn't be sure exactly how many shots Rouillan had left before he'd have to reload. Box magazines were available for Kalashnikov rifles that held anywhere from thirty to seventy-five rounds.

But considering the speed with which Rouillan was peppering the door, the Executioner had to figure he had plenty of ammo at his disposal.

Dropping to the cold concrete porch, Bolan rolled up against the bottom of the door, pressing his shoulder against the wood. Above him, the rifle rounds continued to blast holes in the windows. But every now and then, a volley would work its way through the door just over his head, which told Bolan that the Frenchman was using some kind of fast, penetrative armor-piercing rounds.

The Executioner knew that Rouillan was no dummy. He realized that whoever was after him was trying to determine when he'd have to stop firing to reload. So he was doing his best to confuse the situation.

Bolan turned back to Platinov, still on the steps. With his empty left hand, he waved her toward the back of the house.

The Russian agent nodded, rose back away from the steps, then took off around the side of the dwelling.

The 3-round bursts were coming at slower intervals now, and the Executioner knew it could be nothing short of a miracle that Rouillan hadn't fired at least one volley at the bottom of the door. If he had, Bolan would have died right there on the porch.

But it was only a matter of time before the CLODO leader considered the possibility that the porch floor, right up against the splintered front door, was where his enemy had to be. And when he did, his highly penetrative 7.62 rounds *would* be fired lower.

Bolan waited for another trio of rounds to penetrate the wood above his head, then rose to his hands and feet again. The pause between shots this time was even longer than before, and he hoped that meant that Rouillan actually *was* finally having to reload.

There was another, more deadly possibility, however. Rouillan could be playing possum on a fishing expedition to bait the Executioner with silence, then fill him full of holes as he broke through the door.

There was only one way to find out. Bolan would have to take the bait and, if that's what it was, he'd be forced to rely on superior strategy, speed and accuracy.

The Executioner took a deep breath as he waited for the roar of the AK-47 to die down, then, he again charged forward, driving his shoulder into the front door.

A second later, he had burst through the doorway into the house, and the first thing he saw was the bore of an AK-47 pointing directly between his eyes.

THERE WAS JUST enough room on the right inside the pickup-camper's shell to shove Colette's rug-covered body in next to the final few unmarked cardboard boxes Achille LeForce had just delivered.

Pierre Rouillan saw the man and woman at the end of the block as he lifted one of the boxes, and the sight brought butterflies to his stomach. He continued to watch them out of the corner of his eye as both he and Achille began unloading the boxes and taking them into the house.

The woman was beautiful, blond, and dressed in "touristy" looking shorts and a sweatshirt that barely covered the bottoms of her breasts. The man with her was big and dressed similarly. Were these the same two he had seen through the window back at the Paris safe house? They could be. When he'd peered through the window during the shooting inside, he had caught a glimpse of the man's face but had only seen the woman from the back. Now, the situation was reversed. The man was standing with his back to Rouillan, and the woman faced him.

He knew they could be nobodies, or they could be trouble. What he knew they weren't was friends.

Rouillan tried to calm himself as he walked back and forth from the pickup to the house, carrying boxes. But the anxiety in his chest began to grow rather than diminish. The man and woman were both the right size to have been the ones he'd seen in Paris, but there were plenty of big men and beautiful blond women all over the world, and these two looked little different than the many other tourists who wandered slightly off the beaten path, wanting to see the real Chartres.

Rouillan watched the couple in his peripheral vision as he carried the box toward the house. They continued to face each other, talking, and looking as if they were trying to determine whether this street was worth seeing or if they should head in some other direction. There was nothing unusual about that.

But, dammit, Rouillan thought as he stepped into the house and set the cardboard box on the floor. It looked so *not* unusual that it *was* unusual.

Using his peripheral vision again in order not to draw attention, Rouillan looked at the woman's face once more as he exited the front door. Yes, she was beautiful, but her face had character as well. The man looked no less fit. Tall, broad-shouldered, muscular. But what caught Rouillan's attention even more strongly were the scars on his legs and forearms. Even at the distance at which they were, some of the scars had quite obviously been made by bullets. Others appeared to have been the work of knives.

When they reached the driver's side of the pickup, Rouillan opened the door for LeForce and let his friend slide in behind the steering wheel. A cell phone was weighing down the pocket on the chest of the polo shirt LeForce wore, and Rouillan reached out and tapped it through the stretchy material. "Stay in touch, my friend," he said.

"Always," LeForce replied. Then he backed the pickup out of the driveway and drove away. In the meantime, Rouillan noticed that the man and woman at the end of the block had finally made up their mind to walk down his street, and the fact that they had quickened their pace when they saw the pickup leaving was not lost on him, either.

Now, finally, Rouillan could see the man's face, and the deadpan expression he saw there was more frightening than any scowl or frown he'd ever seen.

It *was* the man and woman from the safe house in Paris, Rouillan realized as he mounted the concrete steps to the front door. Which meant they were cops, or government agents, or perhaps representatives of some other group the world labeled as counterterrorists.

Spinning, Rouillan walked purposefully back up the steps to the house, anxious to get to the AK-47 that he kept fully loaded by the door. Behind him, he heard the footsteps of the man and woman on the sidewalk quicken even more.

Almost out of reflex rather than thought, the French CLODO leader spun around a step away from the front door. He had drawn his 9 mm Kel-Tec "pocket pistol" from his back pocket as he turned, and now he pulled the double-action trigger twice, shooting in the general direction of the man and woman. He felt the lightweight gun kick like an irritated jackass in his right hand, and knew without looking that he had missed both people, both times.

It had not been his intention to take them out with

the little 9 mm pistol—just to slow them down so he could get to his rifle.

And that strategy had worked.

Rouillan saw pistols appear in the hands of both the man and the woman as he whirled away from them. He opened the hardwood door, and, throwing himself through the opening, felt the air pressure and a slight burning sensation on the back of his neck as the gunners fired their weapons.

Hitting the hardwood floor on both knees, the CLODO leader moaned slightly at the pain, but he managed to slam the door shut and lock it at the same time.

A moment later, the Kel-Tec was back in his pocket and the AK-47 was in his hands.

Rouillan pulled back the bolt to chamber the first round, then shuffled on his aching knees to the window next to the door. Peering around the corner of the window frame, he had to squint into the sun to see the man and woman—guns still drawn—creeping toward the porch. Without thinking, he pulled the Kalashnikov back at his side, then drove the barrel through the pane of glass at the bottom left-hand corner of the windows. Looking out toward the yard through the window just above the one he'd broken, Rouillan cut loose with a current of rounds that started in the far left corner of his vision and moved all the way to the right.

But the man and woman were quick and well-trained. Rouillan was surprised to see them drop to the ground below his line of fire. Before he could swing the rifle back and lower his aim, they had sprung to their feet and charged out of sight to the porch.

Rouillan couldn't keep from smiling. He had set the trap, now it was time to spring it.

Still on his knees, the CLODO leader pulled the footstool away from the reclining chair, rested his elbows on the threadbare upholstery and took aim at the door. Aiming the rifle barrel at chest level, he held the trigger back. Full-auto fire exploded from the Soviet assault rifle and, in front of him, he saw a few rays of sunlight begin to shoot back through the near-perfect round holes the penetrative bullets made.

Had he gotten them? He didn't know. He had heard no screams or moans of pain from outside the front door. But the thunderous gunfire itself might have masked such laments. Or perhaps they had both been killed instantly before they had a chance to shriek in pain.

But there was a third possibility, Rouillan knew as he switched to 3-round bursts of fire and continued to make holes in the door. He had caught only a couple of quick glimpses of both the man and the woman. But something he had seen—something in their eyes, perhaps—had told him that neither was the kind to cry out, no matter how bad it got.

The AK-47 in his hands was becoming increasingly lighter as the custom-made 100-round drum magazine continued to empty itself. Rouillan changed his pace again, allowing more time between bursts, hoping to lull the man and woman outside—if they were still alive—

into thinking he has having to change magazines. That was when they would come. That was when he'd suddenly see the bullet-ridden door fly apart and the big man and good-looking woman would appear in front of him.

Totally exposed.

Rouillan fired another volley, then paused. Even if the man and woman outside the house were dead, the neighbors would have called the gendarmes by now. So, everything in this safe house would have to be sacrificed. And it was a big loss. Stored in the center of the house, in a room that had originally been designed to be used as a den, were bomb-making materials such as fertilizer, dynamite, blasting caps and C-4 plastic explosives.

All that material would have to be deserted, and Rouillan knew that a year ago that would have filled his heart with sorrow. But now, as he pulled the trigger back one final time and sent his last trio of rounds into the door, the thought made him smile. He couldn't have asked for a better "red herring" if he'd wanted to. The bombings and other strikes CLODO had conducted during the last few months had been nothing but decoys to keep cops and other agents busy and away from the master stroke.

The smile on the Frenchman's face widened until it was a full-blown grin. The world of law enforcement was focused on a conventional bomb.

And what he had in mind was anything but conventional.

Firing a final 3-round burst through the door, Rouillan set the AK-47 against the footstool with the stock of the weapon on the floor and the barrel still pointing toward the door. Then, swiftly but quietly, he hurried out of the living room and down a short hallway to the den. Passing by the cardboard boxes and other containers, the CLODO leader stopped in the center of the room and lifted the corner of a throw rug similar to the one he had wrapped around Colette's body. Beneath the rug, cut into the hardwood floor, was a trapdoor.

This secret passage would be found. Once he had dropped down into the tunnel to which it led, he would close the door again but he'd have no way of pulling the rug back over it. But that mattered little; he would still have more than enough of a head start. When the man and woman outside the house finally realized it was safe to enter the hole, they'd still have to do so cautiously.

Pierre Rouillan would be long gone before they followed him into the earth below.

Rouillan reached down and grabbed the steel ring set flush into the wood. Popping it out, he added his other arm to the task as he pulled the heavy trap up and open. A crude staircase had been made with pieces of two-by-fours and scraps of plywood, and he lowered himself down several of the steps before flipping a light switch to illuminate the underground passage.

As he reached back up to close the trapdoor behind him, Rouillan heard a crash that was the shattered front door exploding into pieces of wood. A second later, gunshots, and then the crash of glass came from the back of the house.

Ah. His pursuers had split up to cover both exits. They had counted on him attempting an escape through the back door, and planned ahead for it. Good thinking on their part.

But not quite good enough. They had not entertained the possibility that there might be a means of escape *beneath* the house. Or if they had, they had realized that two people could not be in three places at the same time, and that the front and back door had to take precedence over any speculative underground escape route.

The trapdoor closed over his head and Rouillan descended the rest of the steps to the floor of the tunnel. Flipping the single switch earlier had illuminated a string of bare lightbulbs every hundred feet or so, and it was just enough to see the rugged footing and sharp bends and crooks the tunnel took. Enough light to pass safely through the bending, winding tunnel, but not enough to notice small details of what was encountered along the way.

Unless you knew what to look for, and beware of, ahead of time, which Rouillan did. He and some of his most trusted CLODO men had dug this tunnel themselves during a three-month period during which Colette had been in Paris at an advanced nursing school. Ironically, the classes she had attended made her an expert in the field of fungi encountered underground by excavating teams.

She had drawn her last breath still not knowing about the excavating that had gone on in her own house.

As he began to jog, Rouillan was surprised to find that he was breathing hard. It was not from exertion—pulling the trigger on a rifle and climbing down a short set of steps was hardly a workout for a man like him who stayed in good physical condition. The excited breathing, the need for extra oxygen, came from the adrenaline flowing through his veins.

As he jogged through the winding underground tunnel, sometimes leaping into the air, other times ducking, and once even dropping to his belly to crawl several feet before rising and taking two steps with his back arched and his head down, Rouillan's mind drifted back to the first time he had felt such excitement—the television store when he had been a child, the day he and his mother and father had gone to pick out their new TV. He'd watched the news, and the aftermath of the explosion the original CLODO men had caused at the Phillips Data company.

Navigating a sharp turn in the underground passageway, Rouillan came upon a dimly lit passageway. Ahead, he saw an opening that was at least three times as wide as the rest of the tunnel. Hanging from the top of the tunnel was a rope, and attached to the rope was a steel ring not unlike the one that had been installed on the trapdoor back at the house.

Without breaking stride, the French terrorist grabbed the ring as he ran past it, and the feeling of the cold metal in his hand made him smile. He had carefully memorized all of the places within the tunnel where he'd personally installed booby-trapped claymore mines and dental-thread-thin trip lines, and leaped over, or ducked under, these traps as he made his way through the tunnel. But here, at this point, nature itself had set its own trap. All Rouillan had needed to do was install small iron gates on both sides of the underground clearing. The ring in his hand, attached to the cord, would open the gates as he pulled it.

To both of his sides, Rouillan heard a chattering sound. He ran on, letting his forward momentum pull the rope rather than yanking it with his arm. The sound of metal grinding against stone could be heard for a second above the chattering, which rose in intensity as the trip rope was jerked from his hand.

Rouillan slowed his pace to a swift walk. He almost hoped his pursuers escaped the booby traps he'd set between the iron gates and the safe house's trapdoor. It was far more fun picturing them making it all the way to the wider opening and what would await them there.

Ahead, in the underground stillness, Rouillan finally heard the tapping sounds that he knew came from fin-gertips on computer keyboards. He shook his head at the irony of his whole situation. In this day and age, to fight computers one had to *use computers,* and the very thought went against his grain. But the men he had working here in the underground computer lab were vital to his mission. Even now, some of them were scanning the Internet for any new knowledge law-enforcement agencies around the world might have about CLODO. Others were hard at work developing the virus he hoped would be the final strike CLODO would have to perform.

Rouillan gritted his teeth. Now that the man and woman disguised as tourists had found the house, and would inevitably find the tunnel, he would have to shut down this computer lab. Even if the pair blew themselves up there had been enough activity at the house that the gendarmes would soon arrive. They would find the tunnel, too, and eventually discover all of its secrets.

As the keyboard taps grew louder, Rouillan rounded a bend and found himself in brighter lighting. A few more steps brought him to another underground cavern, roughly the same size as the one where he'd pulled the ring and opened the iron gates. But here, he saw three men and three women, all busily tapping their keyboards or maneuvering the mouse that rested on a pad next to each CPU.

All movement, however, stopped abruptly as Rouillan made his surprise entrance into the rocky room.

All six heads turned toward him at once.

"Pierre," one of the women said. "What are you—"

Rouillan held up his hand for silence. "This tunnel has been discovered," he said quickly and simply. "We must be swift, but there is enough time to transfer all of the information on your hard drives to the backup computers at Marseille." Without giving them time to question him, he went on with, "Begin the transfer immediately. And then program your instruments to completely erase the hard drives here as soon as the transfer is complete."

"But, Pierre—" one of the men said.

"Just do it!" Rouillan yelled angrily. "I do not have time to explain more to you now. I will do so after we are out of danger."

All six heads turned back to their keyboards to begin the hard drive transfers and the erasing of all data.

Five minutes later, the tasks were all complete.

"Follow me," Rouillan said, moving out of the room and back into the tunnel on the opposite side from where he'd entered the underground room.

PLATINOV STUDIED the chain-link fence that stood between her and the house's backyard. It was roughly the height of a high hurdle, and hurdles had been her specialty. Still, she saw no reason to bother with the gate and left the ground off of her right foot, her left stretching far out in front of her as her upper body leaned forward.

Pivoting on the balls of her feet as she hit the ground, Platinov turned toward a screened-in back porch. The door appeared to be on the other side of the boxlike area, and the shadows were such that she couldn't see what was inside. As it always did when the adrenaline pumped through her body, her thoughts raced at the speed of light.

What were her options?

Platinov knew she could try to burst through the screen on this side of the porch. But if she did, she was likely to get tangled up in wire and stalled indefinitely. She could pull out her Spyderco Military knife, flip it open and cut her way through the screen. But even if she was able to create an opening with only one downward slash there would be a second or two during which she'd be standing there, nearly perfectly still and in full view of anyone inside the screen. If there was one or more CLODO terrorists on the back porch, Platinov knew she'd be riddled with holes long before she was through cutting the screen.

The third option seemed the most reasonable, the Russian agent thought as she continued to sprint forward without breaking her stride. Go around the porch to where the door had to be. That would accomplish two things. It would get her inside the porch with the minimum amount of trouble, and it would alert her to the presence of any CLODO terrorists who could see her from the shadows. They were bound to shoot at her.

But at least she'd be making them shoot at a moving target.

Reaching for the door latch, Platinov held her Gold Cup pistol close to her body as she pushed through the door. Out of the sun now, she could barely make out several pieces of lawn furniture on the back porch.

There were no CLODO men. If there had been, she'd have been dead by now.

As her eyes began to adjust to dim light, Platinov saw the sliding glass door that led from the porch to the inside of the house. She reached out and grasped the handle, tugging it to the side.

Locked.

Just before she stepped back and fired three carefully placed .45 rounds through the glass, Platinov heard the sound of crashing wood at the front of the house. Good. At least that meant Cooper was still alive, and now they had Rouillan trapped between them.

Sliding the strap of her bag off her shoulder, Platinov covered her head and face as best she could with the thick canvas, then charged forward, her shoulder hitting the glass in the center of the triangle she had created with her three .45 rounds. Glass fell around her in both tiny pieces and razor-edged sheets as she forced herself forward, trying to get out of the way of the deadly cascade.

Platinov didn't stop moving until she ran into the refrigerator on the other side of the wall. Obviously, she was in the kitchen. A quick check of her arms, legs and torso beneath the cut-off sweatshirt proved that she had suffered nothing more than a couple of superficial nicks.

She'd been lucky.

Feeling her pulse slow, Platinov shook her head and shrugged, ridding herself of the splinters of glass that remained. She had to begin searching this house for Rouillan. Although they hadn't talked about it in advance, it only made sense that she would move cautiously forward while Cooper made his way rearward. They would meet somewhere in the middle of the house, and one of them would either have Rouillan in tow or would have killed him.

Platinov checked under the cabinets of the kitchen and in the broom closet. From there she made her way down a short hallway to a bedroom. A bed with a rumpled comforter dominated the room, flanked by two armoires. She checked the closet. Empty.

Another bedroom lay almost directly across the hall. Platinov could hear Cooper's footsteps in the bathroom closer to the front as she pulled back the shower curtain and trained the muzzle of the Gold Cup .45 into the empty shell.

Where the hell was Rouillan?

Platinov saw Cooper standing in the middle of the next room she entered, which was roughly in the center of the house. The big, ruggedly handsome American stood in the middle of the room, his .44 Magnum pistol dangling at the end of his arm, as he watched her slowly pass through the doorway.

"You didn't find him?" Platinov asked as she came to a halt five feet away.

Cooper shook his head.

"How could he get away?" Platinov asked. She already knew what had happened. She had known it since she'd first looked into the room.

A throw rug had been hurriedly and sloppily folded halfway over itself to Cooper's side, and she had seen the ring inside the floor depression at his feet, and the square made by the cracks where the trapdoor had been cut out of the wood.

Cooper held a finger to his lips, then said, "Stay quiet. And ready." He dropped to one knee on the floor beside the opening ring. "For all we know, he's right inside here, waiting."

Platinov took a two-handed grip on her Gold Cup pistol and aimed it at the trapdoor.

A moment later, the big American jerked the ring and

the trapdoor practically tore off its hinges. He aimed his Desert Eagle downward at the same spot Platinov's .45 pointed, but neither pistol was necessary.

All they could see below the floor was a semi-lit set of crudely made wooden steps and what appeared to be more dim light coming from one side of the hole.

Platinov realized she'd been holding her breath and let it out. It was a tunnel, and while they would follow it in the hopes of finding Rouillan somewhere beneath the streets and houses of Chartres, the Russian woman knew that their effort would be futile. Rouillan had several minutes head start on them, and he would be able to travel at top speed while they'd have to negotiate every twist and turn that afforded a place where an ambush could be set up.

Not to mention trying to spot trip wires for land mines and other improvised explosive devices. And while she had been well-trained in booby-trap detection, and Cooper had proved to be just as good or better when they'd worked together in the past, such precautions would slow them to a crawl.

Rouillan would be long out of the tunnel before they were even halfway through.

Platinov looked up at her partner. Although his face remained stoic, she could see both anger and disappointment in his eyes. He had thought their mission was about to be successfully completed, too. He had believed they were about to find Rouillan and end the threat that he and his CLODO organization were posing to the world.

It hadn't turned out that way. Not at all.

Platinov had started to step toward the first of the rough wooden steps leading down into the ground when Cooper held up a hand to stop her. The anger was still in his eyes. But the disappointment had vanished and been replaced with a brand-new resolve. "I'll go first," he said.

Platinov bristled slightly. "Why?" she demanded. "Because you are a man?"

The big American chuckled in what she could see was genuine mirth. "No," he said as he lowered a foot down to the first wooden step. "Because you're a doctor," he said. "If I make a mistake and get an arm blown off, I'd kind of like to have a doctor with all of her own limbs intact to fix me up again."

Platinov felt the tension that had suddenly entered her shoulders relax again. The man had a point. The KGB had sent her to medical school as soon as her Olympic career had ended, and she had come out with the Russian equivalent of an MD. "I don't even have a first-aid kit with me," she said.

Cooper took another step downward. "No, but you've got your brain," he said. "And just like the brain being the best weapon, common sense mixed with medical training is a great tool."

Slowly, and still a little reluctantly, Platinov said, "If, as you said, you get an arm blown off there will be little I can do." She took in a deep breath, then added, "There will be no way to shut off the arteries, and you will bleed to death before I could get you back to the surface for proper care."

Cooper continued to descend into the tunnel. "Well, then, Plat," he said with a tiny trace of irony in his voice, "I'll just have to do my best not to let that happen." A second later he disappeared into the darkness of the tunnel below.

CHAPTER SIX

Behind him, Bolan could hear Platinov descending the rugged wooden steps into the tunnel. The Executioner was amused at the Russian agent's sudden outburst of feminism. All it had done was confirm something that Bolan had known ever since they'd first worked their first mission together.

Platinov was human, and that meant she had weaknesses as well as strengths. Granted, she was one of the most capable partners with whom he'd ever teamed up, but the same competitive spirit that had earned her Olympic gold and made her a top agent could also work negatively. During the days before the fall of the Soviet Union, children who showed athletic prowess were jerked out of the mainstream schools and taught to let nothing stand in the way of their victories.

Platinov had been a product of this system, and that mind-set still remained in the deepest recesses of her brain. The woman had to be first at anything she undertook. Second best would never be enough. *Second* only meant you were the top loser, and it didn't matter whether it came in Olympic competition or who entered a dangerous tunnel first.

Bolan had holstered the Desert Eagle and drawn his Beretta 93-R. In the confines of a tunnel like the one he was about to enter, the .44 Magnum pistol could truly produce permanent deafness. Now, as he waited for Platinov to join him, he reached into his jacket pocket with his other hand and pulled out a small flashlight.

The tunnel ahead was semi-lit with lightbulbs strung together with cheap wiring. They provided enough illumination to walk, but the soldier sensed that the dimness was in place for another reason, too.

Bolan twisted his head to both sides, then looked up at the low roof. Both the walls and the ceiling of the tunnel were an odd combination of moist earth, shale and other rock. In several places, he could see the fresh tool marks where some of the underground boulders had been chipped back, which meant that Rouillan, or more likely some of his CLODO underlings, had built it. It might, or might not, eventually connect to other centuries-old catacombs closer to the cathedral. Chartres had been around since the Middle Ages, when such underground tunnels were common.

As he continued forward, Bolan knew that land mines and trip wires would not be noticed in this half-darkened tunnel. He would have to trust the bright light from the flashlight to illuminate what was nearly invisible in the darkened tunnel.

The soldier thumbed the on button at the butt of the flashlight, turned to Platinov, then said, "You ready?"

"I am ready."

Bolan nodded. "Watch for trip wires or other booby traps." He twisted the ring around the bulb end of the flashlight and spread the spot-beam out to encompass the rest of the tunnel. He had taken only three more steps when he saw the first trip line.

The soldier felt Platinov's breath on the back of his neck as he froze in place to look closer. He pointed down at the spiderweb-thin line that stretched across the rocky floor of the tunnel at ankle height.

"I see it," Platinov whispered.

Bolan stepped over the trip line and the Russian woman followed.

As soon as they had both safely transversed the first booby trap Bolan stopped again. Shoving the Beretta into his waistband, he reached out to his side and grabbed Platinov's arm to keep her from moving on. With the other hand, he cast the flashlight's beam ahead of him. He had set more land mines than he could remember during his lifetime, and he understood that strategic placement was every bit as important as the explosives themselves.

The Executioner felt his eyebrows lower as he put himself in the mind of whoever had set the traps, probably Rouillan himself. The CLODO leader would know that unseasoned warriors would have missed the first line, tripped whatever explosive device to which it was attached and ended their pursuit right there. But the

French terrorist would also know that anyone more experienced would have seen it and stepped over it. Right now, they'd be breathing a sigh of relief and congratulating themselves.

Which also meant they'd have relaxed their guard. They would certainly know that more traps lay ahead. But they would subconsciously believe they wouldn't encounter the next one for at least a few more steps. That meant that an expert land miner would string up another trip wire immediately.

The bright light had illuminated two more near-invisible lines even before Platinov had crossed the first. One ran diagonally from the upper left-hand corner of the tunnel to the lower right side. The second line crossed it from right to left, forming an *X* in the center of the underground passageway.

Bolan let go of Platinov's arm, drew the Beretta again and used it to point at the middle of the thin *X* in front of them.

The Russian woman acknowledged what she saw with another nod.

The soldier tapped the button on the end of the flashlight and allowed the tunnel to be lit by nothing more than the bare lightbulbs. Just as he'd expected, the trip lines became totally invisible. Without the flashlight, he and Platinov would have been blown to bits by a claymore or some improvised explosive devise buried in the soil around them.

The only way through the lines was to belly crawl below the point where they met in the middle. Bolan dropped to his chest and began pulling himself forward on his elbows. Platinov followed.

The Executioner twisted his body sharply to the side as soon as he'd crawled under the X, making room for Platinov to follow. But there was another reason he had stayed close to the crossed trip wires, and he saw it now in the illumination cast by the flashlight.

Still another thin wire stretched across the tunnel at the same ankle height as the first one they'd avoided. Had he kept crawling forward, he'd have tripped it with his head or throat. "Stay close," the Executioner whispered to Platinov.

The Russian agent slid under the X. "I see the next one," she breathed. "Any higher up?"

Bolan moved the flashlight beam slowly up both sides of the wall. "None I can see," he said. "Give me a second to check closer."

Aiming the flashlight beam upward toward the top of the tunnel, Bolan rose slowly to his feet. It didn't surprise him a bit when he saw yet another trip wire directly overhead at shoulder level. "Don't stand up yet," he told Platinov. "Another line above."

The Russian agent froze in place, waiting.

The Executioner had risen to his knees, and found himself between the low wire ahead and the X behind him, with less than three inches on either side. Whoever had set these traps knew his business. If someone got past the X, they faced the next low-line. And even if they saw it before they hit it, they'd be likely to jerk themselves back and away from this new surprise, hitting the

X from the rear rather than the front. For anyone experienced enough to get past that, there was the overhead line that would break on a person's head or shoulders when he or she stood back up.

"You see the next one?" Bolan asked.

The Russian agent nodded. "Ingenious," she said. "Rouillan must have a Russian working for him."

Bolan didn't comment as he shone the light ahead, then stepped over the low trip line while hunching down to avoid the higher one. He then saw that the pathway was clear—at least to the next bend in the winding tunnel.

Behind him, Bolan felt Platinov's presence as she stepped over and under the trip wires, then stopped next to him. "He's probably in Texas by now," the Russian woman said.

Bolan nodded. "Or he could be hiding just around that next corner," he said. "We've got no choice but to go on and hope that we find some sort of lead that'll point toward where he went."

He continued on, the flashlight in his left hand, the Beretta 93-R in his right. He scanned the tunnel for more trip lines but he spotted none. When the soldier reached the next bend, he dropped to a squat and held the flashlight over his head, then duck-walked around the corner with the Beretta aimed slightly upward.

Bolan found no one on the other side. But somewhere, far in the distance, he could now hear a chattering sound. Platinov, just behind him, heard the sound, too. She froze in place, her lips barely moving when she said, "Is that what I think it is?"

"I guess that depends on what you think it is," the soldier said, returning to an upright position.

"It sounds like rats," the woman said with a slight quaver in her voice. "Dozens…no hundreds of rats."

As if to confirm her words something dark and furry suddenly darted toward them in the shadows along the tunnel wall, ran across Platinov's running shoes, then disappeared again into the darkness behind them.

Platinov shrieked at the top of her lungs.

The Russian woman's reaction surprised Bolan. Gently, he reached out and placed his hand on her shoulder. He found the woman's whole body shaking in terror. "Relax," he said. "It's just a rat."

A hand on the shoulder wasn't enough to calm Platinov, and she pressed her cheek against Bolan's chest and wrapped her arms around him. "It may just be a rat to you," she said through trembling lips. "To me it's a phobia."

The Executioner let out a long breath. "Plat," he said softly, "you and I have been together in countless gunfights, fistfights and knife fights over the years. And we've just spent the last forty-five minutes or so trying not to blow ourselves up. In all that time, I've never sensed one iota of fear in you. It doesn't make any sense for you to be afraid of rats."

"That's why they call it a phobia," Platinov snapped back at him, her voice a mixture of fear, loathing, anger and embarrassment. As she spoke she dug her fingernails into the flesh of his back. "I can't go on, Cooper," she said, still trembling. "I've got to go back."

She stopped talking long enough to take in a breath. "We already know Rouillan's had time to get out of this place. There's no sense in going on. We're not going to find—"

Her words were suddenly covered by a deafening explosion that bounced along the tunnel walls from behind them. A few seconds later, dust began to float around the bend in the tunnel.

When the noise had quieted, Bolan said, "I guess the rat didn't know about the trip wires." He waited for a second to let what he'd just said sink into the shivering woman's mind. Then he added, "I'm afraid going back isn't an option. The tunnel will be blocked with rubble."

"I know," Platinov said angrily.

Her face illuminated by the powerful flashlight, Bolan could see that it had faded to a ghastly white. "Look on the bright side," he said. "One less rat to worry about."

"You are not funny," Platinov said, gripping Bolan's forearm with both of her hands as they moved forward. "Just get me out of here and away from these rats. I'll be just fine again."

Bolan felt the warmth of the woman's fingers as she clamped them around his forearm. They moved through the tunnel, avoiding more trip wires as they went. After a few minutes, small clouds of dust drifted past them from the explosion site.

Several more lone rats scampered across their feet, and each time one did, Platinov screamed. "I can't do this," she said after every shriek of horror.

"We don't have any other choice" was Bolan's answer each time.

Carefully rounding a final twist in the tunnel, the Executioner stopped and stared down the passageway to a spot where the tunnel widened into a cave. "Stay here," he told Platinov.

The Russian woman's voice betrayed conflicting desires. Part of her wanted to go no farther, but the other part didn't want to lose touch with Bolan. After a long pause, she finally said, "Okay."

Slowly, and just as gently as he could, the soldier moved away from her.

Bolan walked forward to the wider underground area, and looked down to see that the cavern floor was roughly two feet below that of the tunnel. That accounted for why so few of the rats had come running their way. The vast majority—and even Platinov had been conservative when she'd guessed at "hundreds"—scampered about the shallow pit, running into, and biting, one another.

That told the Executioner that they had only recently entered this pit. He shot the flashlight to both sides and saw rusty iron gates roughly six feet wide and three feet high. Both gates were open, and more rats were trying to squirm under them into the central pit as he watched. The soldier brought the flashlight back to the center of the cave and saw the dangling rope with the steel ring attached. It swayed, ever so slightly, back and forth above his head, as if it was just now settling back into place after being disturbed. Pulling on the ring had opened the gates, and that pull had happened only minutes earlier.

They were closer to Rouillan than he'd thought.

The soldier aimed his light across the rat-infested depression and saw that the tunnel began again on the other side. But between that passageway and where he stood now, were roughly forty yards of near-solid, wiggling, fighting rats.

For Bolan, that posed no big problem. But for a woman with a true phobia for rats, it was going to be a nightmare.

He turned and hurried back to Platinov's side. "I'm not going to lie to you," he said. "There are more rats down there than I've ever seen in one place in my life." He paused. "But just a short sprint away, on the other side of the rats, this tunnel starts up again."

"I don't know," Platinov finally whispered in a voice that sounded like that of a little girl.

Her tone was so out of character that for a moment, Bolan was wordless. This rat thing reflected a side of Platinov's personality he'd never seen before.

"Do you want me to carry you?" Bolan finally asked.

He felt his Russian partner stiffen. "No," she said firmly. "I was a sprinter. I know how to run."

Bolan turned silent again. It was clear that Platinov's self-respect and professionalism were trying to conquer the unreasonable fear that had taken over her brain ever since they'd encountered the first rat. But which part of her psyche would win remained to be seen.

Bolan decided to let her chance things on her own.

"Okay," he said. "Then the plan couldn't be more simple. The pit is roughly two feet below the floor level we're on now so be sure to account for the drop as soon as we leave this tunnel. Keep your balance. We're going to be stepping on a lot of loud, frightened and angry rats. Pump your knees high so they don't trip you up. I'll go first. With any luck, most of these little guys will scatter like fire in the wind after I've stomped a few of them into the ground. That may open the pathway for you." He paused. "But don't count on it."

Platinov nodded.

The soldier took off ten feet from the edge of the rat pit and sprinted to the edge. Launching his body into the air like a broad jumper, he continued to kick his legs to retain balance and stretch every inch possible out of the jump. He came down hard on his hiking shoes, and felt the crunch of bone as his two-hundred-plus pounds smashed two of the rats into the rocky cavern floor.

For a second, the tunnel echoed with high-pitched death screams.

In a matter of only a few seconds Bolan had reached the other side of the rat-infested cavern. If any of the rodents had bitten him, he hadn't noticed it yet. There would be time enough to check that out later, once Platinov had crossed the pit.

Bolan leaped up and into the tunnel, turned and saw Platinov just now taking her first leap into the pit. The sight caused him to frown. He had told her to give him only around a ten-foot head start, which meant she should have been jumping up out of the pit herself right about now. Fear, however, had caused her to pause, delaying her start and allowing more than enough time for the pathway the Executioner had created to fill up again.

It was not a good sign.

Her jump, however, was excellent. Although she had competed in sprints and hurdles in the Olympics, the Executioner could see that she was no stranger to the broad-jump sand pit, either. She sailed up and over the chattering rats below her, then ground more rats into the cavern floor with her running shoes.

But then she froze.

Bolan saw it in her eyes. They took on a vacant, distant stare as she stood looking straight ahead. Her face was even more pale than it had been when he'd checked it earlier, and she didn't even seem to notice when a rat ran up her leg to her shoulder, then fell off again.

"Plat!" Bolan shouted at the top of his lungs. "Wake up!"

If she had heard his words, the Russian agent didn't respond to them.

Bolan didn't hesitate. Jumping back into the pit of angry rats, he ran toward the statuelike woman. But by the time he reached her, he could see half a dozen of the filthy, razor-toothed vermin crawling up her chest and arms.

Bolan barely registered the fact that other rats had chosen him to scurry up, but a second before he reached Platinov, he felt a searing pain in his forearm and looked down to see that one of the rodents had sunk its teeth into his flesh.

Flinging it violently off to the side with a wave of his arm, Bolan ground to a stop in front of Platinov. He leaned forward, grabbed Platinov and threw her over his shoulder in a fireman's carry. Turning, he felt tiny feet running up and down his legs.

As he made his way back to the tunnel entrance, the Executioner saw a large rat on the back of Platinov's thigh. Reaching down as he continued to run through the multitude of vermin, he wrapped his fingers around the rat's neck and squeezed, hearing bones pop beneath his hand. As he prepared to leap up to the tunnel entrance, the soldier slammed the rat against the stone wall of the cavern.

As soon as they were out of the pit again, Bolan lifted Platinov off his shoulder into the air and shook her violently back and forth. Rats that had clung to her legs, chest and back flew from the woman, shrieking and screeching as they struck the tunnel walls and floor. Pulling a final pair of the rodents from where they had bored their way into her hair, Bolan placed Platinov down on the tunnel floor. He brushed several more of the rodents off his legs, back and chest and watched them scamper away—some farther down the tunnel, others back to the pit.

The soldier looked down at Platinov's eyes. The lids were closed. He had stuck the Beretta back in his waistband before he'd started his own run, and now he used that hand to peel open the woman's eyelids. The beautiful brown orbs inside stared straight upward, her brain not accepting whatever messages the eyes were sending to it.

"Plat," Bolan said. "Plat. Can you hear me?"

He got no response.

The Executioner tried calling her out of the trance twice more before he finally slapped her lightly across the face. "Plat, can you hear me?" he asked.

When he started to slap her again, Bolan suddenly saw the woman's arm rise and her fingers clamp down tightly around his wrist. "Hit me again," Platinov said in the old voice with which he was so familiar, "and I'll kill you."

Bolan chuckled in relief. "You back to your old self again?" he asked innocently.

"No," Platinov said, shaking her head as Bolan helped her to her feet. "I am like I was before but embarrassed."

"Forget it. Almost everyone—even the bravest of warriors—has some secret fear."

The color had returned to the Russian woman's face as she stood up. "Perhaps," she said in a slightly irritated tone. "But I had always planned to keep mine confidential."

"It's better this way," Bolan said. "Next time we run into a few thousand rats I'll know what to expect."

"You are still not funny," Platinov said, scratching her arms like someone who felt the need for an immediate bath or shower. "Particularly since it appears that you are one of the few who has no fear of anything."

Bolan shook his head. "That's not true."

"Oh, really?" Platinov said. "Then tell me. What *are* you afraid of?"

"Failure."

"But you always win. I've seen that many times in the past."

Bolan glanced at his watch. There had never been much chance of catching up to Rouillan in this tunnel. But now it was totally out of the question. The best thing to do was continue on as they had been and hope they found some trace of the CLODO leader that might lead them to him somewhere else.

"You didn't answer me," Platinov said. "You always win."

"Maybe the fear of losing, and letting hundreds, or thousands of people fall prey to the evil in this world is the reason I win," the Executioner told her. He shrugged. "It's what keeps me going, I suppose." He stood and pulled the woman to her feet. "In any case, let's get moving. I plan for us to win this one, too."

With the flashlight illuminating the tunnel again, Bolan led the way on through the bowels of Chartres.

Platinov followed. "We have both been bitten several times," she said. "We will need rabies shots."

Bolan nodded. "I knew I'd brought a doctor with me for some reason," he said.

PIERRE ROUILLAN WAITED until the last of his computer team had emerged from the trapdoor, then lowered it and set the final trip wire. It was connected to three claymores hidden in the tunnel walls below, and would take out the man and woman following him if nothing else had so far.

A few moments later, Rouillan led the way down the steps of the building in which that end of the tunnel was hidden. Behind him, almost in military formation, came his six computer experts. They all stopped on the sidewalk, with the six CLODO members crowded around their leader for their next orders. Rouillan was about to speak when he heard the muffled explosion a block or so away. All of the CLODO terrorists' heads, as well as those of the rest of the people in the vicinity, turned toward the sound.

Rouillan had never heard a claymore go off underground, but he knew that could be the only explanation. He couldn't keep the smile off his face. "Go home, pack some clothes and meet me in Marseille," the CLODO leader whispered to his crew. Then he fell in with several curious strangers heading toward the sound of the blast.

Either the man or the woman disguised as tourists had broken one of his carefully set trip lines, and it appeared that they had done so before they'd even reached his rat trap.

Too bad, the CLODO leader thought as he turned a corner and walked toward a crowd of people. As he got closer, Rouillan could see a heap of broken concrete sidewalk, stone and dirt. The soil was mostly damp, but enough of it was dry that the wind was blowing it through the air to create a thin, sinus-irritating fog.

"What happened?" Rouillan heard a voice call out as he approached the crowd around the destruction.

"No one knows," said another faceless voice within the mass.

"It must have been a gas line," stated yet another unseen voice.

"It could have been terrorists," suggested a woman on the other side of the mound of clutter.

"Don't be an idiot," said the man standing next to her. "Why would any terrorist group blow up something underground?"

The woman clamped her lips together, a sad look coming over her face as if she was used to being treated poorly by the man.

Rouillan made his way through the people to the front of the circle. Several attractive young women caught his eye, and each time one did he was tempted to strike up a conversation. But each time, he forced his mind back to the matter at hand.

Everyone had an Achilles' heel of one sort or another, Rouillan knew, and his was beautiful women. For some reason, he associated sex with his pursuit of terrorism against computers and all that used them. He didn't know why, but the relation had been there for as long as he could remember.

Looking downward at the rubble now, his best guess was that his pursuers had trapped one of the ankle-length wires. He found himself frowning. If they had gotten that far, they had encountered and avoided at least a dozen of the traps he'd set, which meant the couple was looking out for them.

So why had they failed to notice this one?

If Rouillan remembered correctly, and he was certain that he did, the line directly below the heap of rubble had been a single ankle-height thread. It was the last explosive on that side of the rat pit, and placed there simply to build false confidence in anyone who had made it that far without being blown up.

"Does anyone know for sure what happened?" Rouillan asked the crowd in general with an innocent face.

The same man who had been rude to his wife spoke up again. "Gas line," he said with the certainty of an expert. "Had to be."

Rouillan nodded, satisfied. A moment ago, someone else had thrown out the "exploding gas line" idea as nothing more than a theory. Within seconds, the loudmouth across the heap from Rouillan had turned that theory into fact.

So went human nature, Rouillan supposed. Most people were as easily led as sheep, and part of his brain said he should abandon his mission to rid the world of computers and simply let them take total control like the various governments around the world had planned.

But that thought left his mind as swiftly as it had come. No. While he might have contempt for the common man in every society, there were a few people, such as himself, who deserved freedom and privacy. And he would never give up his quest to preserve those liberties for those who deserved them.

A police siren sounded in the distance as Rouillan pulled out his cell phone and tapped in a number. Then, as the line began to ring, he turned to walk away. There was no hurry. The man and woman in the tunnel were dead, and the police would assume the explosion had been from a natural gas pipeline, too. Not forever. But at least until it was proved differently.

The seeming absurdity of terrorists blowing something up underground with no casualties would drop that idea to the bottom of the gendarmes' list of possible causes. Besides, most people around the world these days believed the words *terrorist* and *al Qaeda* were synonymous. They had all but forgotten European- and American-based groups like CLODO.

All of which worked in Pierre Rouillan's favor as the time for his worldwide strike drew ever closer.

Rouillan left the scene and walked several blocks to where he'd parked his car. As he got in, he wondered if the bodies of the man and woman would be found, or if they'd been shredded beyond recognition. Either way, they were out of his hair and no longer a threat.

He was winning, Rouillan realized as he drove away.

But the big win was yet to come.

"How MANY TIMES were you bitten?" Platinov asked as they started down the tunnel again.

"I don't know. Several. You?"

"Too many," the Russian woman replied, her voice still shaking slightly. "But my medical bag is packed in the back at the car. We will both take injections just as soon as we can get back there."

"That's nice to know," Bolan said. Then, doing his

best to get the Russian woman's mind off of what had just happened, he added, "I don't think frothing at the mouth would add to your attractiveness one bit."

Platinov laughed, but it sounded forced.

The trap lines and booby traps continued on the other side of the rat pit. But with the help of the flashlight, Bolan and Platinov navigated their way over, under and around them without any more close calls. As they walked on, a faint smell of smoke wafted back toward them from somewhere farther down the underground passageway.

"What is that smell?" Platinov asked.

The Executioner frowned. "Smells like an electrical fire."

The odor grew stronger with each step until they finally reached another larger cavern carved out of the rock-and-mud walls. Bolan stopped at the entrance where the tunnel widened, and Platinov stepped up next to him.

He looked from his left to his right. What he saw were six wooden computer stations, three on each side of the cavern. All of them had burned, and smoke still drifted slowly upward from the remains.

"A little hypocritical," Platinov said. "CLODO is supposed to be so anticomputer."

"Hypocrisy isn't something terrorist organizations ever worry about," Bolan said. "If *they* do something—even the exact same thing their enemies have done—it's always justified." He stepped into the larger cavern and walked swiftly toward the nearest computer on the left.

Some sort of inner explosive device had gone off beneath the thick plastic cover of the hard drive, and the screen had cracked into thousands of tiny pieces, making it look like a hurriedly constructed mosaic. Sparks still crackled inside the wiring, emitting the smoke that they'd first noticed

The Executioner circled the cavern. All six of the computers were in roughly the same condition.

"Is there anything we can salvage?" Platinov asked.

Bolan shrugged. "If my computer expert was here, he might be able to cull something out of this mess, but I doubt it. I don't think it's worth the effort to carry all this stuff out of here and send it to the States for him to look at." He paused for a moment, then said, "But it's worth a call." He reached into his cargo shorts and pulled out the satellite phone. But when he tried to get a tone, the rock and mud overhead prevented contact. "We'll have to wait until we get out of here," he finally said and shoved the phone back in his pocket.

"At least CLODO has lost whatever information it had stored here," Platinov said.

Bolan shook his head. "Not necessarily. They had plenty of lead time that we were coming. I suspect when Rouillan came through here he had all of the information on the hard drives sent somewhere else before destroying these machines and taking whoever it was working them out of here with him."

Platinov looked fatigued.

"We'll find him, Plat," Bolan said, hoping to raise her spirits. He never allowed the possibility of defeat to enter his mind, and he didn't want such negative energy affecting his Russian partner, either. "Just not through these things." He swept a hand across the room, indicating the computers.

Leading the way, the soldier moved out of the computer cavern and on into the tunnel. They made their way through several more thin trip lines. Finally, they rounded a curve in the tunnel and came to an abrupt dead end. In the flashlight's glow Bolan could see another set of crude wooden steps not unlike the ones he and Platinov had descended from the safe house. He stopped just in front of them and aimed the flashlight overhead.

Above, he could see the tiny cracks and hinges of another trapdoor. A small wooden knob was attached to the underside at the front in order to close it from the bottom. But the door itself appeared to open upward, and as far as he could see, there were none of the floss-thin trip wires between him and what had to be an exit from the tunnel.

Platinov was back to her old self again, and she voiced the Executioner's next thought for him. "It could be on the other side," she said.

Bolan knew she was referring to another claymore and trip line.

"Rouillan knew he was being chased," the Russian went on. "He may have rigged this exit up as the final safeguard against pursuit." She took in a deep breath. "I will check it," she said, trying to push past Bolan.

He blocked her path. "I'll do it. You stay here."

Platinov's face clouded with anger. Bolan could see she was still embarrassed, and in dire need of making up for the way she'd behaved back at the rat pit. "There are no rats up there," she said sharply. "And I am perfectly capable of—"

"I know you're perfectly capable of doing it yourself," Bolan said as he turned his back to her and began mounting the steps. "That's not the point." He reached the top, took a deep breath and prepared to pull down on the small wooden rectangle above him. "But like I said before, what if I screw up and lose an arm? I want a medical doctor close at hand. You're more valuable in that capacity right now than you are looking for explosives."

Platinov wasn't completely buying his line of reasoning, but she accepted it.

Bolan grasped the tiny wooden knob, then slowly began to push. The wood creaked with excruciatingly slow squeaks as he edged his face around to stare through the tiny crack as it began to let in a dim light.

The soldier knew that shining the flashlight through the crack to search for a trip line would also serve as an announcement of their presence to anyone watching above. But he had no other ideas on how to handle the situation. So, with the Beretta in his right hand and the flashlight in his left, he aimed the beam through the half-inch crack he had created.

There was no sign of a trip wire.

If Rouillan had, indeed, set one final trap before

fleeing the tunnel, he would have had to have set it in a way that it could be disarmed—he could not be certain that he wouldn't find himself in the tunnel again from the other side, necessitating that he exit this way later. That meant there had to be at least enough slack in the line to get a hand through.

Slowly, the Executioner pushed the trapdoor open farther.

As soon as he'd opened the door enough to squeeze his hand through the opening, Bolan stuck the end of the flashlight in his teeth and reached up, slipping his hand through the narrow space. Slowly, with the gentle touch of a painter putting the final strokes of paint on his canvas, the Executioner worked his hand around the slit above him.

He found the trip wire almost as soon as he'd cleared the front of the trapdoor and was working his way down the side.

"Bingo," Bolan said, glancing down at Platinov.

"You found it?"

"I found it." Bolan moved his hand slowly back away from the wire. "Go back around that last bend in the tunnel, Plat," he said.

Platinov's face turned angry again. "Like hell I will," she said. "If you—"

"Plat," the Executioner said in a slightly exasperated tone, "this has nothing to do with courage or bravery or anything else except for the fact that there's no need for both of us to risk getting blown to pieces. So go, will you? I'll call to you as soon as I've figured out the setup and cleared it. And I'll promise to let you do the very next dangerous thing we come across, okay?"

The expression on the woman's face told the Executioner that she understood his reasoning. Reluctantly, she turned and walked a few yards back down the tunnel.

Bolan let his hand move slowly back to the thin line he'd felt before. This one was different than the trip wires he'd found in the rest of the tunnel. There was no way to go over, under, or around it. His fingers followed the threadlike material a few inches toward the middle of the trapdoor, then he pulled his hand back and reinserted it on the other side.

The line ran all the way across the middle of the door, and even now was resting on the top side of the cover. That meant that opening it any farther would break the line and set off the bomb.

With his hand still extended upward through the crack, Bolan closed his eyes, trying to picture the setup that he couldn't see above him. The trip wire had to be attached to something on both sides of the door and, as he'd thought before, it had to be done in a way that Rouillan himself could dismantle it from below in case he found himself in such a predicament.

Opening his eyes once more, the soldier allowed his fingers to move softly along the line, away from the door this time. A few inches from the side, he felt the cold hardness of a steel rod.

The trip line had been looped around it.

Bolan let his fingers travel from the thread to the rod,

finding that the steel was shaped like an *L* and screwed into the floor next to the trapdoor. Slowly bringing his hand back up the tiny post, he found the loop again and began working it off the end of the post. It took only a few seconds.

"Got it," the Executioner called down the tunnel to Platinov. Then, with a sigh of relief, he started to push the trapdoor upward. Bolan stopped almost as soon as he'd started. He had found the trip line, but where in the rule book did it say there could be only one?

Platinov had come back down the tunnel to where Bolan stood on the wooden steps.

"Go back again," Bolan said. "There could be more."

With a snort of disgust, Platinov did as she'd been told.

There was enough room for Bolan to stick his head through the opening now and, climbing one more step on the scraps of wood that served as steps, he inched his eyes out of the opening. He was in what looked like a very small, semi-lit closet.

But for that, the soldier was grateful. He could just as easily have emerged into a room full of CLODO men circling the overhead and firing bullets into his skull.

Twisting his body and climbing yet one more step, Bolan got the flashlight in his teeth over the partially open trapdoor and suddenly realized where he was. Two of the walls were blank, but a third consisted of a thick curtain.

The side wall toward which he was now facing had

a small sliding door cut into it, which was halfway open, revealing a screened window. Bolan glanced to his side and saw a bench. The trapdoor exit was hidden in a church confessional booth, possibly the Cathedral of Our Lady of Chartres, considering their location.

But what was even more important to the soldier at the moment was what he saw a few inches above the door. A second trip wire, mounted on another set of *L*-shaped steel rods, was set and ready to detonate as soon as he pushed the trapdoor open another few inches— the few inches necessary to get the rest of his, or anyone else's, body out through the hole.

Carefully, he studied the apparatus. It was identical to the first and, returning the Beretta to his waistband, Bolan quickly unlooped the line from the post. Then, cautiously inspecting every inch of the rest of the confessional with the flashlight, he finally opened the door the rest of the way and climbed out.

Platinov followed, with Bolan pulling her up the last few steps by an arm.

The two warriors froze inside the narrow confines of the confessional. On the other side of the curtain, they could hear voices, but it didn't sound as if mass was being said. More like the cathedral was open for tourists to visit.

Bolan pushed the curtain a half inch to the side and saw men, women and children examining the various aspects of the cathedral's sanctuary. He turned back to Platinov. "This is the only way out," he said. "And Rouillan might be out there with the other visitors."

"I doubt it," Platinov said.

"So do I," Bolan agreed, "but we need to keep the possibility in mind. You ready?"

"Certainly," she said. "But what do you think the people outside are going to think we've been doing in here? After all, they didn't see us go in. So they'll believe we have been in here a very long time."

Bolan chuckled softly. "Let's just go," he said. "We've got work ahead of us, and it doesn't make much difference what a bunch of tourists out there think." He turned to face the curtain again.

Only a few of the eyes in the sanctuary even paid them any attention as Bolan and Platinov stepped out of the confessional. "Do you think whoever is in charge of this church is in league with CLODO?" the Russian woman whispered.

"I doubt it. This place is open to the public around the clock. It would be easy enough for any of the CLODO people to just pose as tourists on their way in and out." He paused for a moment, his eyes scanning the sanctuary and finally falling on a priest in a long black robe near the front of the room. "Besides," he said as he started toward the man, "they'd have used the other entrance—the one back at the safe house—ninety-nine percent of the time. This one was just for emergencies."

Platinov fell in behind the Executioner as he moved sideways across a row of church pews, then walked down the center aisle of the sanctuary. The priest was talking to an older man who held an unlit candle in his hand, but they ended their conversation just as Bolan and Platinov arrived.

The priest turned toward them and smiled, his lips barely visible through the thick hair of a long shaggy beard and mustache. "May I help you?" he asked in excellent, if accented, English after sizing them up.

"Father," Bolan said, "I'm going to trust you with some very sensitive information. It can't be repeated."

"No problem," the priest replied. "We've got that confidentiality thing going for us, you know. Do we need to go into the confessional?"

"I don't think so. We were just there."

Deep wrinkles appeared in the priest's forehead as he said, "I'm afraid I don't understand."

Briefly, Bolan explained about CLODO, the tunnel and the booby traps and trapdoor inside the confessional.

"I was aware of the catacombs," the priest admitted. "But we've shut them off from the public for safety reasons." His eyes moved toward the confessional. "But I've been in there myself every day. How is it I didn't blow myself up?"

"For one thing," Bolan said, "you were on the other side. But it's also because, while the claymores were in place, the wire wasn't set until a little while ago today. We were the first to encounter the trap after it became operative. Purely luck on our part."

The priest looked the Executioner squarely in the eyes. "Luck? Maybe, maybe not." He hooked a thumb over his shoulder at the large crucifix behind the pulpit at the front of the sanctuary.

"Could be that, too," Bolan agreed.

The priest frowned as he turned back to face them. "I think I know the answer I'm going to get," he said, "but I feel that I need to ask anyway. Just who are you two?"

"We're two people who are on your side, Father," Bolan said. "That's about all I can tell you."

"That's what I was afraid I was going to hear. But I'm pretty sensitive to good and evil, and I'm getting a 'good' reading from both of you. So, how can I help you?"

"Have you noticed anyone unusual around here today? Within the last couple of hours, for instance?"

"I haven't noticed any unusual *people* around here," the priest said, "but there was an explosion down the street a little while ago."

Bolan nodded. "Thanks, Father."

Then, turning to Platinov, he said, "Let's go."

He and Platinov walked hurriedly down the aisle toward the front door, then stepped out onto the large concrete porch of the Cathedral of Our Lady of Chartres.

Almost immediately, they saw the crowd of people down the block gathered around the spot where the claymore had exploded. Bolan remembered the rat that had scampered past them, only to meet his demise by tripping one of the low lines.

The flashing lights of several police cars, as well as a police helicopter overhead, heightened the excitement filling the air as Bolan and Platinov descended the steps at the front of the cathedral. Besides the crowd already at the scene, other people in the area were hurrying forward, anxious to learn what the commotion was all about. A few men, women and children, however, seemed content to view the spectacle from a distance and stood at various levels of the cathedral's steps or down on the sidewalk in front of the building.

"So where do we go from here?" Platinov asked softly as they stopped just before the steps.

"I wish I knew. I didn't see anything down there—" he let his gaze drop to the ground, indicating the tunnel "—that would lead me to any place in particular where Rouillan would go next. We're going to have to come up with a lead on our own." Even as he spoke the words, however, he caught sight of something familiar in his peripheral vision.

While the attention of the vast majority of people was focused on the rubble down the street, one man stood out among the rest. All the way down at sidewalk level, he stood wearing a blue beret, a short-sleeved tan shirt and brown trousers.

And the man seemed to have no interest in what was going on down the street. He was far too busy staring, openmouthed, at Bolan and Platinov.

As soon as Bolan looked his way, the man turned and began walking swiftly away from the scene.

Platinov grabbed Bolan's arm. "Did you just see what I saw?" she asked.

"I did," Bolan said. "He's wearing the unofficial uniform that CLODO's people wear to help ID one another."

The man in the beret glanced over his shoulder as if some sort of mental radar had warned him that he was about to be followed. When he saw Bolan and Platinov moving his way, he turned back and broke into a run.

But he was simply no match for an Olympic gold medalist sprinter.

Or the Executioner.

CHAPTER SEVEN

The man in the unofficial CLODO uniform was a classic computer geek. He was close to six feet tall but couldn't have weighed more than 140 pounds.

Bolan and Platinov each grabbed a skinny arm as soon as they'd caught him, and ground to a halt next to an alleyway. Pushing him into the alley and out of sight, the soldier slammed him into the cold bricks of the back of a building, then patted him down head-to-toe.

A pocket protector was clipped into the front shirt pocket of the man's tan shirt and held a variety of pens and pencils. Behind that, in the same pocket, was a smartphone, and in his front pants pocket the Executioner found a cell phone. A calculator was in the other pocket.

"You've got a lot of high-tech gear for a guy who's supposed to hate computers," Bolan said in French. Finding no weapons, he spun the man and slammed his back into the bricks.

For a brief moment, the computer nerd gathered his courage. Replying in the same language he'd been addressed in, he said, "I have nothing illegal on me." Then he raised his chin defiantly. "I broke no laws."

Bolan smiled and looked at Platinov. "This is the part that always amuses me the most. When they think we're cops." Turning back to their prisoner, he went on. "I'm afraid you don't quite understand. We aren't the police, and we aren't arresting you."

"Then, if you are not police, I demand that you let me go," the geek said.

"That's not part of the program, either," Bolan said. He shook his head again, then looked deeply into the man's ferretlike eyes. "I sure hope you're willing to talk, because I'm going to feel like the schoolyard bully if I have to beat the information I want out of you."

"It won't bother me," Platinov said as she stepped between them and drove a fist into the geek's chin.

The frail little computer expert crumpled to the ground, unconscious.

Platinov stepped back and looked at Bolan. "Sorry," she said without a trace of remorse in her voice. "I didn't mean to knock him out."

"I just hope you didn't kill him," Bolan said as he knelt next to the man. "I'd rate your punches somewhere around those of the top light-heavyweights."

Platinov smiled. "I will promise never to box with you," she said as Bolan searched for a pulse in the man's neck.

"Thanks."

"Now, *wrestling,* that's another story altogether. No promises there."

The pulse in the man's neck was strong and steady, and as Bolan stood back up he lifted the man over his shoulder. "Actually, there couldn't be a better time to carry him out of here for interrogation," he said. "Anyone who sees us will just assume he was hurt in the explosion."

Platinov nodded. "Let's get him to the car and somewhere private."

Bolan let her lead the way out of the alley. They walked swiftly along the sidewalk, nodding at the few people they passed and telling the ones who inquired about the unconscious man over the Executioner's shoulder that he'd be just fine, thank you, but they had to hurry him to the hospital. When they reached the Nissan, Bolan shoved him into the backseat and took the wheel. Platinov got in the front next to him, but sat sideways in her seat, ready to deal with the CLODO computer man in case he regained consciousness during the ride.

"Where are we going?" the Russian woman asked the Executioner as he pulled away from the parking spot.

"I don't know for sure," Bolan replied. "We need someplace private and out of the way."

"Just before we reached Chartres," Platinov said, "we passed a quaint little inn with cabins. Maria's or Michelle's or something like that."

"Mireille's," Bolan said. "I remember it. The cabins were around a small lake."

"That's the one," Platinov said. "You could go into the office and rent a cabin while I stay here with this—" she paused for a second, trying to find the right word "—nerf?" she finally said.

Bolan turned the Nissan toward the highway and suppressed a laugh. "I think the word you're looking for is *nerd,*" he said.

"Yes, this computer nerd. Or is he a geek? And what is the difference?"

Bolan had to smile this time. "I think the two words are pretty much interchangeable," he said. By the time he had finished speaking they were on the highway headed back toward Paris. But they soon pulled off onto an access road. Bolan halted the vehicle in front of the sign that read Mireille's, then opened his door and exited the vehicle.

The wooden door that led to the front office stood open, but a full-length glass storm door was closed. Bolan pushed through it and a second later, he was inside at the front desk.

A woman on the other side of the counter stood up from her desk and smiled as she approached the soldier. She was almost as beautiful as Platinov, but in a very different way. Long, brown hair fell down past her shoulders and shone in the sunlight gleaming through the storm door. Her blue eyes held an innocent, almost waiflike appeal.

"You must be Mireille," Bolan said in French.

"I am indeed," the woman agreed.

"Do you have any rooms available?"

"Oui." She reached under the counter and pulled out a registration form and pen. As Bolan filled out the form, Mireille handed him a large square piece of wood with a key attached to it. Cabin Six.

"It is on the other side of the lake," the woman told him.

"Thank you," Bolan said as he turned to leave.

Bolan rejoined Platinov and glanced into the backseat. "Our friend is still asleep?" he said.

"Yes, but he's begun to stir. He'll be easy to wake up once we get him inside.

The soldier nodded, threw the car into Drive and began to circle the lake on a gravel road. He adjusted the rearview mirror so he could see the still-sleeping CLODO computer geek in the backseat. The man looked like such a wimp that the Executioner had to remind himself that looks could be deceiving. Regardless of how weak the computer experts in league with him looked, whatever Rouillan had in mind would take thousands of lives.

As Cooper pulled the car to a halt behind Cabin Six and turned off the ignition, the man in the backseat started to regain consciousness. Platinov hurried out of the vehicle and opened the back door, grabbing the skinny man by the ankles and pulling him out. Her companion walked around the car, handed her the wooden block with the key attached, then lifted the man over his shoulder.

The Russian woman stuck the key in the cabin door

with one hand and twisted the knob with the other, then stood aside to allow Cooper entry. As he dumped their semiconscious prisoner on the couch in the small living room, Platinov returned to the Nissan for her medical bag, then returned to the house.

Setting her bag on the coffee table in front of the semiconscious terrorist, Platinov opened it and pulled out two new hypodermic needles and two small vials. Both she and her companion had been bitten by rats who might, or might not, have rabies. But there was no use in taking chances.

"Come here," Platinov said, looking up at Cooper. She tore the paper covering away from one of the needles, inserted it into one of the vials and drew out the serum. "As you Americans say, it is better to be safe than sorry."

"Arm or hip?" Cooper asked as he came to her.

"The usual procedure for this vaccine is an injection in the arm," Platinov replied. "I will inject you first, then you will inject me."

She swabbed alcohol on his upper arm, then administered the injection. He did the same for her.

The CLODO computer man on the couch had come fully awake during the injection process and was staring at Platinov, his attraction to her easy to read.

The Russian agent glanced at Cooper. The big American had taken note of the computer man's reaction, too. The two locked eyes for a second. Finally, her companion nodded and whispered, "Give it a try if you want."

Get FREE BOOKS and a FREE GIFT when you play the...

LAS VEGAS 7

GAME

Just scratch off the gold box with a coin. Then check below to see the gifts you get!

YES! I have scratched off the gold box. Please send me my **2 FREE BOOKS** and **FREE GIFT** for which I qualify. I understand that I am under no obligation to purchase any books as explained on the back of this card.

366 ADL EVMJ

166 ADL EVMU
(GE-LV-09)

FIRST NAME

LAST NAME

ADDRESS

APT.#

CITY

STATE/PROV.

ZIP/POSTAL CODE

7	7	7	Worth TWO FREE BOOKS plus a FREE Gift!
🍒	🍒	🍒	Worth TWO FREE BOOKS!
🔔	🔔	♣	TRY AGAIN!

Offer limited to one per household and not valid to current subscribers of Gold Eagle® books. All orders subject to approval. Please allow 4 to 6 weeks for delivery.

Platinov nodded back. "What is your name?" she asked the man in a low, husky voice.

The man on the couch stammered for a second, then finally said, "Marc."

"It is nice to meet you, Marc," she purred. "I would like to ask you some questions."

Platinov walked forward and lifted her right leg up, resting her foot on the coffee table.

Marc's eyes widened as the shorts rode higher on Platinov's leg.

"Tell me what you were working on down in that horrible dark cave," Platinov said. "I think it was just terrible that Rouillan made you work down there." She leaned back slightly, thrusting out her breasts and flexing the muscles in her thighs. "With all those rats. Ugh."

"It wasn't so bad," he breathed, staring. "I mean… well…yeah, he's kind of mean sometimes I guess…I don't know."

Platinov stepped up on the coffee table, and now she towered over the man on the couch. She stood there with her hands on her hips for a moment, smiling down at him, then sat down on the table with her knees only inches from his. "Tell me what you were working on, Marc," she said as she crossed her legs and gave him a sultry look. "Please."

Marc was breathing hard, his skinny chest moving in and out at twice the normal speed.

Platinov leaned back and rested her elbows on the coffee table.

Marc shifted his gaze from her legs, upward.

"What were you working on, Marc?" she purred.

"A…virus…"

"What kind of virus?" Platinov pressed.

"I…don't know all of the details…." Marc choked out. "It's…complex."

"Oh, Marc," Platinov said, pouting. "Viruses aren't hard to create. Teenagers all over the world set them in motion every day."

"I know," Marc said. "But creating a virus like we're working on…" He paused. "One that can't be killed, ever, isn't that easy."

Platinov uncrossed her legs and Marc's eyes dropped again. "What kind of virus are we taking about, Marc?"

"I don't know all of it," Marc said.

So close, and yet so far away, Platinov thought. "What part do you know?" she asked. She noticed that Cooper had all but disappeared from the room, gradually moving into a corner of the room to Marc's side where he wouldn't be a distraction from Platinov's unusual interrogation technique. He had his arms folded across his chest as he waited to see what she could get out of the computer terrorist.

"You sent all of the information on your hard drives somewhere before you destroyed the computers, didn't you?" Platinov said. "Where did you send it?"

"I…I can't tell you," Marc stammered.

"Of course you can tell me," Platinov said. "Who said you couldn't tell me?"

Marc looked down for a moment, then back up like

a frightened child. "Rouillan," he said. Then, twisting his head away, his eyes fell on Cooper. Quickly, he looked back at the scantily clad woman on the coffee table.

Marc's eyes looked glazed over as they moved up and down Platinov's body, as if trying to decide which particular part to rest on, yet trying to take the whole show in at the same time, too.

"Yes," Platinov purred. "We know of Rouillan, and we know he can be a very scary man. But he isn't here right now, is he, Marc?"

"No." Marc gulped.

"And I am," Platinov said. She had not yet touched the man on the couch and now, when she suddenly reached forward, put her hand under his chin and raised his eyes to meet hers, Marc looked as if a jolt of electricity had just shot through his body.

Platinov stared into his eyes, her face taking on the most seductive expression she could muster. That was not easy to do while looking at Marc. So she thought of her partner as she continued to force the air in and out of her lungs in slow, deep breaths.

Marc was hypnotized by her eyes, and now the orbs in his own head truly did take on a far and distant look of near-ecstasy.

Platinov released his chin and leaned back on her elbows again. She continued to stare at him, while smiling seductively. "Is Rouillan headed to the same place you sent the information on the hard drives, Marc?" she whispered.

Marc nodded. "I think so."

"And where is that?" she asked.

Marc swallowed, and it looked as if a tennis ball was descending his skinny throat. "Marseille," he finally said.

"Now we're getting someplace," Platinov said. "Good boy, Marc. But Marseille is a big place. Where in Marseille is he going?"

"I don't know the address," Marc said. He had lost all control of himself by now, and started to reach for her. "And it isn't really in Marseille, it's just near it."

Platinov lifted her right leg and extended it out to the side like a ballet dancer stretching her hamstring muscle before practice. She caught Marc's hand in midair and guided it gently back to his side. "No touching, Marc," she said as she brought her right leg back in and extended her left. "At least not yet. First, tell me more about where Rouillan's going and what you're up to. We hear there's a big, big thing coming from CLODO." Purposefully, she stared down at Marc's crotch and then breathed out, "And I just love big, big things. Tell me about *your* big thing, Marc."

The CLODO computer man closed his eyes for a moment, and looked as if he might be getting ready to hyperventilate. "I don't know the address," he repeated, and now his voice had a frantic sound as if he were a little boy whose favorite toy might be taken away from him. "And like I said, it's not really in Marseille, proper. But I helped install the computer systems there a few months ago. I can take you there."

"What are we going to find when we get there?" Platinov asked softly as she reached out with both hands and stroked the underside of her thigh. Leaning forward, she turned her head to the side to look at Marc and leaned in, pressing her cheek against her knee.

"It's a virus that will travel worldwide in mere seconds," Marc told her. "It's designed to destroy the hard drives in every computer it touches. Rouillan estimates it'll shut down about ninety-five percent of the computers around the globe."

Platinov glanced up briefly and saw the frown on the face of the man in the corner. She had to fight to keep one off her own face. The world had reached a point where it couldn't survive a computer catastrophe of that magnitude. Not without falling apart and letting chaos take over.

Now, Platinov had to really work to force her smile. "Good boy, Marc," she said again. She reached out and patted him on the head, then stood up, let him have one final look at her front, then moved to join Cooper.

A confused look crossed Marc's face.

"Good thing we didn't bother to unload the car," Cooper said as he stepped out of the corner again.

The sound of his voice brought Marc back out of his trance. "What…what are we doing?" he sputtered.

"We're going to Marseille, Marc," the big American said as he reached down, grabbed one of the man's skinny arms and hoisted him to his feet. "Or wherever it is around Marseille that you helped install the computers."

"I am going?" Marc asked.

"You sure are."

"And if you do a good job," Platinov added, "I might just have a reward for you."

Marc's face could have only been described as a lecherous smirk as he let Cooper guide him to the cabin door. "But if he's not there, how do I explain you two?"

Cooper reached into his pocket, pulled out more than enough euros to cover a night's lodging and dropped the money on the coffee table where Platinov had sat only moments earlier.

The key had never been taken out of the door when they came in, and now they left it in place again as they abandoned Mireille's Cabin Six. "There's a CLODO cell in the U.S., isn't there?" he asked Marc.

"Yes."

"Well, you just introduce us as fellow CLODO computer experts from the U.S.," he said. "That should be easy enough."

Cooper got behind the wheel, Platinov rode shotgun and Marc got into the backseat of his own volition.

The Russian agent hid her face from the backseat as she whispered to her companion, "Do you like my new impromptu form of interrogation?"

"It worked," he said, his lips betraying only a slight smile. "But it's got to be against the Geneva Convention somehow."

Platinov laughed softly, then came back with, "I didn't torture him."

She watched the big American glance up into the

rearview mirror, then turned her head slightly to look at Marc's pathetic face in the backseat. His glassy eyes were still staring at her.

Cooper was still looking into the mirror when Platinov turned back to him. "I'm not sure that wasn't the very worst kind of torture," he told her.

Platinov had been smiling but now she remembered Marc's words about the computer virus. If Rouillan was successful in launching it, every man, woman and child on the planet was in big trouble.

So the smile faded and turned to a grim expression of determination as they headed toward Marseille.

DAWN WAS BREAKING when they reached the outskirts of Marseille. The largest of France's southern seaports, it had a population of nearly one million people. Marc Ajaccio—the little computer geek in the backseat had given them his last name somewhere during the night drive—guided them along the French Riviera, through a series of coastal towns and resorts. They had almost reached the principality of Monaco—the independent little nation completely surrounded by France—when Marc leaned forward and told the soldier to pull over to the shoulder of the highway.

Bolan did as the computer man had directed, then turned and rested an arm on the back of his seat while Marc frowned down at an open map in his lap. "Turn left at the next intersection," the French computer terrorist said. "It's about two more kilometers."

"You sure?" Bolan asked.

Marc shook his head. "No, I am *not* sure. I was only there once, and as I have already told you, it was many months ago." He paused, looking up at Bolan for a second and even smiling. "But I will find it for you. If it is not this turn, it will be another."

Bolan watched the little man turn his attention back to Platinov, with whom he had obviously fallen for. After the excitement of her unorthodox interrogation had finally worn off, Marc Ajaccio had fallen into an exhausted sleep for most of the drive. But as soon as he'd awakened, his eyes had found their way to the back of Platinov's golden head and stayed glued to her every movement since.

The soldier shook his head. He couldn't help but feel a little bit sorry for Marc, even if he was associated with Rouillan and CLODO. In his mid-to-late thirties and already completely bald on the top of his head, the man wore black plastic eyeglasses so thick that they looked like they'd repel a rifle round. He was obviously starved for female companionship, and probably had few, if any, other interests or hobbies to occupy his time when he was away from his computers. He was the kind of man you often saw at the arcades in American malls, playing computerized games next to children at least twenty years younger than himself.

The Executioner couldn't condone Marc Ajaccio's association with CLODO. But he could understand how a man like this, who had probably been bullied all through school by other boys and completely ignored by the girls, might be susceptible to the charismatic personality of someone like Rouillan, who paid attention to his work, and even praised it.

Bolan pulled the Nissan back onto the highway, then turned left at the corner Marc had indicated. As they drove away from the sea now, the soldier felt his jaw tighten as he thought of Pierre Rouillan.

Bolan had never met the man, but he knew him. He had known many like him over the years. Men, and sometimes women, with limitless charisma but black hearts. Such men preyed on individuals like Marc, making them feel important when no one else ever had before. They became like putty in the hand, committing acts of evil without even realizing what they were doing.

The soldier wasn't sure what to do with Marc Ajaccio after he'd led them to this next CLODO safe house. He couldn't just let the man go free—there was far too high of a risk that he'd report everything he knew to Rouillan.

On the other hand, Bolan would not kill a weak and helpless man. Marc was actually a victim of Rouillan's megalomania himself.

The soldier drove on. He didn't need to make that decision yet, so he'd keep his options open.

A few miles later, Bolan saw a sign directing them on to Avignon. But long before they had reached that city, Marc Ajaccio directed the soldier to turn left toward Arles. Yet another left turn—this time onto an old, grassy road that wound through clusters of wild flowers and tree groves—found them heading back south, toward the sea again.

"This had better not be a stall tactic," Bolan said over his shoulder in a threatening voice.

His tone was not lost on Marc. "No, no," he said in a high-pitched voice. "It is a country house. An old villa. In fact…" The computer man stopped talking long enough to stick his long, skinny neck over the seat and peer through the front windshield between Bolan and Platinov. "I think you should stop now. If I remember correctly, and I am certain now that I do, it is just over that next hill."

Bolan had already started up the hill and was near the top. His right foot shot to the brake and he rose off the seat, throwing all of his weight into the stop. The car skidded to a halt but sent a cloud of dirt mixed with chunks of grass on up, and over, the rise.

The soldier turned toward the backseat, clenching his fist to control his anger. The little geek should have warned him earlier that they were that close to the CLODO safe house. But he had failed to do so out of ignorance rather than malice. He was not a field agent of any type.

"You might have told me earlier," Bolan finally said.

His tone had to have reflected his anger because Marc Ajaccio threw himself against the backseat again. "I am sorry," he said. "I did not fully recognize this area until just now." His voice trembled slightly as he spoke.

Silence fell over the inside of the Nissan. Bolan watched as the dirt and blades of wild grass settled atop the hill, wondering if other CLODO terrorists were watching the same thing from the house on the other side.

"Watch him," he told Platinov. "I'm going up and have a look."

The Russian woman nodded.

Bolan glanced at the man in the backseat as he got out of the car. Marc Ajaccio was going to be about as hard for Platinov to control as a newborn puppy.

Raising his T-shirt up and over the grips of both the Desert Eagle and Beretta, Bolan jammed his shirttail into his cargo shorts behind the guns. He walked until he sensed that a few more steps would make him visible from the other side of the hill, then dropped to his chest and crawled the rest of the way to the top.

What he saw on the other side didn't exactly shock him, but it did come as somewhat of a surprise.

The hill dropped down into a valley, and near the bottom was an old but well-kept French château. That, he had expected. But there was only one vehicle outside the house, a small orange Toyota pickup.

Bolan watched the house for a few minutes. The windows were covered by shades, and there was no activity visible around the house, the barn, or several other small outbuildings. For all practical purposes, the place looked as if it had been deserted.

Not for long. The grass around the house had recently been mowed, and pathways were still worn between the various buildings.

Bolan pulled a small case from one of the back pockets of his cargo pants, opened it and produced a pair of folding minibinoculars. He trained them first on the house, then the barn and the sheds. But he saw nothing he had not already seen with his naked eyes.

People had been here until recently, and the pickup meant there might still be at least one person inside the house or somewhere on the property.

Returning the binoculars to the case, and the case to his pocket, the Executioner scooted halfway down the hill backward, then stood again and dusted himself off as he walked back to the Nissan. Opening the back door, he said, "Are you sure this is the right place?"

Marc nodded. "I am certain."

Bolan described what he'd seen in more detail, but Marc nodded more vigorously than before. When the Executioner mentioned the orange pickup, he interrupted long enough to say, "Yes, I know that truck. It belongs to another computer specialist named Charlot. He always arrived and left by himself in that pickup when we were installing the computers."

"Does that mean he's probably alone in the house?" Platinov asked.

"I don't know," Marc said. "Probably."

"CLODO seems to be made up of two specific types of people," Bolan said to Marc. "There are the fighters, and then there are the computer specialists like you, Marc."

Marc nodded, and his skinny chest expanded with confidence at the word *specialist*. Good, Bolan thought. The word had produced the effect he had hoped it would. It was no longer necessary for him to threaten, or Platinov to tease, the man into helping them.

Without even knowing what had happened to him, Marc Ajaccio had changed sides in this war.

"No, he's not a fighter at all," Marc said. "You will see. And yes, I suspect he will be alone." The first smile Bolan had ever seen suddenly came over Marc's face, and he looked from Bolan to Platinov. "But I'm afraid you will not have the power over him that you do me," he said with a small laugh as he continued to gaze at Platinov.

"What do you mean?" Platinov asked.

"You will see." Turning back to Bolan, he said, "I believe it would be safe just to drive down there now. Charlot will see me, and think you two are simply CLODO people he has never met."

Bolan looked at his watch. He didn't know exactly how long they had before this computer virus was perfected and set upon the world, but it could be any second. So they needed to save every moment that they could. Looking up at Platinov, the Executioner said, "I'm game if you are."

"Let's go then," Platinov said.

Bolan threw the car into Drive and topped the hill. The château and other buildings came into view once more.

"This is it," Marc confirmed from the backseat.

The Nissan began descending the road toward the château. Bolan shifted slightly in order to make both the Beretta 93-R and the Desert Eagle a little more accessible in case Marc was wrong about this Charlot character being alone, or a fighter, or both.

From the corner of his eye he could see that Platinov had her hand in her canvas bag, her finger undoubtedly on the trigger and her thumb on the safety of one of the Gold Cups or the Government Model 1911 .45 she carried there.

They were as ready as they could possibly be.

CHAPTER EIGHT

"You lead the way, Marc," the Executioner said as he pulled the Nissan to a halt. "We'll be right behind you."

Bolan killed the engine and pulled the key from the ignition. He doubted that his and Platinov's "tourist" looks would even raise this Charlot character's eyebrows. Particularly since they were posing as computer experts from the American CLODO cell.

Bolan and Marc got out on their side of the vehicle. Platinov exited the door across from them.

Marc reluctantly took the lead, shuffling along toward the front door of the house. "Quit slinking around and act like you know what you're doing," Bolan ordered under his breath, "or I'll put a .44 Magnum right in the middle of your spine."

Marc straightened, lifted his head and mounted the short concrete staircase that led to the porch with the bearing of a king returning to his palace.

Bolan had hooked a thumb into his waistband next

to the Desert Eagle. The weapon still didn't show, but could be produced in less than a half second if necessary.

The steps to the porch were wide enough for two people and to his side, the soldier saw that Platinov still had her hand draped casually into her canvas bag. It was big and bulky—just the type of bag tourist women tote all over the world. He had no doubt that her fingers gripped one of her Gold Cup pistols behind the canvas, and she'd even be able to shoot through the fabric if necessary.

When they reached the front door Bolan leaned forward and whispered, "Do you knock or just go in?"

Marc was nervous again. Even with the fantasies of Platinov he now had dancing through his brain, the survival-of-the-individual instinct still took precedence over survival of the species.

"Like I said," Marc whispered back, "I've only been here once. I'd better knock."

"Then do it," Bolan told him.

Marc raised a bony fist and hammered it against the door. As they waited, the only sounds that could be heard were those of the wind blowing down through the lush green valley and the distant mooing of cattle at some distant farm.

Standing close behind Marc now, and only partially visible through the picture window next to the door, Bolan shifted his feet slightly to block any view of his right side. The hand he'd hooked into his belt now moved across the butt of the big .44 Magnum pistol.

A half minute or so after he'd first knocked, Marc raised his hand to bang the door again. Before his fist met the wood, footsteps sounded on the other side of the door. Then the peephole in the middle of the door darkened for a moment, and a high-pitched voice called out in French, "Who are you and what do you want?"

"Talk to the man," Bolan ordered in a low, rough voice.

"It is Marc Ajaccio from Chartres," the CLODO computer man said. "You remember me, Charlot. I helped install the computers here."

After a short pause, Charlot said, "Yes, I remember you now. But why are you here and what do you want?"

Bolan shoved the barrel of the .44 into Marc's side.

"Dammit, Charlot," Marc spit out more aggressively now. "We have an important message for you."

"Who are your friends?" demanded the high squeaky voice.

"Fellow CLODO computer experts," Marc said. "From America. Now let us in. They have an emergency message from Rouillan."

The CLODO leader's name worked like magic. Bolan heard the clank as a dead-bolt lock slid back from the frame, then a series of snaps as several smaller locking mechanisms were clicked off. The door finally opened.

Bolan gave Marc a small push in the back and the computer terrorist stepped up over the threshold and into the house. The Executioner cut in front of Platinov, his hand resting on the butt of the Desert Eagle. Platinov brought up the rear, her hand still out of sight in her bag.

If they had just walked into a trap, they were about to find out.

Charlot had stood behind the door as they walked in but now he stepped out into view, closed and locked it again. The overhead light was off but several small table lamps illuminated the house's living room. Bolan's eyes swept the area quickly, seeing that two hallways led toward the back part of the house, one doorway on each side of the rear wall. A third opening appeared to lead to a kitchen.

There was no sign that anyone else besides Charlot was in the residence.

Charlot had long blond hair that nearly reached his waist and wore rectangular, bright purple eyeglasses. He was clothed in tight blue jeans and a blue shirt, the tail of which had been tied in a knot halfway up his midriff. After giving Platinov no more than a cursory glance, he looked up at Bolan and broke out in a smile. "My, your friend's a big one, Marc," he said. "Aren't you going to introduce us?"

Lifting his T-shirt, he drew the Desert Eagle and watched Charlot's eyes widen behind the purple glasses.

"I'm going to ask the questions," Bolan said as he leveled the pistol. "You're going to answer them. Truthfully. Because the first time I think you're lying, you're dead."

The little terrorist had tears in his eyes now. Charlot's wet, terrified eyes darted to the side, toward the CLODO man Bolan had used to get them in the front door. "Marc, are you…part of this?"

Marc Ajaccio frowned as if thinking hard. Then he looked from Bolan to Platinov, then back to Bolan. "Yes," he said. "I think I am."

His words confirmed Bolan's intuition that Marc had, indeed, switched sides in this war. Turning back to Charlot, he said, "First question. Where are the computers in this house?"

"In the back," Charlot said. "But they—"

"Shut up and take me to them." He reached down and grabbed Charlot's shoulder and spun the man, then jammed the barrel of the big Desert Eagle into his spine. "Let's go," he ordered.

Charlot was sobbing softly as he walked to the back of the living room, then stepped up off the hardwood floor onto the carpeted hallway. Bolan felt Marc and Platinov fall in behind him.

Still softly sobbing, Charlot led the party into a large rear bedroom, but the room contained nothing other than a half-dozen more computer stations. And, just like they had been set up in the underground tunnel in Chartres, there were three on each side of the room.

Unlike the CLODO computers in Chartres, however, the CPUs had not been burned. With more time to evacuate the premises, all of the CPUs, disks, notes and other paperwork had simply been removed.

All that was left were the screens, keyboards and a large printer on both sides of the room, each servicing three of the stations.

Charlot turned slowly. He leaned down and wiped his eyes with the knotted tail of his shirt. "That's what I tried to tell you," he said in a voice more befitting a toddler than a grown man, "We moved out during the night. In the rush, I forgot some of my clothing and came back to get it today." Tears were streaming down his cheeks now. "It is only through bad luck that you found me here." From the back pocket of his skintight jeans he pulled a handkerchief and blew his nose. Then, looking up at Bolan and Platinov, he trembled visibly as he asked, "Are you going to kill me?"

Bolan let the muzzle of the Desert Eagle rest on the man's nose just to keep his attention. Ignoring the last question, he addressed the statement Charlot had made just before it. "Whether it's good or bad luck depends on which side of this gun you're standing on," he said. "Did Rouillan call to warn you we were coming?"

"Yes," Charlot said. "He told us that a man and a woman had chased him through the tunnel at the cathedral, and that they might very well be headed this way. I must now suppose that you two are that man and woman," Charlot said.

"You suppose right," Bolan said. "The men who left with the hard drives," he went on. "Where did they go?"

Charlot closed his eyes. "I do not know," he said weakly. "Please, you must believe me, there are many other safe houses such as this one. They are not just in France, they are spread all over Europe and one is even in the United States. That is why I believed Marc and let you in."

"Do not kid yourself," Platinov snarled. "We were

coming inside one way or another anyway." She paused, then demanded, "What of the virus?"

Charlot sniffled. "The development of the virus is now complete. But only Rouillan understands how it works, and only he has the code to activate it." Another sniffle and another nose-blow later, he added, "His right-hand man, Achille LeForce, might also know but I doubt it."

"Why would you doubt it?"

"Because LeForce is too stupid," Charlot said, then immediately covered his mouth with his fingers. "Please do not tell him I said that!"

Bolan frowned. He remembered Achille LeForce from Chartres. It was LeForce Rouillan had planned to meet there.

"You're one of the computer experts," he told Charlot, the Desert Eagle still cocked and resting on the bridge of the little man's nose. "Tell me more about your part of the virus."

"Even my part was extremely complex," Charlot said. "Far more complex than any virus or worm or any other destructive computer disease that has ever been seen. And we were all—the computer workers within CLODO—working on different aspects of it. None of us knew, or even now knows, the entire program. It is like the safe houses in that respect. Only one person, Rouillan, knows where all of the safe houses are. And only he understood the whole virus."

Bolan shook his head. "There's something I don't understand about all this," he said. "You, Charlot, and you, Marc, all of you CLODO computer guys have devoted years of your lives to learning about computers." He used his empty hand to indicate what was left of the refuge along one wall. "But now, you're working for an organization that is trying to stamp out this technology altogether. Why?"

Charlot looked to the side of the Desert Eagle's barrel and up into Bolan's eyes. "Because each of us, somewhere along the line, began to understand that what we were doing was evil," he whispered. "We saw how governments around the world were using computer technology to suppress people. And as much as we might enjoy the many good things computers can accomplish, the power they give governments is far too much."

Bolan shook his head. The little man in front of him was serious. His head had been filled with so much CLODO propaganda that he really believed what he was saying.

"You're talking about computers, Charlot," Bolan finally said. "They're inanimate objects that don't have the capacity to be good or evil on their own. They're like this gun. It can be used to rob a bank or murder someone. Or it can be used to stop a bank robbery or murder."

Rouillan had obviously indoctrinated his followers with standard comebacks for such logic. "Men cannot be trusted with such power," Charlot immediately said with all the thought of a parrot mindlessly repeating words which he had been taught. "Eventually, it will be abused."

The Executioner wasted no more time trying to un-brainwash the little man at the end of the Desert Eagle. Pulling his satellite phone from one of his cargo pockets, he cradled it inside the elbow of the arm holding the big pistol and used his other hand to tap in the number to Stony Man Farm. As the call routed itself that way, he looked at Charlot and then Marc. "You two sit down in those chairs," he said, pointing to the closest two computer stations to his side.

The two CLODO men did as they'd been told. Both had quizzical looks on their faces. And Marc even looked disappointed, as if he was being kicked off of his "new team" and returned to the second string.

Bolan turned to Platinov. "Watch them," he said.

The Russian woman nodded, finally pulling her hand out of her bag and training one of her pistols in their direction.

As the call began to ring, Bolan turned back to the computer experts. "I understand a lot about computers," he said. "But I'm a soldier, not a computer expert, and a virus this complicated is above my head." He paused again, letting the compliment sink in and giving a little self-respect back to the two wimpy men. He wanted them both to regain enough confidence to at least be useful. "I'm going to put this on speakerphone, and let you talk to a man who knows your language inside and out. I want you each to explain, in vivid detail, exactly what you've been doing, how you've been doing it and answer any questions he has for you. And believe me—

you try to pull any fast ones or throw double-talk at this guy and I'll throw lead back at you. Got it?"

Both of the CLODO men nodded in agreement, but for different reasons. Charlot knew he'd be killed if he didn't cooperate. Platinov's beauty and attention to Marc had long before rolled him over to their side.

A few seconds later, Barbara Price answered the call. "Hello, Striker," she said.

"Hello. I need Bear."

Price immediately transferred the call to the Stony Man Farm Computer Room.

Aaron Kurtzman's voice was the next one Bolan heard. "Hello, Striker. What's up?"

"I've got two of CLODO's computer men with me right now and I want you to talk to them. I'm going to put you on speakerphone."

"Okay."

Bolan tapped a button, and a second later said, "Can you hear me?"

"Loud and clear."

"Okay. Let me fill you in on what's going down so you'll understand why I want you to talk to them directly."

"I'm all ears," Kurtzman said.

Quickly but efficiently, Bolan explained how the virus had been created in parts at dozens of different lab sites, and how Rouillan was the only one who knew each site.

"Have them each explain what he did, one at a time," Kurtzman said. "I'll try to put the two together, and see if the combination will lead me further."

Bolan held the phone out in front of him. "Marc, you're on first."

The "flipped" CLODO man began explaining exactly what he'd done in relationship to developing the virus, stopping only when Kurtzman interrupted to ask a question.

Bolan looked toward Platinov and watched her shrug. He suspected she was understanding roughly half of what was being said, like himself.

Ten minutes later, Bolan heard Kurtzman say, "Okay, Marc. Put the other guy on but stay close to the phone in case I need to ask you anything else."

Marc had looked at the phone in Bolan's hand the entire time he'd been speaking. But now his eyes rose to the Desert Eagle the soldier still gripped in his other fist. "I don't think there's a chance of me wandering away," he said.

Charlot started in, taking up where Marc had left off to explain what he and his crew at the farmhouse had been working on. As best Bolan could tell from all of the geek-speak, they'd been developing an aspect of the virus that would cause it to spread further every time there was an attempt to kill it.

If successful, the governments around the world would actually be multiplying their own problems every time they attempted to halt the virus.

They'd be fighting themselves.

Since some of their work overlapped, it didn't take Charlot quite as long to explain his part in the development of the virus. Five minutes later, the Executioner heard Kurtzman say, "Okay. Striker, you still there?"

"Here."

"I'll get to work on this, and see what I can put together. It would really help if I could get my hands on at least one of the hard drives, though."

"We'll see what we can do," Bolan said. He looked toward the two CLODO computer experts seated at the computer stations. "Where are we going next, boys?" he asked.

Marc and Charlot looked at each other. Then, almost as if they had practiced the move to come in synchronized harmony, their eyes turned to the big .44 Magnum pistols.

The soldier waited. Marc had already flipped and, at least to a certain degree, could be trusted. Charlot, however, was a different story. Although Bolan suspected that the little man with the long blond hair and purple eyeglasses would go along with whoever was holding a gun on him, he still couldn't be trusted.

"We don't know of any more safe houses," Charlot whined.

"Yes, we do," Marc said.

"Why don't you kill your speakerphone now, Striker," Kurtzman said, "and you and I can have a few final private words."

"Affirmative," Bolan agreed, and began to walk across the room simply to stretch his legs.

"Okay," Kurtzman said. "First one to get more intel calls the other."

"Sure. One more thing."

"Shoot," Kurtzman said.

Bolan reached into the right hip pocket of his cargo

shorts and pulled out a small, computerized Global Positioning Unit or GPU. As soon as he'd turned it on and gotten their exact coordinates, he read them off to Kurtzman. "Relay that latitude and longitude to Jack, will you, Bear? And tell him we're in a good-sized valley. He should be able to land the Learjet without any trouble."

"Roger, big guy," Kurtzman said.

Bolan hung up. Turning back toward the other three people in the room, he let his eyes fall on Marc and then Charlot. "Okay, boys," he said. "We're off to the next place." Pausing a second, he said, "Where's the closest other computer safe house you know about?"

"Belgium," Marc said, standing up. He turned to Charlot.

The little man nodded.

Bolan looked at his watch. Jack Grimaldi had flown him and Platinov to France from the U.S. in one of Stony Man Farm's Learjets, and had been waiting at an isolated airstrip used primarily by drug runners near Paris ever since.

It was time to get the Farm's number one flyboy back into the air.

"Then we'd all better get outside," Bolan said as he and Platinov herded the other two men back out of the farmhouse. "Our ride will be here in a few minutes."

GAUTIER SAUCIER MADE sure the pilot, who had been introduced to him only as André, kept the helicopter high in the air as they passed over the farmhouse. With the binoculars in one hand, his cell phone in the other, he said, "They're going inside. It all looks peaceful."

On the other end of the line, Pierre Rouillan said, "That's because I called the house last night as soon as we hung up the second time. One of the men from the tunnel helped install the computers at that site. I knew that if it was him they had caught, he would lead them there."

"Nice loyal group of guys you've got working for you," Saucier commented.

"My plan requires both warriors and computer experts," Rouillan came back. "It is rare that you find both qualities in one man."

Saucier couldn't resist continuing to taunt his employer. "That's obvious," he said. When he got no reply, he decided to bait Rouillan a little further. "Has it ever struck you or your computer experts as being a little odd that you and your message to the world is that computers are evil…at the same time you're using them yourselves?"

It was obviously a question for which Rouillan was ready, and had probably been asked before—if only by himself. "Sometimes we must fight fire with fire," he said quickly.

"Okay, fine," Saucier replied, tiring of the game. "What do you want me to—" He stopped speaking suddenly as a familiar sound met his ears. When Rouillan started to speak he cut the man off with a quick, "Be quiet for a moment!"

In the distance, Saucier could hear what sounded like jet engines.

Turning to the CLODO chopper pilot, the French mercenary said, "Do you hear that?"

The pilot nodded. "Learjet," he said simply.

"There is a Learjet approaching," Saucier said into the phone.

"It must be theirs," Rouillan stated. "Keep me on the line, but find cover for yourselves somewhere!"

"Get us on the ground and undercover. Do it fast!" Saucier ordered. "This plane has got to be coming for the man and woman in the farmhouse. It's not like this farm is a regular hub for one of the major airlines."

They had flown a half mile or so from the valley where the farmhouse was located, and now the pilot turned the chopper in a quick U-turn.

"What are you doing?" Saucier demanded. "That's where they will be landing." He pointed upward at the top of the helicopter to indicate the approaching Learjet.

"There's a large grove of trees just this side of the valley," André said. "I think there's enough space to set down in the middle of them."

"What is happening? What is happening?" Saucier could hear Rouillan asking over the cell phone.

He didn't bother answering the man.

"You *think?*" Saucier said. "You *think?* I saw those trees myself. And what happens if there isn't enough room?"

Andre shrugged. "Nothing but a rough landing," he said. "We'll be within twenty feet of the ground by the time we reach the top branches. Worst thing that can happen is we shear off the blades. Besides, it's the only place I've seen around here where we can hide this bird."

Saucier looked down at the seat belt across his lap. André was right. If the chopper crashed, it wouldn't be that bad, but it would mean the man and woman inside the farmhouse would escape in the Learjet and he'd lose out on the double payment Rouillan had promised if he killed the Americans today.

Shifting his eyes to the scoped .243 bolt-action rifle that rested on the seat next to him, he decided to put a round through André's brain if that happened.

"Okay," Saucier said, smiling at the pilot.

"What are you doing?" Rouillan asked on the other end of the cell phone.

Once again, Saucier didn't bother answering him.

The Learjet engines were considerably louder by the time the chopper reached the grove of trees. Saucier heard a few snapping sounds as the blades clipped off twigs at the top. But they met no real resistance, and a second or two later the helicopter was on the ground and hidden.

"Stay ready to move out," Saucier said as he opened the door. "I'm going to scout out what's happening. We might have to take off the second I get back."

André shook his head. "It won't make any difference," he said. "If they get into a jet, we'll be left behind within seconds."

Saucier bristled at the man's words. "Just shut up and stay ready," he said again as he exited the chopper, slung the rifle over his shoulder and began making his way through the trees.

The French mercenary had reached the top of the hill overlooking the farmhouse when he moved in against a lone elm tree standing by itself. Unless he moved, he wasn't likely to be spotted by anyone from the plane or the house. His dark coveralls should blend in with the tree's shadows with no problem.

So Saucier remained still as he watched the Learjet pass over his head, bank back and set down at the farthest end of the valley. The landing was not as smooth as it would have been on a runway, but whoever was behind the controls of the Learjet obviously knew what he was doing.

"The helicopter is hidden," Saucier finally said into the phone to Rouillan. "I am out and watching the house. The plane—and it *is* a Learjet—has just landed."

A few seconds later, the shapely woman Saucier had seen earlier backed out of the front door to the farm-house. She carried a large bag, and appeared to be holding a pistol in her hand. Almost right behind her was the same man Saucier had seen her knock to the ground back in Chartres. Then came a new face—either a man or a woman, the French mercenary couldn't tell which—with long blond hair. The big man Saucier also remembered brought up the rear.

Saucier reported all this to Rouillan.

"The blond person," Rouillan said immediately. "Was he or she wearing glasses?"

By now all four people from the farmhouse had disappeared aboard the Learjet.

"Affirmative."

"It was a man," Rouillan said over the airwaves.

"We can never keep up with them in the helicopter," Saucier said into the phone as he finally broke away from the tree and began running back toward where André was waiting.

"It doesn't matter," Rouillan replied. "If the blond-haired man was with them, I know where they will go next." There was a pause on the end of the line, then the CLODO leader said, "Fly the helicopter on into Marseille. I will have an airplane waiting for you at the airport. It will be one André is qualified to fly."

"I'm still expecting the double payment," the French mercenary said.

"Earn it and you will get it," Rouillan stated. "Now, if you will excuse me, please. I have a lot of work to be done. But keep in close touch."

Saucier hung up. By then he had reached the helicopter again. André had removed the magnetic police regalia and fake numbers. Partly out of breath from running, partly from the excitement of the whole chase, Saucier said, "Get us into the air," as he jumped on board.

"We'll never catch—" André started to say.

"Do as I say and quit questioning my orders!"

André took the helicopter straight up into the air again.

"Forget the Learjet for now," the French mercenary stated. "Head for Marseille."

CHAPTER NINE

Ghent, Belgium, had often been referred to as the Florence of the North. Rising up on one of the small islands at the intersection of the Scheldt and Lys rivers, it had become something of an oddity over the years as the modern buildings of the city's thriving textile industry found their way in between medieval houses, narrow walking streets and canals.

From his passenger seat in the Learjet, Bolan looked downward as Jack Grimaldi dropped the plane toward the runway. Below, he caught a quick glimpse of the Cathedral of St. Bavon, a monumental Gothic structure large enough to hold six of the cathedrals he and Platinov had so recently left.

A second later, the sight vanished and the jet's wheels hit the tarmac.

Bolan glanced over his shoulder. Behind him sat Marc Ajaccio, across the aisle and behind Grimaldi. Charlot was directly behind the Executioner. The little man smiled broadly at Bolan, and the Executioner got the feeling that Charlot had been staring at the back of his neck throughout the entire flight.

Grimaldi landed the jet and then followed the motions of a flag man who directed him off the runway onto an asphalt drive that led to the roofed ports where private aircraft parked. "I told you that Hal called ahead to smooth out customs, right?" the Stony Man pilot said.

Bolan nodded as they were turned left into a large aircraft parking area. Directed by yet another flag man, Grimaldi guided the Learjet into a tin-roofed and walled hangar. A man walked across the asphalt toward them with a clipboard in his right hand. A badge reflected light on his left upper chest, and a Browning Hi-Power, along with extra magazines and a half-dozen other pieces of equipment, hung from a black nylon web belt around his waist.

He was smiling widely, showing a perfect row of long, white upper teeth. He arrived at the side of the plane before any of the men on board could get off, opened the Executioner's door, switched the clipboard to his left hand and extended it through the gap.

"I remember you two," he said, grinning. He looked past Bolan to Grimaldi. "You were the guy who flew the plane and bounced us up and down against the deck and top of the aircraft until we achieved zero gravity." Hal Brognola had arranged for this former blacksuit trainee to get the team through customs. Grimaldi smiled. "Hey," he said. "You never know when you might get launched into space and need to know how to operate while you're floating around inside a rocket."

The Belgian customs man chuckled, then looked to Bolan. "And you…" he said, letting his sentence trail off as if he was trying to think of the exact words he wanted to speak next. "You just bounced us off anything that happened to be handy."

Bolan was still grasping the man's hand, and now he smiled as he let go of it. He couldn't remember exactly which class of blacksuits this man had been in. But, among other things, he occasionally taught the close quarters combat section of the blacksuit training.

"LeCoque is my name," the man in the coveralls said next. "Robert LeCoque, in case you've forgotten it, which I'm sure you have considering all of the people you've trained." He looked next at the two men seated behind Bolan and Grimaldi, and the Executioner could almost see the Belgian customs man's brain working through the skin and bone on his forehead as LeCoque immediately sized them up as exactly what they were— informants.

His gaze roved over Platinov appreciatively as he said, "I was told you'd need ground transport." As he led the party out the door of the hangar, he pointed toward the terminal. "And here it comes."

Bolan followed the man's line of sight and saw two vehicles headed their way. One was a civilian version of the ever-popular American military vehicle, the Hummer. The other was a black Toyota Highlander minivan.

"Our friend in Washington didn't know how aggressive or low-key you'd want to look," LeCoque said as the two vehicles neared the hangars. "So I brought you a choice—a Hummer or a minivan. Which one do you want?"

"We'll take them both," Bolan said as the two vehicles slowed and prepared to stop. "We have different needs for each."

The Belgian customs officer glanced back at the open door to the hangar. "There's plenty of room inside there next to the Lear. And you can close the door, lock it if you want to and keep it completely out of sight." He paused and looked behind him at the open doorway. "Your pilot staying with the plane?"

Bolan nodded. "He'll keep an eye on it and the Hummer."

By now both the Toyota and the Hummer had come to a halt just in front of them, their engines idling as the drivers—also wearing customs coveralls—waiting for their next directions.

LeCoque gave them to the men when he held up a hand, palm outward, to the driver of the Toyota, then turned to the man behind the wheel of the Hummer and waved him on in through the hangar door.

Bolan, Platinov and the two CLODO computer geeks began transferring weapons and other equipment from the Learjet to the minivan. As soon as that task was complete, the Executioner turned back to LeCoque. "Anything you need me to sign?" he asked.

LeCoque laughed. "It wouldn't be your real name,"

he said. "Go on. I'll take care of all the paperwork myself."

Bolan nodded and turned back to the Toyota. By now, all the equipment was loaded and Marc Ajaccio and Charlot were settled in the backseat. Platinov had already taken the wheel of the Toyota, so Bolan opened the door and slid up into the passenger's seat.

A moment later, they were driving away from the airport toward yet another of the CLODO computer safe houses.

GAUTIER SAUCIER watched the pilot behind the controls of CLODO's own private Learjet as they prepared to land in Ghent. The man looked as mindless as André, his chauffeur and helicopter pilot back in Chartres. Probably every bit as dull, too, Saucier thought as he felt his abdomen press against the seat belt as they slowed. The two men had not spoken a word to each other during the flight as they followed the jet streams left in the sky by the other Lear. But had they talked, he suspected it would have been limited to the same vacuous CLODO propaganda that seemed to be André's only subject of discussion.

Those modern-day terrorist groups might all have different causes and ideologies, Saucier thought as he watched the pilot out of the corner of his eye. But they all behaved the same, hollow followers of charismatic leaders who used them as much for their own personal gain as they did the moral crusade that propelled them. So he had not even bothered to ask this new pilot's name when he climbed aboard the plane.

It had been somewhat of an effort for Saucier to hide his contempt for the whole CLODO organization ever since Pierre Rouillan had hired him. He had worked for a number of terrorist organizations since leaving the legitimate French military, but he was not—and never would be—a member of any of them. The only "cause" that interested him was his own, and that quest involved nothing more political or complicated than using his unique soldiering talents to make as much money as he possibly could. Already, he was building up a substantial retirement chest that he'd secreted in Swiss and Cayman Island banks under a variety of front businesses. In a few more years he'd hang up his guns for good, assume one of his phony IDs on a permanent basis and live out the rest of his life on the beaches of one of the islands in the Caribbean.

Would he miss the excitement? Saucier wondered as the CLODO plane began its descent into Ghent. Probably. But there would be women, rum, gambling and a variety of other pastimes to take his mind off any boredom that overcame him. And he would have the money to indulge in them all if that's what he wanted to do.

As the wheels of the CLODO plane touched down, Saucier looked across the runway to the hangars that housed the visiting private planes. A man in khaki coveralls was closing the door of one of the hangars as a black Toyota minivan drove away. He was too far away to see through the van's windows, but he guessed it contained the man and woman Rouillan had hired him to kill, and whatever other people they had picked up along the way.

The nameless CLODO pilot followed the directions of the flagmen to the hangar next to the one that had just been closed by the man in the khaki coveralls. Now, the same man was opening the sliding door next to where Saucier highly suspected the man and woman's plane had been hidden. His eyes shot back in the direction where he'd last seen the Toyota. But by now it had vanished from sight.

No matter, Saucier thought as he settled in for this last leg of his trip. It didn't matter where they were going; eventually they would return to their plane. All he'd have to do was wait in his own hangar for their return.

Only one thing bothered him.

He had every type of weapon imaginable on board his jet. And if this customs man who stood waiting on them, clipboard in hand, decided he wanted to check the craft, it would mean trouble.

Not trouble beyond which Saucier could handle, but trouble nonetheless.

As soon as the plane came to a halt Saucier exited the jet, and found himself face-to-face with the man in the khaki coveralls and the clipboard. He noted the badge on the man's chest and the pistol belt around his waist.

He was short, dark-headed and slightly overweight. He looked around nervously to make sure there were no listening ears before he spoke. "It is undoubtedly the two you are looking for," he said in a low, hoarse voice.

Shocked might have been too strong a word to explain Saucier's reaction to the man's words. But highly surprised didn't quite seem quite strong enough, either.

The Belgian customs man was CLODO.

As soon as it had appeared that Ghent was their destination, Saucier had called Rouillan on his cell phone from the plane to give him an update. But he had been the one who obtained valuable information during the call when Rouillan informed him that CLODO had a man on the ground in Ghent who would make contact with him. He had described the short, dark-haired, slightly pudgy man, and revealed that his name was Augestin.

But Saucier had had no idea that the CLODO man was actually employed by Belgian customs.

"The big man, I believe to be American," Augestin whispered, "but, strangely enough, the woman sounded Russian. East German perhaps, but I think Russian."

Saucier had not yet responded to anything Augestin said and now the short chubby man took his silence as a question of identity. Quickly, he reached up to the zipper in his coveralls and pulled it down far enough to reveal the khaki shirt and brown slacks he wore beneath the outer garment. From his back pocket, he pulled a crumpled blue beret.

Saucier just nodded. He had always been a little amused by Rouillan's "unofficial" uniforms, believing they probably did more harm than good. In either case, they could never be relied upon because many men in

France, Belgium and the surrounding countries who had no idea CLODO even existed anymore went around dressed similarly. But rather than laugh, he just nodded. "Where are they going, Augestin?" he asked, using the name Rouillan had given him to insure his own connection to CLODO.

"I do not know," Augestin said as he zipped his coveralls back up. "I know only that they are in a black Toyota Highlander, and that they also have a Hummer at their disposal. It is parked next to you—" he lifted a finger toward the closed door of the hangar "—in there, with their Learjet."

Saucier nodded, then started to say, "I will wait on—"

But the little fat man interrupted him. "There is more that you should know."

Saucier stopped talking for a moment, then said, "Go on."

"My supervisor, Captain LeCoque, I believe he knows them. May even be in league with them." He stopped abruptly for another excited breath. "LeCoque and the big man—as I said, I believe him to be American—acted as if they were old friends when they arrived."

Saucier had found over the years that it was better to say nothing when he was perplexed than to spout out meaningless speculations. But after a few seconds, he said, "Can you lure this LeCoque out here to the hangars on some pretense?"

The customs man nodded vigorously. "The captain had me drive the Hummer out here to meet with them," he said. "I can tell him that I have discovered some malfunction in the vehicle that he should look at."

"Are you sure he will come himself and not just send a mechanic?" Saucier asked.

"He may bring a mechanic with him," Augestin said, "but he will also come himself. He is that kind of man."

"Then get to it," he said. "My pilot and I will remain in this hangar until you return. So leave the door unlocked."

Augestin turned to go but Saucier called him back.

"And do not forget to fill out the paperwork on this plane. What I must do will take some time. And I do not need any other nosy Belgian Customs officers coming out here to check on me."

Augestin nodded, stepped through the door, and took off running, then walking, then running again across the airport toward the customs building next to the terminal.

The pilot had not left his seat behind the controls. But now, as Saucier walked toward him, he opened the door slightly and asked, "What am I to do now?"

This time, Saucier couldn't hide his disdain for the man. "Stay where you are, and out of my way," he said simply. Then, walking back around the tail of the Learjet, he reentered the aircraft and lifted his custom .243 as he passed between the seats.

What he had planned would not call for the perfect long-distance accuracy of this long gun. It would be more of a job for many bullets fired in a short period of time. And quietly fired, so as not to alert the rest of the airport as to what was going on at the private hangars.

Moving to the back of the plane, Saucier returned his sniper's rifle to its padded hard case and unzipped a short, black bag. Inside, he found a Heckler & Koch G-11. The high-tech submachine gun used caseless ammunition. Already loaded with 100 rounds, it also had a sound suppressor fitted onto the end of the barrel.

It would be perfect for what Saucier had in mind when this Captain LeCoque, his mechanic and Augestin returned in a few minutes. He would let them unlock and enter the hangar next to him, then slip out and in behind them once they were inside. Then, he would extract any and all information they had about the man and woman who had become such a pain in the ass to kill.

But, Saucier thought, it would be wise to have the men tied up during interrogation. He dug through several equipment bags until he came to a bag filled with plastic riot cuffs. Grabbing a handful, he paused and frowned to himself. He could not bind the men who would soon return to the hangars and hold the H&K on them at the same time. He glanced back at the CLODO pilot who had flown him here.

It was time to learn the man's name.

Returning to the cockpit area, Saucier asked the pilot, "What do I call you?"

"My name is Louis," the man said.

"Well, get out of the plane with me, Louis," the mercenary said.

Once they were both out of the plane but still hidden inside the hangar, Saucier explained his plan to the man. Then he handed one of the riot cuffs to the pilot, and ordered him to demonstrate that he knew how to apply it.

The man passed the test.

After he had extracted all useful information from this captain and mechanic, Saucier knew it would be time for a good, old-fashioned, down-and-dirty slaughter with the near-silent G-11. He said nothing of this, to Louis, however, because he had not yet decided if he would kill the CLODO pilot along with the others. These first shootings were only a warm-up for the assassination of the big American, the Russian woman and the rest of their entourage when they returned. He would need Louis's assistance in hiding the bodies, and he might even need the man to fly him out of Belgium.

That part of the plan was impossible to predict at this point. So he would keep this option open as long as possible. The one thing he knew he could not do was to escape on the ground without killing Louis. The man was far too stupid to leave behind for interrogation by Belgian authorities.

As he handed the rest of the plastic handcuffs to the pilot, Saucier let a smile creep over his face. What he had assumed would be an easy, simply assassination had turned into an elongated mess. But it was almost over now.

Augestin had closed the hangar door, leaving only a small crack through which he could see what was going on outside. With the Heckler & Koch G-11 caseless sub-machine gun hanging around his neck on its sling, Saucier took up his position at the crack of sunlight coming into the hangar.

Now, it was time to wait. So wait is exactly what he would do.

"I TOLD YOU ALL THIS EARLIER," Charlot whined from the backseat of the Toyota. "We said we'd *heard* about another safe house in Ghent. Not that we knew where it was."

Platinov turned around behind the wheel of the parked Toyota, reached through the space between the front and backseats and slapped Charlot hard on the left cheek.

The Russian agent's fingers left bright red lines across the little Frenchman's face below his purple eye-glasses, and knocked one of the earpieces off his ear. "You said you *knew* of another safe house in Ghent. There is a tremendous difference in hearing of and knowing the location," Platinov spit back at him as the man reached up and set his purple glasses back in place with trembling hands.

Bolan remained silent and watched Marc out of the corner of his eye as Platinov continued to grill Charlot. The computer man who had rolled over to their side looked frightened, as if his turn would come as soon as Platinov tired of hitting Charlot.

Platinov had drawn her hand back to smack Charlot again when the Executioner interrupted. "Tell us what you *do* know, Charlot," he said. "If you can come up with enough things you've heard, maybe we can piece them together." He indicated Platinov's hand with a nod. "And if we can piece them together, maybe she'll let you keep your face in one piece."

Charlot was sniffling, blinking his eyelashes through the tears. Now he turned his attention to Bolan as if the Executioner had just ridden to the rescue. "Please don't let her hit me again," the man in the purple glasses pleaded.

Beside him, Platinov blew air out through her clenched teeth in total disgust. She started to speak, but Bolan caught her eye and shook his head slowly.

Platinov closed her lips.

"Go on," said the Executioner. "Tell us what you know."

It was Marc who spoke first. "I recall Rouillan using my computer to contact someone in Ghent about a week ago," he said. "They e-mailed back and forth several times." Before Bolan could speak, he went on. "The e-mails were encrypted, of course, but I was the one who set up the encryptions."

"Do you remember what they said?" the Executioner asked.

"I'm trying," Marc replied as deep furrows formed above his eyebrows. "It had to do with a trade they were making. Weapons for drugs. Rouillan had somehow come across a large amount of heroin and wanted to trade it to the people in Ghent who had guns. They—the Ghent cell—also had a buyer for the heroin, if I remember correctly."

Now it was Bolan's brows that furrowed as he let the man's words sink in. Such transactions were not unusual in the world of terrorism. All terrorists could always use more guns, and many groups financed their operations by dealing drugs.

Both brought death and destruction, and one was about as lethal as the other.

The guns just worked faster.

"What else?" Platinov asked, stepping back into the interrogation.

Charlot—who was terrified of Platinov now—spoke up quickly, looking directly at her with eyes the size of dartboards. "The guns, if I'm not mistaken, came to our safe house outside Marseille. I didn't see them, but I remember men about that time unloading what looked like rifle crates into the barn."

"Yes!" Marc shouted excitedly, the statement triggering more of his own memory. "I remember now. The country château had more room to store the weapons than we had in the tunnel!"

For a few seconds, the Toyota fell silent. Bolan let these new facts dance around in his head. It was good to have such information, but the weapons had been disbursed from the barn by the time they got there. And it wasn't getting them the address of the safe house they needed in Ghent. Finally, he said, "Do either of you remember anything else about the location here?" he asked. "Anything that might lead us there?"

More silence fell over the Toyota. Then, finally, Charlot said, "I don't know if it makes any difference, but I seem to recall they were delivered in a rental truck."

"Do you remember the name of the rental company?" Bolan asked.

"At the time I had no reason to look for it," Charlot replied. "I was quite busy working on the virus, and only remember seeing the truck through the window." He paused, then seeing that Platinov didn't intend to slap him again, went on with, "Besides, I would not have known how to find the name of the company anyway."

Platinov let out a hiss of disgusted breath. "Perhaps you could have looked on the truck itself," she said sarcastically. "Rental companies do not attempt to hide who they are. They tend more to advertise themselves."

Bolan looked at Platinov to quiet her again, then said, "You don't remember the name of the company printed on the sides of the truck?" he asked.

Charlot shook his head.

"Then maybe you remember a logo. Or even the colors the truck was painted," the Executioner continued.

Charlot brightened suddenly. "There was…a horse's head, I think," he said. "And the colors were blue and yellow." He stopped talking for a moment, then said, "Yes, I am sure of it now. A horse's head and blue and yellow."

"It is not a horse's head, you idiot," Marc said, shaking his own head in revulsion toward his former CLODO brother. "It is the head of a mule. A pack mule like the kind that were used to haul items before trucks were invented."

"You're familiar with it?" Bolan asked, now turning his attention to Marc.

Marc nodded. "It is a Spanish truck-rental company with branches in France and other European countries. Their colors are blue and yellow, and the name of the company is Mulo Español. Spanish Mule."

It was the break the Executioner had been waiting for, and now he pulled the satellite phone from his pocket and dialed Stony Man Farm. A few seconds later Barbara Price had connected him to Kurtzman.

"Hello again, big guy," the computer expert said. "What can I do for you this time?"

"It's hacking time again, Bear," Bolan said. "Two things—first, I need you to get into the files of a truck rental company."

"Like U-Haul or Ryder?" Kurtzman said.

"Like Ryder, but not Ryder," Bolan said. "The company is Mulo Español. Main headquarters are in Spain but they serve all of Europe."

"That should be easy enough. What's the second thing?"

"Check into Ghent, Belgium," Bolan said. "See what kind of Belgian law-enforcement agencies have intelligence and-or counterterrorist squads that cover that area. Then search their files. I'm looking for an address in Ghent from which a Mulo truck was rented sometime last week. The load ended up outside Marseille, but they probably gave a fake destination on the paperwork."

"The address of this Mulo Español office in Ghent I can probably get from a phone book," Kurtzman said. "But to get the exact location of the renter depends on two things."

Bolan suspected he knew what those two things were, but he asked anyway to make sure. "What?" he said simply.

"Mulo will have had to enter the info onto a computer," Kurtzman said.

"I suspect they will have," Bolan answered. "Like I said, they're a big company."

"Then let's hope number two comes through. That the 'renters' gave Mulo their correct address. I'm assuming that's what you're really after. Where the bad guys are actually located."

"It is," Bolan agreed. "Just check anything that looks suspicious to you. Then cross-reference it with Belgian police intel or counterterrorism files. See if we get any matches on the two lists."

"Affirmative. This shouldn't take long. You want to wait?"

"Sure."

Bolan settled back in his seat.

Several minutes went by during which the only sounds the soldier could hear were the keys being tapped on Kurtzman's computer.

Finally, he came back on the line. "Okay, big guy," he said. "I've got one possible for you." He gave out an address in Ghent that Bolan immediately committed to memory. "I found references to that address in both the

Belgian National Police Counterterrorist Unit and their intelligence department files. But the actual reports are sealed in Top Secret jackets."

"Can you get into those jackets?" Bolan asked.

"Sure," the computer genius said. "It'll just take a little longer."

"Okay, Bear," Bolan said. "But I'm not going to wait. We'll head toward that address while you keep hacking."

"Fine," Kurtzman agreed. "I'll call you back once I'm in."

Bolan hung up.

"Either of you know Ghent?" he asked the two men in the backseat.

Charlot nodded. "I used to live here," he said.

"Know how to find this place?" The soldier rattled off the address.

"Yes, it is in Han-sur-Lesse," Charlot said.

"What's Han-sur-Lesse?" Bolan asked.

"A little village, sort of a suburb of Ghent. It's on the northern slope of a hill overlooking the Lesse River."

"How far is it?" Bolan asked.

"It's a ways," Charlot replied.

The ignition was keyed and the Toyota jumped to life.

A moment later, they were on their way to Han-sur-Lesse.

CHAPTER TEN

"I'm going to slow down now and I want you to point out the exact house," Bolan said to Charlot, as they cruised through Han-sur-Lesse. "I don't want any mistakes. You know what will happen if you make a mistake, don't you, Charlot?"

The little man with the long blond hair and purple glasses nodded. His fear was almost palpable.

The Toyota slowed, and soon they were rolling past a small, nondescript frame house that sat at the top of a small rise from the street. Several cars were parked in the steeply sloping driveway, with more sitting along the curb. A ragged assortment of patio blocks had been pushed into the dirt when it had been wet at some time in the past, and they served as a staircase leading up to the front porch.

"If you make a right at the corner, then another right into the alley, you can pull up right next to the back of the house," Charlot said.

Bolan turned to look at him, his face hard. "So you *did* know where this place was after all," he said in a low, menacing voice that sent chills down Marc's spine.

But the big man's words froze Charlot completely as the Frenchman suddenly realized his mistake.

Bolan turned at the first corner, then slowed the car even further. As soon as they'd passed the dwelling on the corner and were out of sight from the safe house, he pulled the vehicle to the curb.

"Okay," said the big man behind the wheel. "It's now time to find out which side you two are on." He nodded to Platinov, who pulled two pistols out of her bag.

Marc recognized them both as being .45s—Rouillan had insisted that all of his people have firearms training. One of the guns was a dull black, and looked almost exactly like the one Rouillan had provided them with to shoot. The other was a sort of rough, nonreflective he assumed, silvery color. But it looked as if it operated the same way.

Both guns had to be cocked before you could shoot them but once the hammer was back, you could use your thumb to push a safety on the side up or down.

"So who's with us?" Bolan asked.

"I am," Charlot said quickly.

"I am on your side," Marc said, looking Platinov directly in the eyes. "Forever." Did he see a softening appear in the woman's dark brown eyes? Or was it just wishful thinking?

Platinov used both hands to deliver the two pistols, grips first, between the seats to the men in the back of the Toyota. At the same time, Charlot took the black gun and Marc grasped hold of the silvery model.

What happened next occurred in less than a second.

Charlot immediately disengaged the safety, aimed his gun at Platinov's face and pulled the trigger.

But seeing what the little man with the long blond hair had in mind, at almost the same time, Marc Ajaccio disengaged his own safety, pointed it at Charlot's and let the hammer fall.

Both hammers fell with a sharp, metallic clicking sound.

And the big man and Russian woman had learned what they'd wanted to know. Charlot had obviously planned ahead for any opportunity to escape or kill them. And even as Marc's click echoed through the Toyota, the little Frenchman had turned the blackened .45 toward the big man behind the wheel. Marc watched him pull the trigger again and again, finally frowning in confusion before his face turned into a mask of realization and fear.

"That's what I thought," Platinov said from the front seat. She reached forward and snatched the black gun from Charlot's hand, pulled back the slide to chamber a round, then pushed the safety up with her thumb and finally dropped the weapon back into her bag.

When she looked at Marc now, the loathing had left her face. "Pull back the slide and get one into the barrel," she said in a far softer voice than the ex-CLODO computer man had heard out of her since her interrogation. "Then thumb the safety up. To shoot it, you have to thumb it back down again."

Marc nodded enthusiastically. "I remember that part," he said, following Platinov's directions.

By then the Russian woman had opened her bag once more and pulled out a large roll of silver duct tape. "Stick your pistol in your belt and take this," she told Marc.

The computer man did as he was told.

"Now, tape your friend's wrists and ankles together."

By now Charlot had come to understand the test he'd just failed and began bargaining for his life. "I made a mistake," he whined. "It wasn't really going to shoot you. I—"

Platinov leaned through the opening between the bucket seats and slapped the man so hard that his purple eyeglasses flew from his face. "Put the first piece of tape on his mouth," she instructed Marc.

Again, Marc followed orders. "Are we going to kill him?" He felt his chest puff out slightly. "I can do it if you like."

Bolan answered the question rather than Platinov. "We'll let him live for now. He may have information we need later."

Marc Ajaccio had offered to kill Charlot in order to impress the Russian, but had not expected to get the "green light" on such an action from the American. Now, he wondered if the sudden nausea he felt in his stomach was revealed on his face.

"Okay," Bolan said. "Here's the plan. I'm going to turn down this alley and drive past the rear of the house. I want to see if there're more vehicles parked there. Then we're going to go back and trade this thing—" he tapped the dashboard of the Toyota with his hand "—with the Hummer. After that, we'll come back and I'll drive the Hummer straight into the back wall of this ramshackle old place. It's old, and from the front the wood looks rotten, and if it's rotten in front it will be in back, too. That simple enough for everybody?"

"So…" Marc said hesitantly. "When we crumple the back wall of the house, we then get out and start shooting people?"

"That's a big negative," said the man behind the wheel. "For you, at least. We're going to let you and your buddy—"

"*Former* buddy," Marc stressed, watching Platinov out of the corner of his eye. "I no longer consider myself part of CLODO."

"You're former buddy, then," Bolan corrected. "We're going to let you both out at the mouth of the alley. Your job is to make sure he doesn't get away."

Marc had been busy taping Charlot's wrists and ankles as they spoke. He finished the task at the same time Bolan stopped speaking. "I've taped him really well," he protested. "He won't get away." He was still watching Platinov in his peripheral vision. "I'd really like to go fight with you."

Bolan turned to the Russian agent. And, again out of the corner of his eye, Marc saw her slowly shake her head.

"We'll see when we get back," Bolan said. "But I'm not sure I want to take the risk with you. You've already established a rapport with my computer man back in the States. And between the two of you, you can ask and answer questions that wouldn't ever even occur to us." He nodded toward the object of Marc's desire.

"How do you feel holding that pistol?" she asked.

"Awkward," Marc came back. "But—"

"But you can make it shoot, right?" Platinov cut in. "Right."

"Well," she said, throwing her head back to get several strands of yellow hair off her face, "that's how we feel at a computer keyboard." Now it was she who nodded back at the big man behind the steering wheel. "We know the basics about computers, just like you know about firearms, and we can make them work. But it's not either of our specialties." She took in a deep breath and Marc watched her breasts rise and fall. "Now that you've seen the light, you're much too valuable to risk getting you killed at this point, Marc."

It was the first time the Russian woman had used his name since her sexy interrogation, and it sent more pangs of desire through the former CLODO man's chest.

"Okay," he said simply. "But I want you to know I'm willing to help. That I'm not afraid to help."

"We know that, Marc," Bolan said. "And we won't hesitate to call on you if we need you."

"You'll be part of our backup plan," Platinov said. "So familiarize yourself with that .45 as best you can between now and then."

Marc nodded, not completely sure whether the two agents were serious or simply placating him, and letting him save face.

Bolan had driven the Toyota to the end of the alley

by now, and turned back onto the street. A few seconds later, they were retracing the route they had taken from the airport to Hans-sur-Lesse.

SOMETHING WAS WRONG.

Bolan didn't know exactly what it was, but he couldn't shake the feeling down deep in his bones.

Dawn was just breaking as he turned onto the drive that led to the private plane hangars. But the tranquility of the early morning did nothing to change the concern he had suddenly felt as soon as the hangars came into view.

Bolan squinted at the closed and padlocked door near the center of the hangars as he turned again, directing the vehicle off the concrete drive and onto the asphalt that led to the structures. Slowing almost to a crawl, he continued to stare at the building that housed their Learjet.

What was it? What was his subconscious mind registering that it wasn't transferring to his consciousness?

Platinov either picked up on his facial expression or the hesitancy radiating from his body. "What's wrong?" the Russian woman asked quietly.

"I don't know," Bolan said. "But something." Four corrugated metal doors away from their own, the Executioner came to a complete halt. He said nothing as his eyes scanned up and down the steel structures; neither did Platinov.

But Marc Ajaccio said, "What are we waiting for?"

Bolan didn't bother answering—he was too busy concentrating on the hangars. Platinov turned in her seat, glared at Marc and held up a hand for silence.

The Russian woman was experienced and battle-hardened. Even though she wasn't experiencing the same phenomena that Bolan was, she recognized it in a fellow warrior.

For a good thirty seconds, the only sounds penetrating the vehicle from the outside were the landings and takeoffs of planes far in the distance. Then it hit Bolan.

The door to the hangar next to theirs was not only unlocked, it had been rolled back a good foot or two. The Executioner bore down on his memory, trying to remember if it had been that way when they'd left. But if it had, that fact hadn't registered with him.

"The door to the hangar next to ours," he said to Platinov. "Do you remember if it was open or closed when we left earlier?"

Now it was Platinov's turn to frown. "No," she said, staring down the line of corrugated metal. "But if it had been open—all the way at least rather than partially like now—I think I would have remembered it." She paused and leaned slightly in toward the windshield. "It would have been only natural for us to look inside."

"My thinking exactly."

"So, do you think someone is in there?" Platinov asked. "Waiting for us?"

"Maybe, maybe not," Bolan replied. "But we take enough chances the way it is. I don't see any sense in taking any we don't have to."

Charlot, whose mouth had been taped shut just as securely as his arms and legs, now began making moaning and gargling sounds, trying to be understood.

"Pull the tape off his mouth for a minute," Bolan ordered Marc.

Marc reached up and did as ordered.

Charlot whined as the adhesive agent jerked off short stubbles of hair and skin with the tape. Then he said, "There is someone waiting in there to kill you."

"And how do you know that?" Bolan demanded.

"It is just a guess," Charlot said. "But I know Rouillan hired an assassin—a professional mercenary who is not really part of CLODO—to kill an American agent and a Russian woman who were working together."

"And how do you know all this?" Platinov demanded.

"Because I was with him when he made the telephone call."

Bolan glanced to Platinov, then turned back to Charlot. "Have you ever met this mercenary?" he asked.

"Yes," Charlot whimpered. "On several occasions."

"Then he'd recognize you?"

"Of course."

"Good," Bolan said. "But tell me one thing. Does you providing us with all this information mean you're coming over to our side like your friend Marc, here?"

"Yes!" Charlot practically screamed in a high-pitched voice. "I want no more to do with CLODO!"

Bolan reached behind him and pulled out the TOPS SAW knife with the three-inch blade. Handing it grip first to Marc, he said, "Cut your friend free."

"Are you sure—" Marc started to say.

"Just do it," Bolan interrupted. While Marc used the knife to separate Charlot's hands and feet, he glanced briefly at Platinov, who nodded that she understood what was going on. She reached into her bag once more and came up with the same blackened 1911 Government Model she had handed Charlot earlier.

"You'll have to chamber the first round," the Executioner said as the Russian woman reached between the seats again and handed the pistol to Charlot. "But don't do it until right before you get to the door."

"What is it I'm supposed to do?" Charlot asked, his voice becoming lower in volume but even more shrill.

"Kill him, you idiot," Platinov said. "He knows you, so he won't suspect you."

Bolan nodded in agreement as Charlot looked to him.

By now, Charlot had twisted the .45 in his hand into a shooting position. He looked down at the weapon. Bolan did the same.

The hammer was down, the safety off.

As if it might be a replay of what had happened earlier, Charlot suddenly turned the weapon in his hand on Platinov and pulled back the slide as Bolan had instructed him to do when he neared the open hangar door. But when he pulled back on the trigger, nothing happened.

A look of horror overtook the blond-haired little Frenchman's face as he turned the .45 sideways and looked down at it again. This time, in addition to the Government Model not being chambered, it held an empty magazine as well. And the slide had locked open just as it would after a final shot had been fired.

"Well, I guess this pretty much answers the question of you changing sides," Bolan said.

"Do you want me to just kill him now?" Platinov asked as she snatched the .45 from Charlot's suddenly limp hand, dropped it into her bag and produced one of her Colt Gold Cups.

Bolan shook his head. "No," he said. "I think what we're going to do is let him lead the way to this mercenary."

"But he will kill me!" Charlot cried softly.

"Probably so," Bolan said. "But you've tried to kill us twice now. And the merc will recognize you, and for at least a second that recognition will cause him to hesitate."

He turned to Platinov. "Give him the empty .45 again," he said.

Platinov had to slap the little man twice, then force his fingers around the butt of the gun to get him to take it.

By now, Charlot's purple glasses had been struck so many times that they rested crookedly on his nose.

"Now," the Executioner said. "We all get out and close the doors quietly. This hired assassin...do you know his name?"

Charlot nodded. "Gautier something," he said. "I do not know the last name."

"Well, whatever his last name is, this Gautier will have heard, maybe even seen us, drive over to the hangars. We're out of his field of vision right now unless he sticks his head out of the door, and I doubt he's stupid enough to do that. So he's waiting for us, wondering if we're the folks he's supposed to kill or just some third party who stopped at one of the hangars."

"So we sneak up on him?" Platinov asked.

Bolan nodded, then, staring straaight into Charlot's

wet eyes, said, "And if anyone makes a sound, which includes sobs and moans, he gets a 9 mm in the head. Is that clear?" From his shoulder rig, he drew the sound-suppressed Beretta 93-R.

Charlot nodded.

Silently, the quartet exited the Toyota and gathered at the front of the car. "If this works the way I hope it will, let me do all the shooting," Bolan whispered. "Any shots fired—either from you or him—will be heard across the airport. And we aren't ready to abandon this hiding place for the plane or the vehicles yet."

Bolan grabbed the back of Charlot's shirt, bunched it up in his left fist and prodded the man along in front of him. The empty .45 was dangling at the end of the little man's arm, and the Executioner whispered into his ear, "Raise that gun and aim it forward or I'll shoot you right now."

The unloaded .45 jerked out in front of the Frenchman as if of its own accord.

Roughly a yard from the partially opened hangar door, Bolan pulled Charlot to a halt. "Call out to him by name," he said quietly. "Remind him who you are, and tell him not to shoot."

"Gauthier," Charlot said in a loud whisper. "It is me, Charlot." He waited a few seconds and when he got no response, he added, "Rouillan's friend."

The voice inside the hangar came back with, "Long blond hair? Purple eyeglasses?"

"Yes!" Charlot said a little louder.

"Tell him you've got information for him from Rouillan," Bolan whispered in his ear.

The CLODO man did as he was ordered. "Rouillan has sent me to speak to you."

"About what?" the voice asked suspiciously.

Bolan nudged Charlot forward slightly.

"May I please come in?" the long-haired Frenchman asked. "Who knows who might hear me out here?"

There was a long pause during which the only sound was the wind whipping past the hangars and rattling the corrugated steel doors. "All right," said the voice inside the slightly opened door. "Come in."

A moment later, Bolan had pushed Charlot into the crack between the door and doorframe. He hunched down behind the smaller man as best he could, but the Executioner knew there was no way he could remain completely hidden behind the slight CLODO man. All it did was give Bolan an extra half second of hesitation on his adversary's part. Almost immediately Gautier opened fire with a sound-suppressed submachine gun.

Bolan had flipped his Beretta to 3-round-burst mode before he'd even taken hold of Charlot, and now he raised the 93-R over the little man's shoulder as the Frenchman shrieked in pain or terror. Inside the semi-lit hangar, the soldier could see a man-shaped form, but his eyes hadn't had time to adjust to the dimmer lighting, and it was impossible to make out any of the subgunner's features.

Pointing the Beretta at center mass of the blurry outline, the Executioner triggered three trios of rounds and watched as the fuzzy man-shape fell to the floor.

A second later he had pushed Charlot to the side and

passed him. Dropping to a knee next to the form on the ground, he pressed two fingers into the man's throat.

There was no pulse.

Not that the Executioner had expected one. Even in the semidarkness, without his eyes having time to adjust, he could easily see that eight of the nine rounds he'd fired had taken the man in the chest. The ninth had probably been the last one to come out of the Beretta, catching Gautier in the center of the chin as he fell.

Bolan stood and heard Charlot crying. The long-haired Frenchman with the purple eyeglasses was leaning against the wall of the hangar, holding his arm.

Platinov did not have her doctor's bag with her, but she was inspecting Charlot's arm just the same. "It is nothing but a flesh wound," she said in a voice that reflected her disgust at the little Frenchman in general, and his current behavior in particular. "Do we need this man for anything else?" She had already drawn one of her Gold Cups from her bag before following Bolan and Marc Ajaccio into the hangar, and now she pressed the nuzzle against Charlot's forehead.

Bolan saw no reason to kill the guy just because his usefulness was over. "Just patch him up and tape him again," he told the Russian woman. "We might need him somewhere down the line. You never know."

Platinov sighed. "In my opinion, he is nothing but deadweight. But I will do as you say." She looked up, past the Executioner, and suddenly squinted. A moment later she had both Gold Cups in front of her as she moved toward one of the rear corners of the hangar.

Bolan's eyes followed her. "Find something?" he asked.

"Yes," Platinov said, stopping in the shadows. "But I think you should come see for yourself."

Bolan hurried toward her. By now, his eyes were growing accustomed to the dim light and haphazardly thrown against the wall he could see three bodies. One wore the khaki coveralls of the Belgian customs officials, but the body did not belong to LeCoque as he feared at first. This man was shorter and far heavier, with dark straight hair.

Another of the bodies wore the striped coveralls of an aircraft mechanic. The third man was dressed in the blue beret and brown slacks of CLODO.

"What do you suppose happened to them?" Platinov asked.

"Hard to tell," Bolan replied. "They got in this merc's way somehow and had to be eliminated. But we don't have time to speculate. Let's go."

Once they had all left the hangar, the soldier closed the door the rest of the way and snapped the padlock that had been hanging open from the latch. A moment later, he had opened the door to their own hangar.

Jack Grimaldi was sitting in a folding lawn chair he'd taken from the plane, reading a paperback mystery novel. He automatically stood up when Bolan and the others entered, ready to fly them to whatever spot on the globe Bolan needed to be next.

"Read any good books lately, Jack?" Platinov asked in a somewhat sarcastic tone of voice.

Grimaldi laughed. "It's not bad," he said, turning and laying the open pages facedown on the chair. "But they all kind of pale compared to hanging around with you guys."

Bolan gave Grimaldi a quick rundown on everything that had happened as Platinov pulled the Hummer outside and parked the Toyota where the heavier vehicle had been next to the Learjet.

As soon as he realized they hadn't come for the plane, Grimaldi removed his book from the chair and sat back down.

Grimaldi, who had been no more than a few feet from the speeding bullets on the other side of the thin sheet-metal wall, hadn't even suspected that a sound-suppressed war had been raging right next to him. This reassured Bolan that no one else around the hangars, or anywhere else at the airport, would have taken note of the battle, either.

A few minutes later, Platinov had dressed Charlot's arm wound, made him swallow two antibiotic capsules and duct-taped his hands. As soon as she was finished, the Executioner led the female warrior, her still-sniveling patient, and one computer-geek-fighter-wanna-be out of the hangar to the Hummer.

As Grimaldi rolled the door shut again, then returned to his lawn chair and paperback novel, the Executioner slid behind the wheel of the Hummer. He turned around once to make sure that Marc Ajaccio was taping Charlot's ankles together.

Then, a few seconds later, they were headed back toward the safe house in Han-sur-Lesse to resume the war.

CHAPTER ELEVEN

The feeling that something was wrong returned to the Executioner as soon as he turned the corner toward the safe house in Han-sur-Lesse. In such a high profile vehicle as the Hummer, he decided not to even slow as he passed the house at the top of the sloping bank.

"What's wrong?" Platinov asked. Like all partners the world over, be they police officers, military or civilian intelligence, or members of any other occupation that required its members to stare death in the face, she and Bolan were in tune.

Bolan didn't answer until he was a block past the safe house. Stopping briefly at a stop sign, he moved on through the empty intersection before he said, "Same thing as before. I don't know what's wrong. But something is different."

For a seasoned veteran like Platinov, that was all the explanation that was needed. She said nothing more.

Adjusting the rearview mirror slightly, the Executioner now saw the face of the blacksuit-trained Belgian customs man, Robert LeCoque. They had picked up LeCoque up on their way away from the airport and he'd been excited about getting away from his humdrum job to see some action. Bolan needed another gun, and he wouldn't find one better than a man or woman who had been through the Stony Man Farm blacksuit program.

They had also solved the mystery of the three bodies in the assassin's hangar. According to LeCoque, the overweight customs man with the dark hair had tried hard to get him to come out to the hangars with the mechanic, but LeCoque had been awaiting a telephone call and refused to accompany them.

Now he knew that if he had, he would have probably made a fourth body.

Bolan turned in his seat and looked at Charlot who was, again, directly behind him. The little man had begun whimpering again during the drive back from the airport, whining that his gunshot wound hurt, that the tape around his wrists was cutting off his circulation and anything else he could think of to complain about.

"You lied about knowing this place before," the soldier said. "Are you sure this is the right house now."

"I am sure," the Frenchman replied. "Marc encrypted the e-mails, remember?" He turned toward the former CLODO computer man. "That is the exact address that they gave Rouillan for the drug and gun exchange. Look—you can even see the numbers."

As they passed, Bolan glanced quickly up the slope

to the house and saw the black numerals nailed to the dull yellow siding next to the front door. Charlot was right. This was the right house.

But something was still wrong.

Bolan closed his eyes. For several seconds, he didn't speak. Rouillan was the leader of CLODO. So why would this cell in Ghent even need to give him an address in an e-mail? Wouldn't he already know it? The Executioner felt his facial muscles tensing into a grimace. There were other possibilities, he supposed. The Ghent CLODO men could have been holed up at another location but decided it was getting too hot, that the police were beginning to take notice of the type of men who came and went. If that was the case, they might have just moved into this new safe house and were passing the information on to Rouillan for the first time.

Believing that, or any of the other reasons the Ghent cell might have had for giving Rouillan the address, was a stretch. Still, such things did happen. Once in awhile, coincidences actually did occur.

The soldier still wasn't satisfied with any of the ex-planations that had crossed his mind. But he knew of only one way to find out the answer to why the Ghent CLODO terrorists had found it necessary to remind, or inform, Pierre Rouillan of the safe house address.

Attack.

"Okay," Bolan finally said, still sitting sideways in the Hummer seat and looking at Charlot. "There's something missing in all this, but the only way to find out what it is, is to go on with the plan." He turned to Marc. "Do you want in on this?" he asked bluntly.

Marc glanced at Platinov. "Yes. I want to make up for the harm I have done."

Bolan nodded. That wasn't the real reason and he, Marc and Platinov all knew it. The reason he really wanted in on the fight was to prove to Platinov that he was more than just a computer geek.

The soldier knew that Marc would be a marginal fighter at best. More than likely, he would do nothing but get in everyone else's way and probably get himself killed in the process.

The trick would be to give him some duty that he thought was dangerous and important but which wasn't. Charlot had proved twice now that he couldn't be trusted. So Marc Ajaccio was their key to Computer guy, and he was far more valuable in that role than he was getting himself blown away in a firefight during which he'd be more hindrance than help.

"Then here's what we're going to do," Bolan said. "I'm going to let LeCoque and you—" he nodded at Marc "—off at the corner right before the alley. I want you both to stay out of sight until you hear the crash at the rear of the house. Then, LeCoque, I want you sprinting in the front door just as fast as your legs will carry you."

Marc Ajaccio had started to speak, but Bolan turned back to him before he could. "Marc, you're our rear guard. You stay hidden and watch for any CLODO men who might be returning to the safe house during the time it takes us to strike."

The man started to speak again, but again the Executioner cut him off. "You've got to stay vigilant," he said in a commanding voice. "If they sneak up behind us, we'll be defenseless." He paused for a moment, then finished with, "Are you up for the job?"

In his lap, Marc still had the .45 pistol Platinov had given him. Now she handed two extra magazines over the seat to him, smiled and said, "I think he's our man."

Suddenly, Marc's face rivaled the sun for brightness.

"Any questions?" Bolan asked.

"One," LeCoque said. "Are we trying to take anybody alive?"

"If it's possible, yes," Bolan replied. "But don't get yourself killed doing it."

"Affirmative. Death's not on my list of things to do today, anyway."

"Where am I supposed to go?" Charlot whined out.

"Nowhere," Bolan said.

"Just sit where you are and shut up," Platinov added. "And if you're lucky, you won't get hit by a stray bullet."

Charlot began to sob, but he did so silently, his eyes a mask of fear as they stared at the Russian woman.

Bolan backed the Hummer out of the parking space where he'd parked, then turned out of the lot itself. A few minutes later, he was back at the corner where he'd turn toward the alley. He stopped while first Marc, then LeCoque, exited the vehicle.

The Executioner grabbed the 9 mm Vigneron M2 submachine gun LeCoque had brought along with him just before the man's feet hit the ground.

LeCoque turned toward the Executioner.

"Make sure he stays behind and safe when you go in," Bolan whispered.

LeCoque winked his understanding, then turned and led Marc toward a chest-high hedge growing at the edge of the lawn between them and the safe house across the side street.

Bolan turned the corner and started down the alley. As he neared the back of the safe house, he said, "Everybody ready?"

"Ready," Platinov said, a Colt Gold Cup pistol in both hands.

"No," Charlot whimpered.

"Your vote doesn't count," Platinov said scornfully. "Sit back and relax."

But before either one of them could say anything else, the Hummer was exploding through the ancient, termite-infested back wall of the safe house.

PLATINOV BRACED HERSELF for the impact with the house by putting both forearms on the Hummer's dashboard. While she had removed both index fingers from inside the trigger guards of her twin Colt Gold Cup pistols, she wasn't about to holster them or set them on the seat next to her.

The Russian agent knew that while a vehicle suddenly shredding the back wall of the small house would be unnerving, and cause an extra moment of confusion on the parts of the CLODO terrorists inside, they would not be far from their weapons.

So she wasn't going to let go of her own firearms "for love or money" as she'd heard Americans say.

A tornado of splintered wood, cheap siding, glass and other broken bits of building material blew into the Hummer's windshield. Much of it hit at an angle that propelled it up and over the roof of the vehicle. The rest bounced off. Although it seemed like minutes, Platinov had been in enough life-or-death struggles to know that only two or three seconds could have passed before the Hummer came to a halt. And when it did, she found that the vehicle had penetrated the house into the kitchen. It was now wedged with the driver's side standing just in front of a doorway to a bedroom and the right side smashing what was left of the refrigerator almost in two.

Cooper was out of his door before the Hummer had even quit rocking up and down, but when she tried the latch to her own door, Platinov found it had jammed.

Gunfire drove the Russian woman below window level as bullets broke glass and zipped over her head. She tried the door handle again with no more success than she'd had before. Trapped on the floor of the Hummer, she looked past the steering wheel to see that Cooper had left his door ajar.

That could be her only way out of this shooting-fish-in-a-barrel situation she was in—another Americanism she had picked up. The trick would be staying low enough to keep from getting shot as she exited the barrel.

The Gold Cup pistols still cocked and locked in her

hands, Platinov used her elbows to lift her canvas tourist bag off the floorboard, and place it on the driver's seat. Then, she pulled herself back up off the floorboards. Scooting forward, inch by inch, she soon realized that at least part of her had to be visible from outside the Hummer.

Because Platinov felt the heat of bullets skimming the area just above her buttocks.

She flattened back down onto the seat. While she waited for the volley of rounds to end, she double-checked the push-button snaps at the top of her canvas bag, then pushed it on out the Hummer onto the floor.

The volley of gunfire that had been aimed her way suddenly stopped. That either meant the man behind it had run his weapon dry and was reloading or he wanted her to think that was the case and show herself again. The way she saw it, she had little choice.

Platinov rose to her elbows and knees again, ready to chance being shot, when two big hands clamped around her wrists. Before she had fully comprehended what was happening, she was suddenly jerked out of the driver's-side door and onto her belly on the floor.

The Russian agent looked up to see that Cooper had holstered both of his pistols in order to save her. In the world of combat—where seconds counted as much as hours—he had endangered his own life to save hers.

Greater love hath no man than he lay down his life for a friend went quickly through Platinov's head and she remembered her mother—a staunch Russian

Orthodox church member—reading those words to her from the Bible when she'd been a little girl.

In one lightninglike move, Cooper's left hand drew his Desert Eagle and his right grasped the Beretta 93-R. Then, dropping to his knees next to him, Platinov twisted and watched through the Hummer's windows as a dark-skinned man sporting a neatly trimmed beard fell to the scream of the Eagle and the soft cough of the Beretta. She had still not lost her grip on either of her .45s, and now she used her thumbs to drop the ambidextrous safeties into the "fire" position. Aiming through the Hummer, she pulled both triggers at the same time and saw the 230-grain bullets make a single hole in the center of another CLODO man's chest.

The Hummer was a civilian model rather than one made for the military and now return fire—this time from what sounded like an Uzi submachine gun— drilled holes through the big vehicle's windows and body. Platinov squatted behind the engine block, hip to hip with the big American, who was doing the same. As soon as the burst ended, they rose to their feet again and sent 9 mm .44 Magnum and .45ACP rounds back at more enemy gunners. Some wore the same trimmed beards as the first man Platinov had watched Cooper kill. Others had mustaches, while still others were clean shaven. But the feeling that something was wrong that Cooper had expressed earlier suddenly hit Platinov with as much force as 12-gauge shotgun slug. And along with that feeling, came the answer as to what that "something wrong" actually was.

Before she could speak, Cooper turned to her. "Stay here and keep shooting," he said. "How are you fixed for reloads?"

"I've got a full bag of magazines," Platinov said, sliding the shoulder strap over her head and across her body. "Where are you going?"

Her companion inclined his head toward a partially blocked doorway that had been struck by the Hummer as it sailed into the house moments earlier. "There have to be more men through there," he whispered. "And unless I miss my guess, there's another bedroom down that hall with another doorway that leads into the living room."

"They'll have a clear shot at LeCoque as he comes through the front door," Platinov said.

"They'll see him long before he sees them," Bolan agreed. "Unless I get to them first."

Platinov nodded her understanding. She was about to answer when another terrorist sprinted from the room on the other side of the battered refrigerator, a British Sterling submachine gun in his hands.

The man leaped up into the air, twisting to the side, planning to land in a position from which he could pepper both Cooper and Platinov with automatic fire through the Hummer's windshield. He was successful in both his aerial twist and his landing.

But what he hadn't planned on was having two .45s and a pair of .44 Magnum rounds in his chest when he hit the glass.

The attacker came to rest with his cheek on the windshield and blood pouring from his open mouth as if he were regurgitating. Slowly, he began to slide back down the glass to the hood of the Hummer, leaving a red streak of blood as a trail.

Then another pair of men had leaped up onto the Hummer's windshield, screaming, *"Allah Akhbar!"*

THE EXECUTIONER had realized what had happened a second after they'd crashed through the back wall of the house. It was not anything he saw, or felt, or heard, or tasted. It was something he smelled.

The strong odor of curry and other seasonings used far more often in the Middle East than in the Western World.

Someone was cooking, he realized as the Hummer zoomed past the stove and he saw steam rising from several pots.

And it wasn't the French-like cuisine of Belgium.

Whatever it was, it was Arabic.

One thought led to another as the Executioner jumped out of the Hummer and drew his Desert Eagle. There was a time for the near-silence of the Beretta, and there was a time for the deafening thunder of the .44 Magnum. And right now, Bolan wanted to prolong the shock and awe that had started with the Hummer taking out most of the house's back wall for as long as possible.

So he tapped two rounds from the Desert Eagle into the heart of a dark-complected man reaching for an M-16 leaning against the wall. By the time Bolan pulled the trigger the first time, the man had wrapped his fist around the pistol grip and clutched the fore end with his other hand. By the time the Executioner pulled the trigger again, the barrel of the American-made rifle had almost risen to gut level.

The rifle fell to the floor much faster than it had risen, as did the dark-skinned terrorist, out of sight on the other side of the Hummer.

A fusillade of fire now came from the door next to the refrigerator, forcing Bolan down and out of sight. But from this new vantage point, he could see back into the Hummer. Platinov had tossed her carry-all onto the seat he'd just vacated and was attempting to crawl beneath the fire toward his open door.

The door on her side had to have jammed shut sometime during the collision.

The Executioner didn't hesitate. Holstering both pistols, he reached in, grabbed Platinov's wrists and hoped that she'd look up to see who it was before she took the safeties off her pistols and shot him.

She did.

After both warriors moved to the relative safety of the cover provided by the Hummer's engine block, Bolan looked over his shoulder. Behind him, he could see what looked like a hallway. But it was partially blocked by the debris that the Hummer had left in its path.

That didn't make it safe, however. There was more than enough room for someone to sneak down the hall, hide among the rubble and pump bullets into his and Platinov's backs.

He was about to make his way through the ruins and then double back around the house when a man screaming something leaped up onto the windshield. Both he and Platinov drilled slugs into the man, and he slithered down the windshield, then down the hood and onto the floor.

"You know these aren't CLODO men, don't you?" Platinov said after he'd whispered to her his plan to circle the house.

"I know," the Executioner said. "But as long as we're here, we might as well stay for the party." He moved toward the partially blocked doorway, then heard two more voices shouting, followed by what sounded like .45-caliber double-taps from both of Platinov's Gold Cup pistols. Then the shouting ceased.

Bolan frowned to himself. Although it made little difference at this point, he couldn't help wonder which of the Islamic-based terrorist groups were using this ancient structure as a safe house. Hezbollah or Hamas would be his guess.

But again, it didn't really matter. Whoever they were, they'd be delighted to murder both the soldier and Platinov in the name of God.

Bolan moved closer to the rubbish that had once been a hallway. The Islamic extremists had guns for sale. Rouillan had come across a load of heroin that he was willing to trade the Muslims for weaponry. CLODO would then be better armed than ever, and the Islamic extremists would sell the heroin to help finance their ongoing acts of terror around the world.

Not to mention the fact that they'd be creating more chaos and death for the Western world of "infidels" who ended up with the white powder liquidized and injected into their arms.

All of these things were on the Executioner's mind as he did his best to keep from making noise as he navigated through the splintered wood and broken boards on the floor in the hallway. The wainscoting had pulled up some of the old linoleum tile as it was forced forward by the Hummer, and the speckled squares that had once covered the concrete foundation were now in ragged pieces.

After what seemed like an hour but could have been no more than a minute, the Executioner found himself at the entrance to another bedroom. And he had been correct. Another open door gave way to the living room, and Bolan arrived just as LeCoque booted the front door and came crashing in.

Bolan jerked the Beretta out of his shoulder rig and thumbed the selector to 3-round-burst mode. A total of five men were in his field of vision, and all had been waiting for a frontal attack, paying little attention to what had happened in the kitchen on the other side of the caved-in hallway wall.

Bolan followed the old shooter's axiom of taking the enemy out in order of threat. One man—he could see him through the doorway in the living room—held a sawed-off double-barreled shotgun. It was aimed at LeCoque, waist level, as the Executioner held the trigger back and pumped three 9 mm RBCD fragmentation rounds through the man's armpit and into his heart.

LeCoque was no rookie and took out a target hidden from Bolan's sight on the other side of the bedroom wall. A second later, the man—again with Arabic features but dressed in jeans and a T-shirt—fell forward, a 7.62 mm FN FAL rifle falling to the carpet in front of him.

Bolan's quiet 3-round burst had gone unheard or perhaps unnoticed by the three men still in the bedroom. And he was behind them all.

So it should have been easy, but easy rarely came to the Executioner.

As the three Islamic terrorists sensed his presence and started to turn, Bolan saw that the fifth man he had initially seen—another shotgunner with a Franchi SPAS-12—had set the versatile scattergun's sights on LeCoque. And even though the blacksuit-trained Belgian was swinging his Vigneron M2 that way, Bolan could see that he'd be a fraction of a second too late.

Which, in turn, meant he'd die.

Ignoring the three terrorists turning their weapons his way, the Executioner fired another 3-round burst into the living room. At least one of the rounds hit the sub-machine gun, because sparks flew through the air and the weapon jumped out of the man's hands. Raising the Desert Eagle—which was still in his other hand—Bolan pumped out a .44 Magnum round as his adversary fumbled for a pistol in his belt.

The big .44 round hit the "kill zone" long before the

terrorist could gain control of his pistol, and he suddenly dropped to the ground and froze in death.

While the Executioner had been holding the Beretta's trigger back, one of the men not three feet away from him had turned far enough to shoot. The gunner held a Browning Hi-Power in his hand, and his desperate, hurried shot sailed over Bolan's shoulder and lodged itself harmlessly in the wall.

Bolan cut loose a second later three more 9 mm RBCD rounds, which took the man with the Hi-Power in the head and throat. He had been sitting on the corner of the bed. Now he fell forward on his face to the floor.

The other two men seemed to freeze at the sight of their comrade's bloody demise. But then one of them—a short stocky Arab who had been standing on the other side of the door to the living room—turned his old Cetme 7.62 mm Model 68 toward the Executioner, who lived up to his name.

The stocky man fell on top of his rifle, much as his friend had just done.

The firing had died down in the kitchen, but Bolan heard two more short volleys from LeCoque's Vigneron in the living room, then silence.

Before he even had time to turn the Beretta his way, the third man in the bedroom dropped his AK-47, lifted his empty hands high in the air and said something in Arabic. Bolan couldn't make out the words, but the man's body language screamed that he was giving up.

The Executioner holstered the Beretta but kept the

Desert Eagle in his other hand. He kept the huge pistol trained on the man as he walked to the door to the living room where LeCoque stood over the three dead bodies. The Belgian used his subgun to point at the man with the Franchi. "Thanks for the help," he said. "I didn't even see him. He'd have killed me for sure."

Bolan nodded. Then, turning back to the terrorist with his hands in the air, he said, "Come on," as he waved the man forward.

With Bolan pushing the terrorist forward with the Desert Eagle and LeCoque bringing up the rear, they marched through the other bedroom and saw the front of the Hummer jammed in the doorframe down the hall.

Platinov was sitting on the roof of the vehicle, her legs crossed, with one foot dangling down the windshield. Her arms were crossed in front of her breasts, and she held a Gold Cup .45 in both hands.

The kitchen floor around her was as littered with dead terrorists as the rest of the house.

"I found the heroin," the Russian agent said, pointing at a row of cabinets near the top of the kitchen wall. The doors had been left open and inside Bolan could see plastic freezer bags filled with white powder stacked on top of one another.

He'd leave the drugs where they were. The Belgian cops could take care of them.

"Have you checked on Charlot?" Bolan asked.

Platinov's eyebrows rose, and it was obvious that she'd forgotten all about the blond-haired Frenchman.

She pulled herself up onto the roof of the Hummer, then slid down off the side.

As Bolan and the other men climbed over the Hummer's front grille, which was still jammed in the doorway, Platinov opened the rear door and said, "Uh-oh."

Bolan slid down next to her and looked inside.

Charlot had taken a round squarely in the forehead. His lifeless eyes stared straight ahead.

"Maybe we should have left him out there with Marc," LeCoque said as he rounded the Hummer and looked inside.

"He tried to shoot us twice," Platinov said, indicating Bolan and herself with a thumb and a forefinger. "He couldn't be trusted." She jerked open the Hummer's door next to where the man's lifeless body still sat, grabbed his arm with both hands and jerked him unceremoniously out of the Hummer to the floor of the kitchen.

"LeCoque," Bolan said, "go get Marc and bring him in. We're going to have to get this thing—" he kicked the tire of the Hummer "—running again or find alternate transportation. And we've got the same old reoccurring problem we always have after we take down a safe house like this."

"What's that?" LeCoque asked, frowning.

"The cops," Platinov said. "They'll be on their way by now."

LeCoque took off through the bedroom, and Bolan heard the front door open and close again. But then, as if to lend credence to Platinov's words, the first police siren sounded in the distance.

Bolan got behind the wheel of the Hummer. He twisted the key, and the engine jumped immediately to life. The Executioner shook his head in wonder. "I guess once in a while everyone gets a lucky break," he said.

"It takes a licking but keeps on kicking," Platinov said, smiling.

"I think what you meant to say was it takes a licking but keeps on *ticking*," the Executioner corrected. "That's from an old American watch commercial."

"I wasn't talking about the commercial," Platinov said. "I was talking about us."

Bolan backed the Hummer out of the house.

EVENING TRAFFIC SLOWED the Hummer to a crawl, and sometimes even had to stop as Bolan did his best to thread their way back to the airport and the waiting pilot and Learjet.

Platinov had traded seats with LeCoque, and now sat in the back between Marc and the Islamic terrorist who had surrendered a split second before Bolan would have killed him. Ever since they'd driven away from the dilapidated safe house, the Russian woman had kept up an almost steady dialogue with the Arab, but their voices had rarely risen above a whisper.

Bolan smiled inwardly. Marynka Platinov was a master of many covert skills, and intuitively knowing what approach to take with an individual during interrogation was one of those talents. Somehow—call it feminine intuition or anything else you wanted to—she had known that Marc was so attracted to her that she had conducted his questioning in a rather provocative manner.

The Executioner didn't know exactly what course of action she was using on the terrorist in the backseat, but he knew it was working. And luckily, the man spoke English.

So far, they had learned that his name was Ali, that the group at the safe house had been a Hezbollah cell and, yes, they had traded a cache of rifles, submachine guns and other weapons and ammunition for the heroin. The leader of the cell—a man named Shuaib who had died during the battle back at the house—had a drug connection who was willing to pay them top dollar for the dope.

As Bolan continued to creep along in the traffic, he was tempted to break into the conversation behind him and ask Ali where, and when, that buy was scheduled to take place. But he didn't want to chance breaking the bond Platinov seemed to have created with this newest, unwilling member of their ongoing "search and destroy" troupe.

Besides, the soldier thought as a Honda from the lane to his right cut him off and forced him to stomp on the brakes, tracking the buy would lead him in the wrong direction. Under other circumstances, he'd have been more than happy to follow the transaction and destroy both the drugs and the drug dealers, but that wouldn't get him to Rouillan, or the rest of CLODO, or this super virus they were putting together to shut down the world's computers.

Platinov was speaking a little louder now, and Bolan heard her say, "Ali, you seem to be a fine young man. Whatever possessed you to become a terrorist like this?"

Platinov was taking sort of a "mother" or "big sister" approach with Ali, but paying the man so much attention in any way wasn't going over very well with Marc. Bolan could see the anger and jealousy on Marc's face in the rearview mirror.

Traffic picked up a little as they got farther from the center of the city, but then halted abruptly once more. A minute or two later, both a fire engine and an ambulance raced past on the grass divider between the Hummer and the oncoming lane, which meant there had been a traffic accident of some sort ahead.

Which in turn meant more delay.

"Ali, tell me what you know about CLODO," Platinov asked gently. "Do you know what they were going to do with the guns?"

In the rearview mirror, Bolan watched the terrorist shake his head. "No," he said. "Except that they had some big plan. Something that had nothing to do with guns or bombs. What we traded them for the heroin were weapons that they simply planned to use as distractions for their bigger plan."

"And you don't know what that bigger plan is?" Platinov probed.

Ali shook his head again. "Just that it probably has to do with computers," he said. "That's their big complaint. They hate computer technology."

"Don't you hate technology, too?" Platinov asked. "When I am in your part of the world, it seems little has changed for many years."

"That is true," Ali said, raising his taped wrists and scratching his nose with both hands. "But I do not hate computers or technology myself, and I believe we are foolish not to take advantage of new inventions and other things."

"Then what in the world are you doing as a member of this Hezbollah cell?" Platinov asked.

Ali shrugged. "I was raised to become what I have become. From the cradle I was taught that there is but one God, his name is Allah, and Mohammed was his prophet. And I have been taught to hate Christians, Jews, Buddhists, Hindus—anyone who is not of the faith. And not only am I allowed to steal from them, swindle them, or otherwise act toward them in ways that would be sinful toward my Muslim brothers, I am bound to kill them whenever possible, as well."

"Well," Platinov said. "Isn't that nice."

Ali caught her sarcasm. "No," he said, "it is not nice, and it is not right. I cannot believe in a God who wants me to kill my fellow man, regardless of his beliefs. Convert, persuade, even pressure him to adopt my religion if necessary. But kill women and children and innocent men? I cannot accept it."

"Then I'll ask you again," Platinov said. "If you

don't believe in it, why are you here, doing what you are doing?"

Ali leaned down and brought his taped hands up to cover his face. "And I must answer you the same way I did before. Since birth, I have known no other way. How could I possibly have turned out any other way when you consider that fact?"

Bolan sensed that Ali was nearing a breaking point from the contradictions between his brain and heart, and he knew Platinov would have noticed it, too. And if there was one thing the Executioner had learned about the Russian woman, it was that she never let an opportunity slip by her.

Platinov leaned between the bucket seats and whispered, "The trade has already taken place."

"I heard," Bolan whispered back.

"It will do us no good to go to where it happened."

"Probably not," he replied. "But then again, we might pick up some lead as to where they went from there. In any case, I don't have any better ideas. Do you?"

Platinov shook her head, then returned to Ali. Softly, she squeezed the arm of the man and said, "Ali, do you know anything that might lead us to Rouillan or more CLODO cells?"

Without speaking, Ali shook his head.

"Do you know where the trade took place, then?" Platinov asked.

Ali finally looked up, a grimace on his face. "Yes," he said. "I was there as a guard when they made their exchange."

By now, the traffic congestion had thinned out and Bolan was racing the Hummer down the highway toward the airport. "Where was the exchange?" he asked over his shoulder.

"It was in Spain," Ali said. "Near Barcelona."

The soldier pulled his satellite phone from his pocket and tapped the automatic call button for Grimaldi. "Jack," he said as soon as the pilot answered, "get the bird warmed up. We'll be there in just a few more minutes."

"Fair enough," Grimaldi said. "Where we going?"

"Spain."

"What part?" the pilot asked. "I may need to gas up."

"Barcelona area," Bolan said. "So it won't be that far."

"No sweat, then. We can make that easy. Then I'll fill 'er up while you do whatever it is you're going to do."

"All right," Bolan said, and hung up.

The interior of the Hummer went silent as they continued toward the airport.

CHAPTER TWELVE

Pierre Rouillan and Achille LeForce exited the old deserted Moorish-style castle through a side door. The small castle was not far off the beach, and as they walked toward their vehicle their shoes kicked up a mixture of grass, dirt and sand. Rouillan opened the driver's door and slid behind the wheel. He glanced through the windshield as he inserted the key into the ignition of the sport Renault.

He loved the castle. It was hardly bigger than a modern house, but it reminded him of simpler times. Times before computers had taken over everyone's lives. Times when human beings lived real lives rather burying themselves in virtual existence.

Rouillan twisted the key and started the engine. The old castle had been a neglected wreck when he'd bought it, he remembered as LeForce got into the passenger's seat, which meant he had picked it up "for a song" from the Spanish government when the former owner defaulted on taxes. He, LeForce and other CLODO warriors had cleaned and restored it themselves and, in that way, avoided questions and suspicions as to some of the newer features and arrangements behind the old stones.

Someday Rouillan would retire to this small castle. It was close enough to the village of Sitges, Spain, to be handy. But it was also isolated enough to be private, and if he ever needed anything only a big city could provide, Barcelona was only about thirty miles to the north.

As he threw the Renault into Drive, Rouillan took one last mental picture of the castle. He had left an even dozen men behind to watch the place. After his master plan was successfully completed, he intended to renovate the rest of the rooms and make it a retirement home instead of CLODO's headquarters. And again, he would do the work himself; he would not trust any contractors to do the job. They would not only try to overcharge him, they'd constantly be trying to cut corners to increase their profits. He and LeForce would clean the stones, and do the rest of the work, themselves. It would be a labor of love, and when he was finished the castle would be no different than the way it had looked when originally built by Moorish invaders from Morocco.

Of course he would also have electricity, running water, a telephone, television and a few other modern conveniences. He had grown up with these things, and was comfortable with them. Not all modern conveniences were evil.

Just computers.

The Renault hit a grassy road that led to the landing strip, and Rouillan drove on in silence. To his followers, he preached a philosophy of simplicity, and did his best to explain and demonstrate how e-mail, instant messaging, the Internet and all other aspects of computers had narrowed their lives rather than expanded them. He said these things because he was afraid that the rest of CLODO could not handle the truth.

Satan himself really did live inside computers, and Rouillan did not mean that figuratively. It was true. He could feel the truth of it in his chest.

As the landing strip appeared in the distance, Rouillan drove on. He was not a religious man. He had never accepted Christianity or Islam or Judaism or any other religious belief. But he knew there was an evil force at work in the world, and he knew he had to stop it.

As Rouillan parked the car and they started to get out, LeForce suddenly broke the silence with a loud, "Dammit!"

Rouillan looked across the hood of the automobile at his old friend. The sun was bright, the breeze was cool, and in the distance the Mediterranean's waves lapped lazily onto the sand next to the road. "What could possibly have caused you such consternation on a day as beautiful as this?" Rouillan asked. "Particularly since we are about to complete our life's work?"

"The blueprints," LeForce said, his shoulders hunching as he shifted uncomfortably in his seat. "I left them back at the castle. On your desk. We will have to go back for them I guess."

Rouillan laughed. "Do not worry, old friend," he said. "We have a complete set at the offices in New York. We have no need for the copies you left behind."

"But if they should fall into the wrong hands—" LeForce started to say.

"They won't," Rouillan interrupted. "You have forgotten the men we left behind." He paused, remembering that his lifelong friend had never been the smartest kid on the block. "No police or other outsiders would understand the blueprints if they did see them."

LeForce relaxed slightly. "I suppose you are correct," he muttered.

Rouillan put his arm around his friend's shoulders as they walked to the plane. "Of course I am correct, Achille," he said gently. "I am always correct."

LeForce nodded.

The two top CLODO men entered the plane, with Rouillan sliding behind the controls. After a quick safety check of all electronics and the fuel gauge, Rouillan started the plane down the runway. It was barely long enough to get a Learjet into the air, but Rouillan was an expert pilot, and soon they were off the ground and rising.

As soon as they had reached the altitude Rouillan desired for this flight across the Atlantic, he pulled a cell phone from his shirt pocket and tapped in a number. A moment later, a voice on the other end said, "Hello."

Rouillan gave the voice his code number, then said,

"Please alert everyone that we are on schedule. I will contact you again once we reach New York." Then he hung up.

A tune had been dancing around in Rouillan's head ever since they'd left the castle, and now he found himself humming it. A glance at LeForce told him the man was asleep, so he allowed himself to hum slightly louder. What was the name of the tune? He knew it— it was on the tip of his tongue….

Yes. "Take Me Out to the Ball Game," Rouillan finally realized, and when he did he began to sing quietly instead of just hum.

Soon, the whole Barcelona area was far behind him, and Rouillan could see Portugal below. His eyes automatically went to the fuel gauge again. They would be fine.

A few minutes later, the CLODO leader and his number-one henchman were looking down at the waves of the Atlantic Ocean as they made their way to New York, Rouillan's master plan, and, yes, Rouillan thought, history.

Rouillan was about to turn the world upside down and while he knew the immediate reaction of the people might not be good, eventually he would be looked upon as the man who had saved the human race.

The little voice in the back of his head that had bothered him before spoke up now, accusingly: You're crazy, Pierre. Satan is in you, not the computers.

But Rouillan killed the voice.

And then he smiled.

"THERE IS A LANDING STRIP near the small city of Sitges," Ali said as the Stony Man Farm Learjet flew over Barcelona and began to follow the Mediterranean coast. "It was there that the weapons-for-heroin exchange took place."

Bolan had turned sideways in his seat within the plane in order to speak to Ali, who was behind Grimaldi. Marc was directly behind the Executioner, and Platinov, as she'd done before when Charlot had still been with them, was watching both men from the third row of seats inside the plane. But this time, she had the added help of Robert LeCoque, the Belgian customs officer, sitting across the aisle from her.

Now, Bolan turned back to Grimaldi. "You know the place he's talking about?" he asked.

Grimaldi shook his head. "Nope," he said, "but I'll find it. I've flown over this area a million times. Drug dealers are constantly building new landing strips, deserting them when they get too 'hot,' and then building more."

Bolan nodded as the Learjet moved in a half mile or so from the water. Below, the Executioner could see Sitges, and the beaches to the side.

Then, suddenly and without prompting, Ali practically screamed out, "There! That is the place!" He waited only long enough to draw in more air and then added, "I remember that old Moorish castle. It was not far away." By the time he had finished, the Learjet was well past the landing strip and the castle. But Bolan had seen it, as well as a half-dozen cars and pickups parked around it.

Grimaldi banked to the left and performed a tight, aerial U-turn in the sky. But the pilot was frowning.

"What's wrong, Jack?" Bolan asked.

"It's a fresh landing strip, all right," Grimaldi said. "Ask our new buddy what kind of plane Hezbollah was in when they landed."

Bolan did as Grimaldi had asked.

"I am not sure," Ali replied. "I do not know very much about airplanes."

"Ask him if it was like this one or if it had propellers," Grimaldi said.

This time, he had spoken loud enough for Ali to hear. "Is that word you used—prop-something—that thing like a windmill on the front?" he asked,

Grimaldi nodded. "Considerably faster than a windmill, however," he said.

"Then it was like that."

"How about the CLODO plane that met you here?" Grimaldi asked.

"It was like this one," Ali replied.

Grimaldi had almost reached the landing strip by then. "The reason I asked all that, Striker," he said to Bolan, "is that it's going to be a pretty tight squeeze landing."

"Can you do it?" the Executioner asked.

"Oh, I can do it all right," Grimaldi said, turning his head and smiling. "But not every pilot could." As they flew over the strip again, he added, "What it means is that someone in CLODO is not just a pilot—he's a *very good* pilot."

By this time the Executioner had risen from his seat and started back between the seats. From the storage area, he grabbed two parachutes off the deck, then opened one of the lockers bolted to the wall and pulled out four smoke grenades. For a moment, he considered arming himself and Platinov with fragmentation grenades as well. But while they'd certainly come in useful, they were just as likely to ruin evidence that would lead them on in this mission.

So Bolan closed the locker door again.

The soldier dropped one of the parachutes and two of the smoke grenades in Platinov's lap as he returned to the front of the plane. "You're going to have to do this short landing without Plat and me," he told Grimaldi. "If we land now, whoever's in that place will have shot this plane to pieces before you can even get us stopped."

"It's a HALO, then?" Grimaldi asked, referring to a high altitude low opening jump. He pulled the Learjet higher into the air.

"You got it," Bolan said as he began slipping the chute's straps over his shoulders. "Give us thirty minutes at least before you set her down." He snapped the belt around his waist. "If you can still see fireworks going on below, then stay in the air until they've quieted down."

"Will do," Grimaldi said. "But once in a while, I'd really like to actually get in a shot or two at the bad guys, you know." He tapped the grip of his S&W Model 66.

"And once in a while, you do," he said, recalling

dozens of times when Grimaldi had helped shoot it out with criminals or terrorists either from the plane or on the ground. "But did you ever notice how the quarterback in a football game who drops back to pass, can't find an open receiver and is forced to run it, does his best to run out of bounds as quickly as possible?"

"Yeah, yeah, yeah," Grimaldi said with feigned irritation.

"That's because he's too valuable to the team in other ways to risk getting hurt just to gain a few more yards. And quite frankly, you're my quarterback. I need you to fly us around more than I need your 6-shot wheelgun."

Grimaldi nodded, chuckling. "Thanks for the half-time pep-talk, Coach," he said.

Bolan grinned, then moved back between the seats and joined Platinov at the closed door. "Give us the word as soon as you see the castle, Jack," he called over his shoulder. "This is wide open country and I want to fall fast in case anybody's watching out the window."

"You've got it," Grimaldi called back.

And a few seconds later he had slid back the Learjet's door and was following Platinov into the open sky.

DUSK WAS SETTLING over the Mediterranean coast as Bolan and Platinov free-fell through the sky. Both had tucked their arms at their sides and shot headfirst toward the ground. The Executioner lifted one arm, causing him to veer slightly to his left, more toward the castle.

Even with the HALO jump, there was going to be a period of seconds during which their approach might be noted by anyone in the castle. So, if it really was CLODO men inside the ancient Moorish castle, he and Platinov would be like ducks flying over a blind.

During hunting season.

It would only be a few seconds, but those few seconds could be deadly.

Bolan glanced at the altimeter gauge. Then, at the last possible moment, he pulled the ripcord. Roughly a hundred feet to his side, he saw Platinov do the same.

Both chutes blossomed like flowers in the spring and, for just a moment, both the Executioner and the Russian women actually reversed direction, jerked upward before starting back down, considerably slower.

By the time he was roughly a hundred feet above the ground, the Executioner could see that if he steered the risers slightly farther to the left, he could come down directly on top of a flat section of the roof itself. He turned to see Platinov about fifty feet to his right. She'd hit the ground behind two pickups parked side by side.

Bolan caught her eye, then pointed to his chest, then straight down.

The Russian woman nodded, pointed to her own breasts, then down, then at the castle.

The Executioner nodded. There was bound to be a door of some kind that led into the depths of the old castle, and he'd attack from above while Platinov entered on the ground floor of the three-level structure.

They would then shoot their way to being reunited on the middle, or second floor.

At the same time as his feet hit the ground, the Executioner saw a trapdoor open less than a yard in front of him. It was a slight surprise as he snapped off the chute canopy. He had been right.

The enemy had seen him coming.

But this close, sudden encounter came as an even bigger surprise to the man dressed in an OD green T-shirt and faded blue jeans, wearing a traditional French beret and holding a Heckler & Koch 93.

That surprise, however, didn't last long. In less than a second the expression of shock was swept off his face—and along with it went his nose and right eye as a .44 Magnum hollowpoint round from Bolan's Desert Eagle sent him tumbling down the steps.

Both the Executioner's physical actions and thought process immediately shot into high gear, his mind taking in the fact that while the trapdoor itself was old, the folding steps leading up to it were new.

The roar of the Desert Eagle could be heard for miles, and there was no sense in using the sound-suppressed Beretta at this point. So the Executioner started down the steps, the big bore weapon in his right hand. He had taken only one step when another man came into his field of vision and knelt next to the CLODO man he'd just shot.

This new man's T-shirt was white, but another tap on the trigger as he turned his face upward turned it a bright crimson as blood spurted directly out of his exploded heart.

For a split second, the Executioner hesitated. By now, anyone in the room below would have figured out that someone was attacking from the roof. That fact was confirmed by a loud explosion and a bullet that struck the folding ladder an inch from his left foot. As his brain accelerated, he realized that only his boots were visible.

But he had a decision to make. Should he jump back or dive into the room? From the roof, he would have limited vision but maximum coverage and he could lie on his belly, take quick looks downward and basically snipe at the enemy.

As he considered the option, the Executioner heard gunfire break out below and the easily recognizable .45-caliber barks of Platinov's pistols at work. In a nanosecond, Bolan made his decision. Sniping from the roof was far too limiting. Besides, he thought as he dived headfirst at the bodies of the two men at the other end of the wooden steps, one definition of the word *warrior* was someone who runs toward the gunfire rather than away from it.

The Executioner raised his hands slightly as he fell through the air, landing first on his elbows and forearms, then his knees. The dead men lying at the foot of the ladder cushioned his fall, and he heard bones break beneath his weight.

Rising to one knee, Bolan fired a double-tap of .44 Magnum rounds at yet another man who wore a loose khaki BDU blouse over his jeans. In his hands was what looked like a sawed-off, double-barreled Rossi 12-gauge—both hammers cocked.

The Executioner's rounds hit the *X* on the man's chest, less than an inch apart, knocking him back against the gray stone wall of this upper room. As he fell, the Rossi's barrels twisted upward and back toward him, and when the muscles in his hand contracted in death, his fingers instinctively pulled both triggers. The double dose of 12-gauge buckshot left him practically headless.

Bolan did a quick 360-degree sweep with his eyes, noting that the large room had been turned into a barracks of sort. Single beds—at least twenty of them—were lined up and down both sides of the room. A footlocker rested at the end of each bed, and the arrangement made the room look more like the inside of a U.S. Marine Quonset hut than an ancient Moorish castle. As the gunfire on the floors beneath him continued, the Executioner dropped to his chest on the bare wooden floor. Some of the beds were neatly made while others looked as if someone had just awakened in them. Using his elbows to pull him along, Bolan crawled down the line, looking beneath each bed and lifting covers and sheets when necessary to ensure none of the CLODO men were hiding there.

He found none.

The bunk room on the top floor of the castle was deserted, but distant gunfire from somewhere below drew his attention.

The Executioner turned toward the centuries-old stone steps that led downward. He had taken out two CLODO men up here, but it sounded as if there were plenty more below. Platinov was good, but she wasn't so good that she couldn't use some help.

Dropping the magazine from the Desert Eagle, Bolan jammed a fresh load into the big grips and pulled the slide back slightly to ensure that a round was chambered.

Then he started down the steps.

PLATINOV HIT THE GROUND, releasing her canopy behind her as she sprinted between two pickups, a .45 in each hand. As she neared the front entrance to the castle, she saw tiny red and orange flashes in the doorway and felt bullets zip past her on both sides.

Holding both Gold Cup .45s in front of her, Platinov peppered the doorway with return fire as he raced into the castle. She had heard one long moan in between her shots, but she knew there were more of the enemy just waiting for her. So she would give them their chance.

"Kill me if you can," Platinov muttered in Russian beneath her breath. She stepped inside the doorway and found herself in what had probably once been a ballroom, Now, it had been turned into a giant living room.

Bullets kept whizzing past her from behind every couch and chair she could see.

Platinov dived behind the nearest couch. Immediately, it began to rattle and shake as gunfire drilled into it. A few of the rounds penetrated cleanly through, and one—which must have hit steel somewhere in the padding and slowed down—actually made it out the back and hit her lightly on the arm. It felt as if someone had passed their middle finger against the pad of their thumb, then flipped it against her sleeve. The mangled piece of lead fell to the stone floor, wobbled in circular motion a few times, then stopped.

Rising to a squatting position, the Russian agent suddenly darted from behind the couch toward a large marble statue—a fairly well-done copy of Michelangelo's *David*. She felt her hamstrings tighten as she ran, then loosen again as she dropped to her knees at the feet of the sculpture.

Now the return fire began chipping away at the marble. It wasn't an ideal location from which to launch an attack, but it was better than the couch. And from this new vantage point, Platinov could see most of the hiding places from which the CLODO men were shooting.

Pressing the magazine release button on the .45 in her right hand, Platinov let the box fall to the ground. From one of the pockets of her blacksuit, she pulled out a 10-round magazine loaded with .45-caliber armor-piercing rounds. Shoving it up into the butt of her Gold Cup, Platinov leaned slightly around the side of David's calves.

As she did, a rifle round from one of the other sofas struck the statue on the knee, ricocheting off to the side but sending a sharp shard of marble onto the top of her head. Again, the bullet had lost its power, but it reminded her that while she was formidable she was not invulnerable.

Platinov fired the chambered round—still one of the hollowpoints—at the sofa from behind which she thought the last bullet had come. She couldn't be certain, but she suspected it had "flowered out" and been stopped somewhere in the couch like the CLODO men's rounds had when she'd been behind the couch.

But the next round up was an all-steel, high-velocity armor-piercing load, and while it wouldn't have the penetration power that Cooper's .44 Magnum had, she knew these needle-tipped missiles should do the trick.

Platinov began firing randomly. First a double-tap into the same sofa, then two more rounds into a stuffed armchair. She couldn't be sure, but she thought she heard whines and other cries of pain as he moved on around the room, pulling the trigger again and again until her pistol locked open, empty.

At least one of the CLODO terrorists had been counting her rounds, and a second after she'd ceased fire and was reaching for another magazine of the penetrative rounds, a man wearing khaki chinos and a torn shirt revealed himself and started toward her.

Platinov almost wanted to laugh as she dropped the magazine, picked up her other Gold Cup with her left hand and shot him through the heart.

She had the fresh armor-piercing magazine inserted in her right-handed .45 pistol before the corpse hit the stone floor.

For a second, the gunfire ceased. But she heard the telltale blasts of Cooper's Desert Eagle far above her. He seemed to be fighting his own war almost directly above her head, and it was her job to dispatch the rest of the CLODO terrorists down here, then meet up with him on the second floor of the three-story castle.

Platinov repeated here performance with the armor-piercing rounds, taking out two more men who had hidden behind armchairs. Then, suddenly, all firing stopped.

Had she killed all of the men in this area? Or were some of them just playing possum, as she'd heard Americans say?

It was impossible to know unless she checked it out visibly. And the only way to do that was to get to the other side of the furniture.

Platinov took a seated position behind the statue and began stretching her hamstrings. Who better to check behind these couches and chairs than an Olympic sprinter and hurdler? In one quick motion, the Russian agent rose to her feet, and with a .45 in both hands, she sprinted toward the nearest couch. A step away, she lifted her right leg into the air, stretching it out in front of her and extending her arm almost to the toes. As she vaulted over the barrier, she looked down to see a dead man lying on his side, blood still pouring from a head wound.

Two more steps and Platinov went airborne again, but this time when she looked down, she saw a cringing little man holding an AK-47. The man directly below her looked more like one of CLODO's computer geeks than a fighter. He was even cradling the rifle more like you would a baby than a weapon.

But the little man's face turned to an ugly scowl as Platinov's feet hit the ground, and he started to turn the AK toward her.

In one fluid movement the Russian agent whirled and put a .45 round squarely between his eyes.

Two more hurdles, and she had reached the other end of the huge living room. The rest of the bodies she could now see were just that—bodies. Switching partially spent magazines for a pair of 10-rounders, Platinov turned to the stone stairs.

It was time to go help Cooper.

They met each other coming up and down the centuries-old stone steps. A quick recon of all the rooms on this middle level confirmed that none of the CLODO men were hidden there. What they did find, however, was puzzling.

A complete set of blueprints lay open on the desktop, and when he read the caption at the bottom of the drawings, the Executioner frowned.

The document was for the new Yankee Stadium.

Platinov looked over Bolan's shoulder, and he could feel her warm breath on his neck. "Unbelievable. They're planning an attack on Yankee Stadium."

DARKNESS HAD FINALLY FALLEN over the old castle by the time Jack Grimaldi was convinced that the gunfight was over in the castle below. He had circled the old castle for the better part of an hour, seeing the periodic flash of orange muzzle-flashes through the open windows. It had been a lot like popping a bag of microwave popcorn, where you had to watch and listen, then stop the appliance when there was finally two seconds between pops.

Of course, his time element for landing was longer on this mission—not to mention more deadly if he landed too soon. But when he passed the castle twice without seeing any more light, he knew it was time to take her down.

The Learjet's wheels hit the loose mixture of grass, dirt and sand as they touched down at the extreme end of the landing strip. The Learjet tried to fishtail on the soft surface, but Grimaldi lived up to his promise to land them safely.

The plane had barely halted by the time Bolan and Platinov came sprinting out of the castle. The two warriors jumped on board the plane as Grimaldi said, "Where to, Striker?"

"New York," the Executioner said as he and Platinov buckled their seat belts. "Specifically, Yankee Stadium in the Bronx." He paused for a breath. "I think I finally know exactly what Rouillan has in mind, and if we don't stop him he really will turn the world upside down."

"Then let's get at it," Grimaldi said, thrusting the Learjet's control forward to begin the takeoff.

"THEY'RE RIGHT about one thing," Aaron Kurtzman's voice said in the Executioner's ear. "The only way to fight a computer is with a computer. Sort of like fighting fire with fire."

"Except that this 'fire' is going to spread faster than any the world has ever seen before," Bolan returned.

"It sounds like it," Kurtzman answered. "You're sure we're talking about a computer virus and not a nuke or some physical disease like smallpox?" Kurtzman asked.

"I'm talking about a computer plague, Bear," Bolan replied. "A disease that'll make the black plague look like a case of indigestion by comparison. They're going to attach it to a news item containing the final score of the final World Series game, which is one of the most widely distributed pieces of information in the world every year. And if it feeds on attempts to kill it like we think, it'll spread faster than any disease the world has ever known."

There was a short pause on the other end of the line, then Kurtzman said, "Okay, Striker. I've heard rumors about the development of a virus like this. I'll get busy trying to run it down. Then, with a little luck, I may be able to write a program that actually will kill it."

"Tonight's the final game," Bolan said. "The Rockies are in New York. Can you find this thing and get your program done before the game's over?" Bolan asked.

"I don't know," Kurtzman told him. "I'd say doing all that would pretty much be on a par with the parting of the Red Sea. But the longer I talk to you the less time I've got to try. Anything else I need to know?"

"I don't think so. At least not right now. I'll get with you if anything new develops."

The two men disconnected the call.

Bolan sat back in his seat and took a deep breath.

Once again, he was seated next to Jack Grimaldi. They had flown from the landing strip near Sitges to Barcelona to fuel up for the trip back to America. The Executioner's first call had been to Hal Brognola, who had gone through several contacts and pulled the right strings for them to land, obtain the fuel they needed, and not be arrested for their illegal entry into Spain.

It hadn't hurt to have LeCoque, still wearing his Belgian customs coveralls and carrying the proper ID, with them, either. The low-on-the-totem-pole Spanish bureaucrats had not even come on board the Learjet. They had been made to feel like they were part of some top-secret spy mission before it was all over.

And that was not only good for their egos, Bolan thought as he closed his eyes, hoping to get at least an hour or two of rest before they reached the U.S. again, but it was also good for him, Platinov and the rest of the crew. If the Spanish customs agents had boarded the Learjet, they'd have found enough guns, ammunition and other weapons to outfit a small country. Not a good situation.

Silence had fallen over the aircraft, and the only sounds were from the Learjet's engines. But Bolan's eyelids refused to stay closed, and a moment later he found himself dialing Stony Man Farm and being transferred to Kurtzman again. As he waited for the call to be transferred, he looked through the window to see the Iberian Peninsula thousands of feet below.

As soon as Kurtzman was on the line again, the Executioner said, "You've got photos of Rouillan, right?"

"Right. And I'm running them through my facial recognition software while I search for the virus. Rouillan's mug's getting compared to anyone and everyone who's entered the U.S. in a private plane at any port of entry during the last three days. Three days takes a little longer."

"Okay. Get back to me as soon as you find a match. Now, pass me along to Hal, would you?"

A moment later, Hal Brognola was on the line. "Sounds like things are finally breaking, big guy," the Stony Man Farm director said. "What else can I do for you?"

"Get us ready at New York customs. As soon as we land, things will go hell-bent for leather, and I can't afford getting tied up because of the weapons or because one of my foreigners doesn't have his passport."

"That's no sweat," Brognola said. "Much easier than doing it in Barcelona."

"Affirmative, then. That's all for now. Striker out."

"Stony Base out," Brognola said, and then the line clicked.

Bolan unbuckled his seat belt, stood up and walked toward the rear of the passenger seats, where Platinov and LeCoque were watching Ali and Marc. Neither had been a problem so far. Ali's common sense had finally broken through the way he'd been raised and tutored, and Marc was still fixated on Platinov.

But Bolan knew that could change at the drop of a hat. Both men had been members of terrorist organizations only hours earlier, and the lies they'd been fed could always suddenly reappear in their brains and make them dangerous.

Taking the seat behind Platinov and across the aisle from LeCoque, the Executioner motioned that they should all put their heads together. When they were close enough to whisper, he said, "Here's what I think's going on. All this work, all these different CLODO cells of computer experts, have been working on different aspects of this super virus. According to my sources, there are other people working on the same kind of thing. Evidently, every time you try to kill it, it multiplies. So you do more harm fighting it than just leaving it alone."

"Then why don't we put out the word for everyone to turn off their computers until this is over?" LeCoque asked.

"Because not everyone will do it," Bolan said. "A lot of countries, organizations and individuals will think it's a trick of some kind. Every place in the world where there's any kind of war going on, big or small, both sides will think it's part of some massive operation by their enemy. A way to cut or at least slow down communication so they can strike."

"And any country that is not at war will blame the United States," Platinov said.

Bolan was slightly surprised. "I'm glad you said it and I didn't have to," he told the woman.

Platinov shrugged. "No need to thank me," she said. "I was part of making the rest of the world believe such things back in the old days of the Soviet Union."

"Okay," Bolan said. "Here's what's going to do. I've got all the confidence in the world that the Bear will match up Rouillan's face with someone who passed through a customs entry point under an assumed name. When he finds out what name Rouillan was using, we're going to have to gamble that he's using the same passport at whatever hotel he'll be staying at. And that's where we'll find him."

BY THE TIME the Learjet had touched down on the tarmac, the sun was beginning to drop over the horizon. But not all of the occupants of the plane could see it. Bolan and Grimaldi were the only two members of the crew who didn't have black hoods over their heads to keep Stony Man Farm's location top secret. Marc and Ali had been surprised when the Executioner tied the hoods around their necks. But they hadn't put up any resistance. LeCoque had been through it all during blacksuit training, and knew it was to be expected. Platinov made a low, guttural comment about the cold war never ending, and tied her hood in place herself.

Marc and Ali were taken to a secure area of the farmhouse, while Bolan, Platinov and LeCoque made their way to the War Room. Bolan saw that Platinov recognized Hal Brognola, who was seated at the head of the table.

"Hal," she said, smiling.

"Nice to see you, Marynka," the big Fed said, and nodded to LeCoque. He cleared his throat, then looked down to the side of the table where the Russian beauty had dropped her large carryall. "Now, may I have it, please?"

Bolan repressed a chuckle. If Brognola hadn't asked that question, he would have.

"Have what, Hal?" Platinov asked innocently.

"You know what I'm talking about," Brognola said politely. He held out his hand, palm up. "Please?"

"Ah, yes!" Platinov said in a tone that turned surprise into mockery. "The GPS?"

"Yes, the GPS." Brognola nodded.

Platinov reached down to her bag and lifted it up onto the table. A moment later, she was digging through its contents, finally coming up with a small handheld device that looked little different than the remote control for a television.

But both Bolan and Brognola saw it for exactly what it was. A Garmin GPS 72 Handheld Global Positioning System. "Do us all a favor, Plat," the Executioner said quickly. "Don't look at it before you give it to him."

Platinov had pulled it out by the wrist strap and now held it upside down, away from her eyes. She chuckled as she extended her arm down the table to Brognola.

Brognola took the GPS unit, turned it over so he could read the face, then said, "Your longitude is a half degree off." He cleared the instrument of the latitude and longitude it showed, then erased all of the GPS's memory before handing it back. "But it's not bad for an economy-based unit."

Platinov smiled as she dropped the GPS back in her

carryall. But before she could return the bag to the floor, Bolan said, "Now, let's have the real one."

This time, Platinov's face was not as happy. With a slightly grudging expression, she reached back into her bag and pulled out a similar instrument. This time, when she handed the other GPS to Brognola, she didn't smile.

Nor did the Stony Man Farm director. "Ah," Brognola said. "The NUVI 250 W Wide model," he said. "Much more accurate." He repeated his erasing techniques, then gave the second GPS back to the Russian woman. "Do we need to check the rest of your purse and clothing, Marynka?" he asked.

Platinov said a simple "No" to Brognola, then turned to Bolan.

The phone on the table rang.

"Yeah," Brognola said into the receiver against the side of his face. "Okay. I'll tell him." He hung up and looked to the Executioner, seated to his right. "Aaron's got a match," he said. "A Mr. Robert Green, British passport, entered the U.S. in a private Learjet only a few hours ago." Behind him, against the wall, a printer began to spit out a photograph.

Bolan stood up, walked around Brognola and waited for the page to print out. A moment later, he had a full-sized sheet of top-quality cotton paper, which was divided into four separate photographs obviously pulled from a continuous video recorder. The first showed a man fitting Rouillan's general description standing in front of a U.S. customs booth, talking to a uniformed customs man. In it, "Mr. Green" wore brown plastic sunglasses.

In the second photo, the customs agent had looked down at an open passport on the counter, and Mr. Green had pulled his sunglasses to the top of his head to show his eyes. In the third picture, Green-Rouillan was stuffing both his passport and sunglasses into the front pocket of his sport coat, and in the fourth he had turned full face and was looking almost directly into the camera without knowing it.

Bolan studied the pictures for a moment, then handed them to Platinov and picked up the phone next to Brognola. A moment later, he had Kurtzman on the line again. "You're sure it's him?" he asked.

"Almost one hundred percent," Kurtzman said. "Although he's lost a little weight. But the things that are hard to change—the ears for instance, or the distance between the top lip and the bottom of the nose—they're dead on. It's him, Striker."

"Any idea where he's gone?" Bolan asked.

"Right now, your guess is as good as mine. He's had plenty of time to leave the airport since these were taken, so it's anybody's guess. I'm already doing some checking, however."

"I'd start with the luxury hotels nearest the Bronx," Bolan said. "The man likes his comforts. Can you tap into their computers?"

"Striker, Striker, Striker," Kurtzman said in a mock-scolding voice. "Hacking into a hotel registry is about on the same level of computer manipulation as a baby finding the nipple on his formula bottle." He paused a second, then said, "But do you suppose he'll be using the 'Robert Green' moniker again?"

"I don't know. There's no reason for us to think he knows that we know that he's here. So he might, just to get receipts and other papers to match up for his return flight. On the other hand, he may be using a dozen different IDs while he's here."

"Well, just do what you can," Bolan said. "In the meantime I'm going to head out to Yankee Stadium and—"

Before he could finish the sentence, Kurtzman interrupted him again. "Wait a minute, Striker," he said in a slightly excited voice.

A second later, the computer expert was back on the phone. "Looks like we're in luck," he said. "A Mr. Green from Liverpool just checked in to the Constantine. That's not exactly the Bronx, but hey, this is New York and the World Series is about to be decided and—"

"And he probably had to pay one of the desk clerks double on the arm to get a five-star room anywhere in the Big Apple," Bolan finished for him.

"He may have paid more than that," Kurtzman came back. "He's in the Constantine's Presidential Suite. Right in the heart of the arts and theater district, Central Park. Getting to Yankee Stadium won't be hard. Not with the crazy cabbies they've got up there."

Bolan frowned silently for a moment. Then he said, "He won't take a cab, Bear. He'll have hired a car and driver or rented a vehicle or provided some other means of transportation for this. He'll want to be in control. Total control. I'm beginning to understand how he thinks, and he wants to watch his master plan go down, but from a safe distance."

"I'll start checking for rentals," said Kurtzman. "Anything else?"

"Yeah," said the Executioner. "Any more info on the computer virus itself?"

"Nothing earth-shaking," Kurtzman said. "But the second the game is over this evening, the score is going to go out from almost every news agency in the world. It'll be splashed all over the Internet. Anyone who checks out a site with the score will download the virus, which will infect everyone listed in that person's mailbox. With all the social networking going on, it'll spread like wildfire. If you try to kill it the normal ways, it overrides those attacks and turns them back on themselves, but brings the virus with it."

"Let me put this into laymen's terms so I'll understand it," Bolan said. "It's as if you were going around stabbing people. I came at you with what I thought was a bigger knife and better training, but you were able to take that knife away from me and then stab me with both of them."

"A decent analogy," Kurtzman said. "But add to that the fact that I'd also be able to immediately stab everyone else you knew—everyone who's ever sent that computer an e-mail or instant message—then multiply it all by a couple of billion." He stopped talking to take a long, tired-sounding breath. "That's a lot of computers."

For a moment, the Executioner's mind saw plane crashes, train derailments and anarchy in the streets. The world had become so dependent on computer technology that most people had forgotten how to live without them. Finally, he said, "It sounds like if I don't get this stopped before it's programmed in there's not much hope."

"There isn't," Kurtzman said. "If I had a few more days I might be able to come up with something that would override it. And don't worry—I'll keep trying. But we're racing against the clock. And time's going fast. Anything else?"

"Not at the moment," Bolan said. "But I'm sure I'll be getting back to you." He hung up.

Brognola stood up. "If I interpreted this end of the call right, our Mr. Green is in one of the downtown hotels?"

"The Constantine," said Bolan.

"Phoenix Force and Able Team are tied up at the moment," Brognola stated. "Want me to send a couple of the blacksuits to check on him?"

The Executioner looked at his watch, then he glanced toward Platinov, who had sat quietly in her seat across from him ever since she'd gotten her second GPS unit back. "I think I've got a better idea, Hal," he said.

"What's that?" Brognola asked.

Bolan told him.

When he'd finished speaking, Brognola let out a short breath, then turned toward Platinov. "Are you sure he won't recognize you from Chartres?" he asked.

"I am sure of nothing," Platinov said. "But he could have gotten only quick glances, and I can do wonders with makeup. And I am willing to try it."

Brognola looked her up and down. Then, in a very clinical voice, he said, "Well, it'd probably work on me."

Platinov was smiling again, her busted GPS scheme to pinpoint Stony Man Farm for Russia no longer on her mind. "It would work on any man," she breathed out.

Then, without another word, the team headed back to the Learjet. Marc and Ali would remain behind.

CHAPTER THIRTEEN

Pierre Rouillan held the door as the two bellmen rolled the luggage carrier into the Presidential Suite at the Constantine. He had stocked up on American cash before leaving Europe, and as soon as they'd lifted his and LeForce's suitcases off the carrier and set them on the floor, he gave both men hundred-dollar bills.

Even at the posh high-rolling hotel, it was enough to raise both workers' eyebrows.

"Thank you, sir!" said the shorter of the two. "Is there anything else we can—"

"Yes," said Rouillan with the indignity only the French can muster. "You can leave."

The venom in his words, coming so soon after the overgenerous tip, shocked both bellmen, but they were certain that they had just met the "goose who laid golden eggs," even if that goose was a bit grumpy.

So they weren't about to give up. At least not quite yet.

"Perhaps you fine gentleman would like some

female companionship for the evening," said the taller bellman. "I happen to know that there are two extremely attractive young ladies staying on the floor right below this one who have expressed an interest in the baseball game tonight. But they are hesitant to go unescorted."

For a moment, Pierre Rouillan considered the possibility. He had accepted the fact that he was a "wine, women and song" man long ago. But he had also learned to temper those pleasures when he had important CLODO work to perform. He stared into the eyes of the bellman who had spoken, then looked at the other one briefly. The two men, he suspected, were working on their own. The hotel might be willing to turn a blind eye toward their pimping, but it would never actively participate in prostitution. The prestige, and expense, however, of the Constantine meant that only the wealthy would stay there. That, in turn, meant that the call girls would be of the highest quality.

It was tempting.

As Rouillan continued to weigh the pros and cons of taking a brief break with a beautiful woman or two, he was reminded that sex and violence had always been connected in his mind. Could it be that the sight of the running girl's garters and panties during the CLODO bombing so many years ago had stayed with him all these years? Manifested itself in his subconscious, and remained there long after puberty? Perhaps. He was, after all, just beginning to form his own sexuality at the time.

But, Rouillan thought as he glanced down at his watch, if he took the bellmen up on their offer it would have to be a hurried affair. He could not afford to be chained to some call girl—no matter how beautiful—once he arrived at Yankee Stadium. It would have to be what the Americans called a "slam, bang, thank you, ma'am" affair before he kicked them both out of the suite.

No, he finally decided. He had the most important event of his life coming up. He was literally about to change history. Not to mention the meeting of the American CLODO cell whose members would arrive to assist him and LeForce any minute now.

He needed no distractions like beautiful women. At least not until after the game.

"No, thank you," he said, taking the bellman by the arm and pushing him gently toward the door. "That will be all."

The two bellmen left the room.

Achille LeForce had been standing quietly next to the luggage rack during the brief conversation. But now he took a seat in one of the elaborately carved mahogany chairs in the living room. "Some girls might have been nice, Pierre," the man said in a slightly disappointed voice.

Rouillan felt a moment of sadness for his old friend. Achille LeForce had never had much luck with women. He was far too stupid and "ape"-looking for any lady of class, and unless he paid for it he had been forced to settle for ugly and stupid women all his life. "Relax, Achille," Rouillan said in the most lighthearted voice he could muster. "There will be plenty of beautiful girls in your future. Don't you see?"

From the puzzled look on his face, LeForce obviously did not.

"By this time tomorrow, the entire world will be in chaos," Rouillan went on. "And while I have no intention of trying to reunite any nation, or other group of peoples, women will be reduced to the scale of 'chattel' as is always the case when pandemonium rules. We will have our own airplane at our disposal, and will return to Spain where even the most beautiful and desirable females will be available for sale or rent. For months, probably years, we will have our pick of any women we desire, whenever we desire them."

LeForce's usual confused expression cleared, but then it turned to dismay. "But eventually," he said, "the world will figure out a way to return the computers to working order. Once again, they will be used to oppress and control the people. What are we to do then?"

To Rouillan, his old friend often sounded as much like an ape as he looked like one, repeating his own words back to him as if he had never had even one original thought in his life. But that was one of the things that made him valuable.

He did as he was told without questioning.

Had Achille LeForce not contained such stupidity and complete loyalty, Rouillan realized, he would have had to kill the "ape man" long ago.

"Achille," Rouillan said in the voice he always used when explaining things to his less-intelligent friend, "CLODO's work will not be finished tonight. The different cells we have in Europe and America will continue to function, as well as draw in new recruits who are craving some kind of order to their meaningless lives. CLODO will remain, but our mission will change. We will constantly be sabotaging efforts to reconstruct the Internet and other computer facets." He glanced down at his watch. "I think it is more than safe to say that we will never see another computerized society like we have now. At least not in our lifetime." He walked to the minibar, unlocked it with the key one of the bellmen had given him, then took out a bottle of Perrier.

LeForce still looked confused.

"But come now," Rouillan said as he sipped at the bottle while bringing his other hand up to indicate that LeForce should stand. "We have just enough time for a drink at one of the bars downstairs before we proceed further."

Rouillan finished the small bottle of Perrier, then checked to make sure the 9 mm Kel-Tec was still in place in the waistband of his slacks. He had carried it through customs and immigration without a thought, knowing that the CLODO man he had planted within U.S. Customs had done his job as well as the Belgian customs CLODO member.

But that thought made him frown for only a moment. The Belgian had not called in after Saucier had killed the man and woman who followed him, he realized Had something gone wrong? He shrugged. At this point, it did not matter. If they had somehow survived the mercenary's attack, they would still be looking for him in Europe. And he was an entire ocean away.

Rouillan's thoughts turned to another man, now. A man whose job was the most crucial in the entire plan— the CLODO man who would be in the press box at Yankee Stadium, tonight, ready to attach the super virus to the final score and unleash it upon the world. Of course he could not do that until he got the final code from Rouillan. And the French terrorist leader would not give it to him until right before the game began.

PIERRE ROUILLAN continued to think about the man in the press box as he opened the door to the hall for Achille LeForce. It had taken almost four years for this key player in Rouillan's scheme to rise up through the ranks of the New York Yankee organization. But now he finally had a man in a position where he could spend the game in the press box. That thought led Rouillan on to the many other men he had planted among the other major league teams. Some of them had risen in their organizations, too. Others had not. But now, they were irrelevant.

The Yankees had won the pennant, and his CLODO man would be in position to send out the virus attached to the final score. Rouillan grinned to himself. It was only appropriate that this involve baseball. As the Americans liked to say, "Mom, apple pie and baseball." Baseball was a symbol of America and, therefore, his final irony.

Rouillan tapped the side of his jacket again and felt the security of the compact 9 mm Kel-Tec. Yes, his man in the press box was one of his best. He would do a good job. It was a shame that Rouillan would have to kill him later, but one never knew who one could trust. Rouillan knew that eventually the police would interrogate everyone in the press box, and he had no intention of leaving behind a trail that might eventually lead back to him—even in Spain.

The bellmen had barely left when the first knock on the

door came. Rouillan took a seat in another of the embellished mahogany chairs and let LeForce answer. He didn't bother rising to his feet when René Menigon entered the room and crossed the carpet to shake his hand. Menigon's dark brown hair covered the tops of his ears, giving him a sort of "seventies look" that Rouillan couldn't stand. But the man had been loyal, and once again Rouillan regretted that he would have to kill him later that evening.

"You are ready?" was all that Rouillan said.

"I am ready," Menigon answered. "I will be working the computer to the scoreboard, as well as sending out the final score to the news stations and various Internet providers at the end of the ninth inning. And along with that score, of course, I will send the virus." He paused to see if Rouillan had anything to interject. When nothing came, he went on. "Running the scoreboard is beneath my station within the organization, of course, but no one even raised an eyebrow when I requested the task." He paused, unbuttoned his jacket, then said, "It is, after all, the last game of the World Series."

When Rouillan still did not respond, Menigon smiled. "All I need is the code," he said as he brushed an imaginary dust spot off of his thousand-dollar suit.

Rouillan reached into his coat and pulled out a sheet of paper. "I have it written down for you here," he said. "But as a security precaution, I will keep it to myself until right before the game." He returned the paper to his coat. "I am sure you understand that it is nothing personal."

"Of course not," Menigon said. "As you said, it is a security precaution."

"We will meet again in Paris after we have accomplished our task. Exactly when, is impossible to predict. My plane is ready to go, but there will be chaos in the streets." He paused, then added, "Which is why I have arranged different transportation for Achille and myself."

Menigon frowned. "Would it not be wiser to just meet at the airport?" he asked. "I could ride with—"

"No, it would not be wiser," Rouillan interrupted, "and that is all that you need to know."

Menigon nodded and turned to leave, but before he reached the door there was another knock.

LeForce opened the door and five far more fierce-looking men than Menigon entered the Presidential Suite as the press box man exited.

Rouillan motioned for them to take seats around the living room. They were all dressed in suits, but the material and cut was a step or two down from the top-of-the-line Brooks Brothers that Menigon had worn. Few people, however, could tell the difference.

One of the men spoke in French as soon as he'd taken his seat. "You are ready, I assume?" he said.

"I am ready," Rouillan replied. He was glancing at his watch once more when the phone on the stand next to his chair suddenly rang. Rouillan frowned as he picked it up and held it to his ear. He listened for several seconds, then said, "I understand. Thank you," and hung up. "We're about to have an unexpected visitor."

LeForce frowned. "Do you know who it is?" he asked.

Rouillan thought back to the man and woman who had been only a half step behind him for the last few days. Agents of some kind or another who were trying to stop him.

"Not precisely *who* she is," Rouillan said. "But I have an idea *what*."

"And?" asked one of the recently arrived American CLODO men.

"Trouble," Rouillan said. He drew the 9 mm Kel-Tec from his waistband as he stood up. "Trouble we should have been dealt with some time ago."

The other men started to draw guns but Rouillan suddenly stopped them, and shoved his weapon back out of sight in his belt. "Let us keep our weapons hidden for now."

A second later, there was yet another knock at the door. Rouillan nodded for LeForce to get it, and the Frenchman lumbered over, pulled off the safety chain and opened the door.

In the hallway, Rouillan saw one of the most beautiful, sexy and desirable women he had ever seen in his life.

The problem was, he had seen her before.

MARYNKA PLATINOV HAD HEARD the term *little black dress* more than once in her lifetime, and knew it to be one of those carefully thought-out garments that revealed all without actually revealing anything. As she entered the revolving door to the Constantine Hotel, she heard a faint swish as her well-developed runner's thighs, covered now in nylon, rubbed together with each step. Beneath the long coat she wore, she knew the hem of the little black dress she had just purchased a few blocks away on Madison Avenue barely covered her silk thong panties.

Walking directly to the front desk of the five-star hotel, Platinov let her coat fall open. A young man and woman stood behind the desk, both working on computers. There were no other customers on her side of the barrier. Good. Her first show of the evening was about to begin.

Quickly, Platinov looked at the young woman. Dressed in a female-cut blue blazer and striped tie, she was punching the keyboard in front of her. She wore conservative makeup, and had long well-kept hair that came down past her shoulders. Everything about her said "heterosexual." So Platinov looked to the other end of the counter at the young man.

He was in his early twenties with short hair. Again, a blue blazer and striped tie. His skin still sported a few pimples left over from his teenage years, but he had covered them as well as he could with a flesh-colored antibiotic. He, too, was typing away. And even to well-trained and sensitive eyes like Platinov's, his sexuality was not as obvious.

She hoped he liked girls. Because if this kid was gay, she was going to have to change her whole battle plan.

He wasn't, and Platinov knew it the second she shrugged out of her coat, standing just far enough away for the youth to catch a view of her short skirt, long legs and black stiletto heels.

The young man's eyes grew large as he looked her up and down. "May I…" he sputtered out as Platinov stepped on up to the counter and rested her elbows on the surface. "May you…I mean may I…help you?" he asked.

Platinov gave the kid the most sexy smile she could muster. "Oh, I'm sure you could, young man," she said in a husky voice that made her Russian accent even stronger and more exotic. She leaned in closer and felt the low cut *V* of the top of her dress fall outward, away from her braless breasts.

"Well…what…er…" the young man continued to sputter, his gaze glued to her chest.

"What can you do for me?" Platinov finished for him.

He bobbed his head up and down.

"You can give me the room number and a key to Mr. Robert Green's room, honey," the beautiful Russian woman said.

After a few more mindless sputters, the desk clerk finally responded, "I'm sorry, it's against hotel policy to give out the room numbers of our guests. Let alone keys."

Platinov leaned in another three inches and felt her breasts about to fall completely out of the front of her dress. "Couldn't you make an exception, sweetie? I so want to surprise him."

The clerk's eyes stayed on her chest as he tried to speak again. "I'm sorry…" he said before Platinov interrupted him.

"Be a good boy," she said with the purr of a kitten. "And there might be a really nice tit left over for you when I leave." Immediately, she forced her face to redden. "Oh!" she said in mock surprise at herself. "Did I misspeak myself? Sometimes my English is not so good. I meant to say there might be a nice *tip* in it for you when I leave." She paused and continued to smile as she lowered her voice. "But what I said first would be a part of it, of course."

It was all more than a young man in his early twenties could handle. He tapped in a few keys on his computer, then reached under the counter and pulled out a key card. "I, uh…get off in about three hours," he said as he put the card in a small envelope and wrote the Presidential Suite, top floor on the front.

"That should be perfect," Platinov said. "By then, Mr. Green will be tired out. But I'll just be getting warmed up."

The young man closed his eyes as he handed her the key card, but she could feel his gaze on her as she walked to the elevators.

Two elderly couples, all four decked out in Yankee baseball caps, T-shirts and team jackets got off of the elevator as the doors opened. They chattered excitedly about someone's batting average and the number of home runs that had been hit by New York compared to Colorado during the series as Platinov got on. She pushed the button for the Presidential Suite's floor and waited as the doors closed. As soon as they did and the car started to rise, the Russian woman pulled a cell phone from her purse and tapped in the number to Cooper's satellite phone.

"He's in the Presidential Suite like your man said," she told the big American as the elevator continued to rise. "I'm going up now."

"No," she heard in her ear. "Wait for us."

"No reason for you to get 'burned,'" Platinov said. "I'll check it out, then call you back."

"Plat," Cooper said. "Stay where you are. LeCoque and I are on our way in."

The car suddenly stopped on the third floor and more baseball fans got on. These people, however, were dressed in Rockies regalia. "I've got to end the call now," Platinov said as the middle-aged men crowding in gave her lecherous looks and their wives stared hatred through her forehead. "I'll call you back as soon as I can." She hung up, dropped the cell phone back into her purse and smiled at her new fellow passengers.

Several men got elbows in the ribs, which changed their expressions, but they continued to look.

As soon as the elevator reached the Presidential Suite's floor, Platinov got out. As the doors closed behind her, she heard the word *whore* come out of a woman's mouth. It made her laugh.

It seemed she was playing her part well.

Now, Platinov thought as she walked down the hall, following the arrows toward the Presidential Suite, she would recon things by continuing to play the part of a whore. She would knock on Rouillan's door, and give him and anyone with him a free eyeful as she determined how many CLODO men were in the room. She had changed her makeup, fixed her long blond hair atop her head and was dressed completely differently than she had been when Rouillan had caught glimpses of her before. If things went well, he and anyone else in the suite would think she was just another high-priced call girl like the youth at the desk had believed. She would apologize for coming to the wrong suite, then leave and apprise Cooper and LeCoque of how many guns they were likely to face.

Then, they would attack. They would crash Pierre Rouillan's party before it even got started. That would be the end of things. Somewhere on Rouillan or in the suite, they'd find the code for the virus and get CLODO stopped before the world "shut down."

MARISSA BERRY WAS NOT yet twenty years old, but she had figured out at least one fact of life.

When it came to sex, all men were fools.

Still tapping the keyboard on her computer, she had watched what had taken place at the other end of the desk between Victor Matthews and the prostitute. The woman's ploy had been so obvious. Yet Victor, being a man with a man's ego, had fallen for it hook, line and sinker.

Marissa waited until the prostitute had gotten on the elevator and then walked down the desk to Victor's side. "You're going to get fired over this," she said bluntly.

Victor's face was still red with lust when he said, "Right now, Marissa, I don't care. Besides, you're not going to rat me out."

Marissa shook her head in disgust. She and Victor both attended NYU but had never met until they were hired by the Constantine. They had become fast friends, but never lovers. Theirs had become a brother-and-sister relationship, and Marissa cared for him very much in that way. "You may not care now," she said. "But when tuition time comes again and you haven't been working you will," she told him. "And while I won't 'rat you out' as you called it, Mr. Green sure might. I overheard the bellmen saying he and his friend in the Presidential Suite must be gay. They refused their offer of women."

"There's nothing I can do about it now," Victor said, staring at the closed doors to the elevator. His mind was obviously still on the woman in the black dress and, in a way, Marissa couldn't blame him. She *was* beautiful, and beautiful in a far more "healthy" way than the other good-looking prostitutes the bellmen pimped out. The fact was, if she had not been alone and behaved as she had, Marissa would have believed she was just another wealthy woman on her way to meet her husband in one of the hotel's bars for cocktails. She definitely had more class than the others.

"Well, there's something *I* can do about it," Marissa said. She picked up the phone in front of them.

"What are you doing?" Victor asked.

"Covering your butt for you, you ignorant, horny idiot," Marissa said. She glanced behind her to the back wall behind the desk and saw the names of the hotel's different shift managers. Mrs. Coker was on duty now. But her office was way in the back, and she couldn't hear anything that went on in the lobby or at the desk.

Marissa tapped in the number to the Presidential Suite. Her call was answered on the second ring.

"Mr. Green," Marissa said before the man could even say hello. "This is Mrs. Coker, the shift manager for the Constantine. I'm afraid a terrible mistake has been made. I might as well be blunt with it. I've just caught one of the desk clerks…" She paused dramatically for effect, then went on. "I'm trying to think of how to tastefully say it, but I'm not sure there is such a way." She paused again, then said, "One of the desk clerks just gave a keycard to your suite to a prostitute. He was fired on the spot, of course, and I hope you'll accept our most sincere apology. If you'll stop by the front desk and ask for Marissa, she'll give you a pass for a free night here the next time you're in town." She pointed under the counter as she glared at Victor, indicating he should get one of the free night passes from the lower shelf.

"I understand," Mr. Green said. "Thank you."

"Thank *you* for understanding, sir. And again, please accept my apology," Marissa said, and hung up.

Looking back at Victor, she shook her head again in disgust. "Now Mr. Green has the choice of either taking her or leaving her, and he thinks the management knows all about it so he won't be tempted to report it to them."

Victor's face had fallen, which made Marissa laugh. Somehow, it was impossible to stay mad at someone so naive. "You weren't going to get any of that anyway," she told Victor. "She was just using you to get the key."

Victor's face looked even more disappointed now. "Yeah, I guess you're right," he said. "I knew it had to be too good to be true."

"Well, it's not like it's the end of the world as we know it or anything," Marissa said. "Just start thinking with your brain instead of your crotch."

Victor finally grinned. "Okay," he said. "But it's hard."

Marissa laughed again as she walked back down to

her end of the counter. "I wouldn't touch that comment with a ten-foot pole," she said.

"If I had a ten-foot pole I'd—"

"Victor, just shut up," Marissa said as she went back to work.

PLATINOV REALIZED HER mistake the second the door opened.

There were at least seven men in the suite, and the man standing in the middle of the room staring at her was squinting as if trying to remember her from somewhere.

He couldn't know who she was working for—she wasn't even sure of that herself. But she wished now that she'd taken Cooper's advice and waited for him and Robert LeCoque to arrive.

"I'm sorry," Platinov tried anyway. "I must have been told the wrong room number. This isn't the Governor's Suite, is it?"

The man in the center of the room with both hands behind his back shook his head. "You know that it isn't," he said as he pulled his arms around to the front of his body and she saw that he'd drawn a pistol. "It's the Presidential Suite. Just as you were told."

There was no longer any doubt in the beautiful Russian woman's mind as to whether or not Rouillan recognized her. All the makeup, the different hairstyle and little black dresses in the world hadn't fooled the man.

Platinov had her long coat in her right hand, her purse in her left. Suddenly, she opened the coat and threw it out in front of her. The arms and body of the garment spread out like wings, covering her for a split second. She used that time to take a step to the side of the open doorway and pull one of her Gold Cup .45s from her purse.

The first 9 mm shot zipped past at chest level, exactly where she'd been a moment before.

Platinov leaned slightly around the door and fired a double tap of .45s from her pistol, kicking off her high heels as she did. More gunfire—sounding as if it came from a variety of pistols—exploded inside the suite. Platinov saw holes appear in the wall across the hall from the open door as she sprinted back down the hall toward both the elevators and the stairs.

There was no way she was going to outgun that many men by herself. At least not for long. Her only chance was escape.

Another volley of shots blew past her as she ran, meaning that some of the men were out in the hallway now. She came to a corner and ducked around it, thanking God that her dress didn't bind her. There was no way she could wait on an elevator. But if she could just reach the stairs before they got her, she still stood a chance.

But Platinov was wrong that escape was her only possible salvation. She realized there was another way when she was still a good ten yards from the stairwell door.

Suddenly, the door opened on its own.

And Matt Cooper, followed by Robert LeCoque, stepped out into the hallway holding guns of their own.

There was no such thing as cover or concealment in the narrow hallway, so Bolan used the next best strategy. As the Beretta 93-R burped out 3-round bursts, he pulled the trigger of the semiautomatic .44 Magnum Desert Eagle as fast as he could with the other hand.

A volley of lead and copper blew down the hallway, driving the CLODO men chasing her back around the corner they had just turned. Platinov had dived to the carpet, giving Bolan's guns and LeCoque's Browning Hi-Power more target space. By the time she had rolled back to her feet and turned her Gold Cup the other way, the only targets left were two men on the floor.

And even from the distance at which she, Bolan and LeCoque now stood, it was obvious they were no longer a threat.

"Reload!" Bolan shouted, making sure it was loud enough for the men around the corner to hear. He had already switched the Beretta back to semiauto mode. Now, while both Platinov and LeCoque did as ordered, dropping their spent magazines from the grips of their pistols and shoving new ones into their weapons, the Executioner picked off two more of the CLODO terrorists who were foolish enough to fall for the trick and stick their heads around the corner.

The Executioner still had a round chambered when he thumbed the Beretta's magazine release and stuck in a new fifteen-round stick. Then, seeing that both Platinov and LeCoque had "reloaded" their own pistols, he whispered, "Fire a round that way every few seconds. Just enough to keep them honest."

"What are *you* going to do?" Platinov asked as she aimed her Gold Cup pistol down the hallway again.

"Watch and see. And do your best not to shoot me."

Platinov looked puzzled but nodded.

Keeping his back against the wall, and the Desert Eagle pointed toward the corner of the hallway beyond where he knew there were still at least five terrorists, Bolan glided as quietly as he could across the carpet. Each time LeCoque or Platinov fired a round, he used the noise as cover for a longer, faster step. It took only seconds to reach the corner, and as soon as he did the Executioner dropped to both knees.

In the relative quiet between the cover fire Platinov and LeCoque were giving him, Bolan could hear excited and frightened voices on the other side of the corner. They were speaking almost incoherently in French.

And their confusion meant that, at least for the moment, they didn't know how to handle what was happening.

Which, in turn, told the Executioner that now was the time to strike.

Still on his knees, Bolan propelled himself forward past the corner. He landed on his left side, with his right arm—and the Desert Eagle—held up and in front of him.

If they'd been expecting an offensive retaliation, the CLODO men didn't act like it. For a split second, they seemed frozen in place, which was enough time for Bolan, shooting upward from the floor, to pull the trigger three times. A large, bulky man who looked like a power-lifter forced into a suit far too small for him, took Bolan's first round through his open mouth. The

RBCD total fragmentation round took out several teeth as it passed, then moved on through the softer, water-based tissue of his upper palate and into his brain.

The CLODO man's head didn't explode so much as disintegrate with blood, tissue and pieces of skull flying through the air to splatter the walls and the other two men.

As the nearly headless man slunk to the carpet, the CLODO man next to him—a man wearing a long black ponytail with his suit and tie—screamed. He wiped frantically at his face with his free hand, trying to get the blood and tissue out of his eyes.

Bolan's next .44 Magnum round made that problem inconsequential, providing the man with his own nearly severed head.

The third gunman stood a couple of steps behind the others, and the time it took for Bolan to take out the duo gave him time to react. Aiming a Glock 21 pistol at the Executioner, he pulled the trigger.

But Bolan had seen the man in his peripheral vision, and a split second before the Glock exploded he rolled backward. The .45-caliber round dug into the carpet where his chest had been only a moment earlier.

Raising the Desert Eagle slightly, the Executioner drilled another huge Magnum round through the chest of the man with the Glock.

Suddenly, the hallways were silent.

During the gun battle, Platinov and LeCoque had moved forward, and now they joined him as Bolan rose to his feet. The Executioner stared down the hall to the open door of the Presidential Suite. "How many men left?" he whispered to Platinov.

"At least two," she whispered back. "Rouillan and that sidekick of his who looks like a monkey. But there might have been more men in the other rooms I couldn't see."

"Well," Bolan said, "there's only one way to find out."

With the Beretta 93-R in his left hand, the Desert Eagle in his right, Bolan strode quickly across the carpet, stopping just to the side of the Presidential Suite's open door. With both guns ready, he snapped his eyes quickly around the corner and looked into the living room.

Empty.

Moving more cautiously now, and waving LeCoque and Platinov to follow behind him, Bolan brought his pistols up at a forty-five-degree angle to the ground and moved on into the living room. Doors opened on both sides of the suite, and he went right, again signaling LeCoque and Platinov with a wave to go the other way.

Quickly, the soldier gave the large dining room a quick scan, then moved on to the bedrooms on that side of the suite. By now he knew what he was going to find, yet he still had to go through the motions just in case he was wrong.

Behind the closed door of the first bedroom he came to, he found only the slightly musty odor all rooms get when closed too long. But in the second bedroom—whose outside balcony faced the alley—he saw what he expected.

The sliding glass door was still open, and the tails of the light, gossamerlike curtains had been sucked out onto the porch by the vacuum that had been created. Hurrying through the open doorway, Bolan stopped at the railing around the edge, looking down at the alley as well as the people he could see walking past it on the sidewalks at both ends.

The fire escape was right next to him, and he could see it all the way to the ground. Rouillan and his buddy, Achille LeForce, were nowhere to be seen. Bolan holstered his weapons. The two men would have had to flee immediately upon hearing the first gunshots.

Which meant he wasn't going to find them anywhere around the hotel.

The Executioner looked at his watch. The game at Yankee Stadium would probably be in the second or third inning by now.

Hearing Platinov and LeCoque enter the room behind him, Bolan stepped back into the bedroom.

"Clear on our side," LeCoque said.

The Executioner nodded. "Here, too. They took the fire escape."

"Then we have only one last chance to stop them," Platinov said.

LeCoque nodded. "Take me out to the ball game," he mimicked in an American accent.

"That's exactly what I intend to do," Bolan replied.

As they retraced their steps back to the elevators, Bolan heard a faint but audible moan from one of the bodies in the hallway.

All three of the warriors aimed their weapons at the man, who was just barely alive.

"Wait," Bolan said to keep any of them from putting

the man out of his misery. Kneeling next to him, he pulled a Czech-made .380-caliber pistol from the man's hand, then said, "You're dying."

Slowly, almost imperceptively, the CLODO terrorist nodded.

"So be honest for once in your life. Tell the truth and save the lives of hundreds of people. Is Rouillan going to be at the game himself?"

Slowly, the dying man shook his head. "Our man... in the press box...Rouillan is giving him the code. He... Rouillan...will be in a helicopter overhead."

With that, the man on the floor drew his last breath and died.

CHAPTER FOURTEEN

"I assume you haven't found a way to kill the virus once it's entered?" Bolan asked.

"Not yet," Aaron Kurtzman replied. "We're still working on it, and we'll come up with something eventually. But I've gotta be straight with you, Striker. That's not going to happen by the time the game's over tonight."

"Okay," Bolan said into his satellite phone as he, LeCoque and Platinov took the steps to the Constantine's roof two at a time. "Then I need you to hack in to any and all places that rent or sell helicopters, Bear. See if you can pick up on Rouillan's trail."

"With all due respect, old friend," Kurtzman said, "what makes you think he rented or bought a helicopter?"

"Right before he died, one of his men back at the hotel told me he'd be in a chopper. Also, that there's a man in the press box ready to send out the virus as soon as he gets the code from Rouillan. By now, he'll have that code. I'm beginning to know this guy, Bear," he said. "He's wants to be close enough to the action to see his plan come off. But basically, he's a coward, and he'll also want to be far enough away not to get hurt. And the best way to do that is from the air."

"Okay," Kurtzman said on the other end of the line. "You want to wait? This should only take a minute or two."

"I'll wait," Bolan said as he reached the door to the roof. "But while I do, transfer me to Hal, will you?" He opened the door and held it as Platinov and LeCoque hurried onto the roof spotted with metal exhaust outlets, antennas, power and support lines, and other objects.

Kurtzman wasted no time answering. The next thing Bolan heard was Hal Brognola's voice saying, "We're cutting things mighty close, big guy."

"I know," Bolan said as he followed Platinov and LeCoque onto the roof. "And believe me, I don't like it any more than you do. But these are the cards we were dealt, and we've got to play them."

"So what can I be doing?" Brognola asked.

"Someone—either NYPD or a team of blacksuits or both—needs to get to the stadium, pronto," Bolan replied. "One of the Yankee administrative personnel is really a CLODO plant, and he's going to be attaching the virus to the score as soon as he gets the final code from Rouillan. Then he'll send the score and virus out to every news agency and Internet provider, which in turn will upload it to their opening pages." He drew in a deep breath. "You know the rest."

"Let's keep this in the family as much as possible," Brognola said. "I'll outfit a team of blacksuits with Justice Department credentials, dress them in regular suits and make a phone call to NYPD to leave them alone."

"You going to face any turf-war problems?" Bolan asked.

Brognola laughed softly. "Probably. But nothing I can't handle. The new NYPD commissioner is an acquaintance of mine," he said. "What do you need?"

"I need—" Bolan got out before suddenly Kurtzman was on the line again, making it a conference call. "Striker, Hal," the computer wizard said, "I didn't find any record anywhere of a Rouillan or Green renting or buying a helicopter. But I did come across a rental under the name of Tomas Breton. It was rented for yesterday, flown away by Breton, who had the proper license and papers, but never returned. They—the rental company— reported it as stolen this morning."

"You check on the license?" Bolan asked.

"Sure did," Kurtzman said. "No record of anyone named Tomas Breton possessing a chopper license either here or in France."

"He's just got more than one fake ID," Brognola said. "So, again, Striker. What can I do for you?"

"You can send Jack my way in a chopper. Make sure it's fully loaded. My guess is that Rouillan has outfitted his stolen helicopter with teeth by now, too."

"As soon as you asked Aaron to check chopper rentals, I sent Jack packing," the big Fed stated. "He should be arriving in NYC anytime now. Where do you want him to land?"

"The top of the Constantine Hotel," Bolan said. He was still on the line when distant helicopter blades sounded, and Grimaldi entered the conference call, too.

"I'm maybe three minutes away," the Stony Man pilot said. "Just hang loose."

Bolan turned in the direction of the rotor noise and saw a tiny speck in the sky. "Striker out," he said into his phone.

The rest of the men signed off as well.

"Marc and Ali don't know what they're missing," LeCoque said as the trio waited.

"What will you do with them?" Platinov asked Bolan. "Marc and Ali?"

He shrugged, his mind turning to Rosario Blancanales, the psych-op expert of Able Team. The Executioner knew that Marc and Ali were scheduled for some long, grueling interrogation by Blancanales as soon as Able Team had finished its current mission. Blancanales would do his best to determine if Marc and Ali's "team change" was for real, or simply an act.

"What will you do with them?" Platinov asked again as their helicopter began descending straight down onto the hotel's roof.

"They'll be evaluated by one of our men who's good at that sort of thing," said Bolan. "If their change of heart is for real, they'll be returned to their country and released."

Platinov shook her head as she slid back the helicopter's door and pulled herself up and in. Looking back at the Executioner, she said, "You Americans. I wouldn't be surprised if you didn't form a support group for them. And come up with some kind of colored ribbon-lapel pins and bumper stickers to commemorate them." The Russian woman shook her head in dismay. "I am glad that the cold war is over," she said. "But how you beat us will forever remain a mystery in my mind."

"What would you do with them?" he asked as he let LeCoque board next.

"Kill them," Platinov said. "Just to be sure."

The Executioner didn't answer as he crawled up and into the helicopter and strapped himself in next to the M-60 machine gun mounted just behind the doorway. He could explain what Blancanales would be doing with Marc and Ali, and then she would understand. But the bottom line was that Platinov didn't need to know any more about American, or Stony Man Farm, business than necessary.

IT WAS THE BOTTOM of the eighth inning, and the Yankees were at bat, trailing the Rockies 4-1 by the time the Stony Man chopper reached Yankee Stadium. Following Bolan's orders, Grimaldi made a mile-wide circle of the site. When they spotted no other aircraft in the air, the ace pilot cut the circle by half and reversed directions.

It was then that they finally saw the stolen chopper making similar circles in the sky.

Bolan tapped the Stony Man number into his satellite phone. "We've got visual," he told Barbara Price when she answered the line. Bolan heard a click and Hal Brognola said, "Location, Striker?"

"We're almost directly over the stadium," Bolan said. "If I shoot them down now, they're going to land just foul of the left field line and kill hundreds of the people seated in that section."

"Then you've got to lure them out of there somehow," Brognola said. "Somewhere away from people. You might see if you can raise them on the radio. Maybe cut a deal?"

"Hang on and I'll try, but don't count on it," Bolan said, reaching forward to pull the microphone off its hook.

Grimaldi maneuvered the helicopter to a spot in the chopper's tail wind. Making his own "call number" up on the spot, Bolan said, "SMF One to unidentified helicopter over Yankee Stadium. Come in, helicopter."

There was a long pause, and finally a French-accented voice said, "Who are you and what do you want?"

"Not important. But be aware that I have all the firepower I need to blow you out of the sky," said the Executioner, thumbing the red button on the microphone again. "I want you to land in the parking lot and exit with your hands on top of your heads."

An immediate sound of laughter came over the radio, and the chopper ahead of them suddenly turned in the air to face them. A blast of full-auto machine-gun rounds ground into the bullet-resistant glass in front of

Bolan and Grimaldi before bouncing off again. Other rounds struck steel, causing sparks to light up the sky like sparklers.

A roar from the crowd below them made the Executioner look downward. It looked as if the crowd was on its feet, cheering. It was the World Series, after all, and they thought the helicopter fight in the sky above the field was all part of the show.

Platinov pulled the sliding door all the way open as Bolan grabbed the grips of the M-60. He looked down at the baseball diamond far below. Rouillan's chopper wasn't armored like the one Grimaldi piloted, but he couldn't take it out here without it falling directly down into the stadium. He would have to find some other way to neutralize it.

Rouillan fired again, and more 7.62 mms skidded off the glass bubble. Bolan looked to LeCoque and said, "Come over here and man the belt."

The blacksuit-trained Belgian slid in next to him and lifted the belt over his lap with both hands. "Land your chopper, Rouillan," Bolan said into the radio. "We know who you are, and your plan in the press box has already been shut down."

His answer was another burst of fire.

Bolan aimed the M-60 at the other chopper and held the trigger back. A carefully aimed automatic burst of rounds flew from the mounted weapon and took out a chunk of glass in the windshield. A split second after the bullets struck, the Frenchman did what all cowards do.

He ran.

"Take her down, a bit, Jack," Bolan shouted as Rouillan's helicopter suddenly dropped through the air, directly at the ballpark below. For a moment, the Executioner had a sinking feeling in the pit of his stomach. Had some of his rounds accidentally struck some vital part of the other craft? If so, the deaths of hundreds of people below would be on his head.

But just before it struck the scoreboard, Rouillan's helicopter suddenly resumed flight and took off laterally again. Now, as Grimaldi sped after him the crowd grew silent, finally realizing that this was something more than just a show put on for their benefit. But almost as quickly as the helicopter battle had begun they had zoomed away from the stadium and were following Rouillan's flight across the Harlem River.

Bolan twisted the M-60 on its mount until the other chopper was in his sights again. But by then they had crossed that river and were above houses and other buildings. The Executioner had to relax his finger on the trigger yet again, and wait.

Far to his left, Bolan could see the lights of Columbia University. Rouillan cut sharply to the left when they neared Grant's Tomb, then suddenly they were over the wider waters of the Hudson River.

Bolan cut loose with a long blast as LeCoque fed the belt for him. Rouillan's chopper jerked up and down, back and forth, with smoke beginning to rise as it lost altitude.

But it stayed in the air.

The Executioner continued to hammer the other chopper with rounds until it suddenly cut south again, flying back in over Riverside Drive and forcing him to let up on the trigger yet again.

Again, they were over a heavily populated area, which meant hundreds, or perhaps even thousands, of deaths if they crashed. Smoke and flames were now visible from Rouillan's chopper, and it didn't look like it had too many miles left in it whether Bolan continued to shoot or not.

Grimaldi was not only an ace pilot, he knew aircraft like the back of his hand. And now, he spoke up, saying, "It's gonna crash, Striker. Real soon. And when it does, it's going straight down on Riverside Drive." Bolan watched him frown at the smoke and flames. "I'd say it'll hit somewhere between the Lincoln Tunnel and Times Square."

"We've got to get them back over the water," Bolan shouted from his seat in the doorway. "Can you give them a nudge, Jack?"

"Not without taking a very big chance of shearing off our blades," the pilot said. "But I'm game if you are."

Bolan looked behind him to Platinov. "The question is," the Russian woman said, "which is more valuable? Our lives, or the lives of so many more below?" She paused, then raised her hand, inspecting a cuticle. Then she said, "Let's go for it" with an emotionless voice.

LeCoque nodded. "Too many innocent people will die below if we don't try it," he said. A grim smile came over his face. "Besides, like I said before, I'm sick of where they've stuck me in Belgian customs, anyway."

"Do it," Bolan told Grimaldi.

Stony Man Farm's ace pilot dropped slightly below the altitude at which Rouillan's craft was still flying, then pulled up on the side without the mounted M-60. Slowly, he began inching nearer and nearer to the other chopper, as well as angling his own helicopter sideways to the left.

Grimaldi's helicopter was finally leaning at the forty-five-degree angle he desired, which meant the rotary blades could have been no more than a foot from the blades of the CLODO chopper. All it would take, as Grimaldi inched closer to the other craft, was a tiny miscalculation and both choppers would crash.

Finally, Bolan felt a jolt and heard the crash as the Stony Man helicopter's landing rails struck Rouillan's chopper, and began pushing it away from land and toward the water. Then, as Grimaldi herded the other craft through the sky, Bolan grabbed the grips of his own M-60 again. Grimaldi suddenly cut their speed, backing off and away from Rouillan now as the Executioner swiveled the M-60 one final time.

A second before he pulled the trigger, Bolan saw the terrified face of the man flying the stolen helicopter.

Pierre Rouillan was about to die, and he knew it.

A second later, the Executioner pulled the trigger back and Rouillan's chopper finally burst into one huge orange-and-red fireball. Chunks of steel and glass began to fall from the sky.

Grimaldi let the Stony Man helicopter hover over the area while Bolan once again tapped a number into his satellite phone. "Mission is complete," he told Barbara Price. "How'd the blacksuits at the press box do?"

"They did fine," Price said. "Two CLODO terrorists were killed, but they took the man running the scoreboard and the rest alive. They'll be handed over to the FBI."

For a moment, the helicopter went silent, then Price asked, "Is Agent Platinov still with you?"

"Yeah. She's still here. Want to talk to her?"

"No, just click on the speakerphone so she can hear."

Bolan punched another button on his satellite phone and Price said, "Agent Platinov?"

The Russian agent frowned, then said, "Yes?"

"I have a message to relay to you. You're needed back in Moscow immediately."

Platinov looked at Bolan.

"Tell them I will take the first flight there in the morning," she said, smiling at the Executioner.

"Negative," Price said. "They said immediately, and they must have meant it. There's a private plane waiting for you in D.C. Jack, can you swing by and let her out on your way?" Price asked.

"No problem," Grimaldi said.

Platinov looked angrily at the ceiling. "No problem for you, perhaps," she said. Then she looked Bolan in the eye and said, "I suppose there is always next time."

The Executioner nodded. "There's always that."